PRAISE FOR *APRIL FOOLS*

"I laughed, gasped, and cried (all out loud)."
—Catriona McPherson, author of *Hop Scot*

"Mira James, along with her sidekick, Mrs. Berns, and the ragtag denizens of Battle Lake, are up to their usual hilarious and increasingly heart-wrenching tricks."
—Linda Joffe Hull, author of *The Big Bang*

PRAISE FOR *MARCH OF CRIMES*

Jess Lourey named to Book Riot's "10 Funny Mystery Authors Like Janet Evanovich" list

"I laughed my way through this small-town mystery."
—Book Riot

"Earthy language, quirky suspects, and much related tomfoolery."
—*Kirkus Reviews*

PRAISE FOR *FEBRUARY FEVER*

Lefty Finalist for Most Humorous Mystery

"The best outing yet for Mira!"
—*Kirkus Reviews*

T0314457

"Lourey skillfully mixes humor and suspense . . . and the mile-a-minute pace never falters. Another excellent addition to Lourey's very entertaining Mira James Mystery series."

—*Booklist* (starred review)

"[An] incredible series . . . [*February Fever*] is a charming story with great dialogue [and] there are more months coming, so readers definitely have something to look forward to."

—*Suspense Magazine*

"I can't wait to see what Mira does next."

—*Crimespree Magazine*

PRAISE FOR *JANUARY THAW*

Lefty Finalist for Most Humorous Mystery

"Who can resist a mystery that includes a daredevil octogenarian sidekick; a flashy, plant-whispering mayor; some really bad villains; and a little girl ghost?"

—*Booklist*

"Those looking for an engaging, multigenerational small-town mystery that tackles contemporary issues can't miss with this entry."

—*Library Journal*

"Good, high-calorie fun!"

—*Mystery Scene*

PRAISE FOR *DECEMBER DREAD*

Lefty Finalist for Most Humorous Mystery

"Lourey creates a splendid mix of humor and suspense."
—*Booklist*

"Lourey, who keeps her secrets well, delivers a breathtaking finale."
—*Publishers Weekly*

"Lourey pulls out all the stops in this eighth case."
—*Library Journal*

PRAISE FOR *NOVEMBER HUNT*

"It's not easy to make people laugh while they're on the edge of their seats, but Lourey pulls it off, while her vivid descriptions of a brutal Minnesota winter will make readers shiver in the seventh book in her very clever Mira James mystery series."
—*Booklist* (starred review)

"Clever, quirky, and completely original!"
—Hank Phillippi Ryan, Anthony, Agatha, and Macavity Award–winning author

"A masterful mix of mayhem and mirth."
—Reed Farrel Coleman, *New York Times* bestselling author

"Lourey has successfully created an independent, relatable heroine in Mira James. Mira's wit and fearlessness enable her to overcome the many challenges she faces as she tries to unravel the murder."

—*Crimespree Magazine*

"Lourey's seventh cozy featuring PI wannabe Mira James successfully combines humor, an intriguing mystery, and quirky small-town characters."

—*Publishers Weekly*

"Lourey has a knack for wholesome sexual innuendo, and she gets plenty of mileage out of Minnesota. This light novel keeps the reader engaged, like one of those sweet, chewy Nut Goodies that Mira is addicted to."

—*The Boston Globe*

PRAISE FOR *OCTOBER FEST*

Lefty Finalist for Most Humorous Mystery

"Snappy jokes and edgy dialogue . . . More spunky than sweet; get started on this Lefty-nominated series if you've previously missed it."

—*Library Journal* (starred review)

"I loved Lourey's quirky, appealing sleuth and her wry yet affectionate look at small-town life. No gimmicks, just an intriguing plot with oddball characters. I hope Mira's misfortune of stumbling over a dead body every month lasts for many years!"

—Donna Andrews, *New York Times* bestselling author of *Stork Raving Mad*

"Funny, ribald, and brimming with small-town eccentrics."

—*Kirkus Reviews*

"Lourey has cleverly created an entertaining murder mystery . . . Her latest is loaded with humor, and many of the descriptions are downright poetic."

—*Booklist* (starred review)

PRAISE FOR *SEPTEMBER MOURN*

"Once again, the very funny Lourey serves up a delicious dish of murder, mayhem, and merriment."

—*Booklist* (starred review)

"Beautifully written and wickedly funny."

—Harley Jane Kozak, Agatha, Anthony, and Macavity Award–winning author

"Lourey has a talent for creating hilarious characters in bizarre, laugh-out-loud situations, while at the same time capturing the honest and endearing subtleties of human life."

—*The Strand*

PRAISE FOR *AUGUST MOON*

"Hilarious, fast paced, and madcap."

—*Booklist* (starred review)

"Another amusing tale set in the town full of over-the-top zanies who've endeared themselves to the engaging Mira."

—*Kirkus Reviews*

"[A] hilarious, wonderfully funny cozy."

—*Crimespree Magazine*

"Lourey has a gift for creating terrific characters. Her sly and witty take on small-town USA is a sweet summer treat. Pull up a lawn chair, pour yourself a glass of lemonade, and enjoy."

—Denise Swanson, bestselling author

"A fun, fast-paced mystery with a heroine readers will enjoy."

—*The Mystery Reader*

PRAISE FOR *KNEE HIGH BY THE FOURTH OF JULY*

Lefty Finalist for Most Humorous Mystery

"*Knee High by the Fourth of July* . . . kept me hooked from beginning to end. I enjoyed every page!"

—Sammi Carter, author of the Candy Shop Mysteries

"Sweet, nutty, evocative of the American Heartland, and utterly addicting."

—*The Strand*

"[The] humor transcends both genders and makes for a delightful romp."

—*Fergus Falls Journal*

"Mira . . . is an amusing heroine in a town full of quirky characters."
—*Kirkus Reviews*

"Lourey's rollicking good cozy planted me in the heat of a Minnesota summer for a laugh-out-loud mystery ride."
—Leann Sweeney, bestselling author

PRAISE FOR *JUNE BUG*

"Jess Lourey is a talented, witty, and clever writer."
—Monica Ferris, author of the Needlecraft Mysteries

"Don't miss this one—it's a hoot!"
—William Kent Krueger, *New York Times* bestselling author

"With just the right amount of insouciance, tongue-in-cheek sexiness, and plain common sense, Jess Lourey offers up a funny, well-written, engaging story . . . Readers will thoroughly enjoy the well-paced ride."
—Carl Brookins, author of *The Case of the Greedy Lawyers*

PRAISE FOR *MAY DAY*

"Jess Lourey writes about a small-town assistant librarian, but this is no genteel traditional mystery. Mira James likes guys in a big way, likes booze, and isn't afraid of motorcycles. She flees a dead-end job and a dead-end boyfriend in Minneapolis and ends up in Battle Lake, a little town with plenty of dirty secrets. The first-person narrative in *May Day* is fresh, the characters quirky. Minnesota has many fine crime writers, and Jess Lourey has just entered their ranks!"

—Ellen Hart, award-winning author of the Jane Lawless and Sophie Greenway series

"This trade paperback packed a punch . . . I loved it from the get-go!"

—*Tulsa World*

"What a romp this is! I found myself laughing out loud."

—*Crimespree Magazine*

"Mira digs up a closetful of dirty secrets, including sex parties, cross-dressing, and blackmail, on her way to exposing the killer. Lourey's debut has a likable heroine and surfeit of sass."

—*Kirkus Reviews*

PRAISE FOR *THE TAKEN ONES*

Short-listed for the 2024 Edgar Award for Best Paperback Original

"Setting the standard for top-notch thrillers, *The Taken Ones* is smart, compelling, and filled with utterly real characters. Lourey brings her formidable storytelling talent to the game and, on top of that, wows us with a deft stylistic touch. This is a one-sitting read!"

—Jeffery Deaver, author of *The Bone Collector* and *The Watchmaker's Hand*

"*The Taken Ones* has Jess Lourey's trademark of suspense all the way. A damaged and brave heroine, an equally damaged evildoer, and missing girls from long ago all combine to keep the reader rushing through to the explosive ending."

—Charlaine Harris, *New York Times* bestselling author

"Lourey is at the top of her game with *The Taken Ones*. A master of building tension while maintaining a riveting pace, Lourey is a hell of a writer on all fronts, but her greatest talent may be her characters. Evangeline Reed, an agent with the Minnesota Bureau of Criminal Apprehension, is a woman with a devastating past and the haunting ability to know the darkest crimes happening around her. She is also exactly the kind of character I would happily follow through a dozen books or more. In awe of her bravery, I also identified with her pain and wanted desperately to protect her. Along with an incredible cast of support characters, *The Taken Ones* will break your heart wide open and stay with you long after you've turned the final page. This is a 2023 must read."

—Danielle Girard, *USA Today* and Amazon #1 bestselling author of *Up Close*

PRAISE FOR *THE QUARRY GIRLS*

Winner of the 2023 Anthony Award for Best Paperback Original

Winner of the 2023 Minnesota Book Award for Genre Fiction

"Few authors can blend the genuine fear generated by a sordid tale of true crime with evocative, three-dimensional characters and mesmerizing prose like Jess Lourey. Her fictional stories feel rooted in a world we all know but also fear. *The Quarry Girls* is a story of secrets gone to seed, and Lourey gives readers her best novel yet—which is quite the accomplishment. Calling it: *The Quarry Girls* will be one of the best books of the year."

—Alex Segura, acclaimed author of *Secret Identity, Star Wars Poe Dameron: Free Fall,* and *Miami Midnight*

"Jess Lourey once more taps deep into her Midwest roots and childhood fears with *The Quarry Girls*, an absorbing, true crime–informed thriller narrated in the compelling voice of young drummer Heather Cash as she and her bandmates navigate the treacherous and confusing ground between girlhood and womanhood one simmering and deadly summer. Lourey conveys the edgy, hungry restlessness of teen girls with a touch of Megan Abbott while steadily intensifying the claustrophobic atmosphere of a small 1977 Minnesota town where darkness snakes below the surface."

—Loreth Anne White, *Washington Post* and Amazon Charts bestselling author of *The Patient's Secret*

"Jess Lourey is a master of the coming-of-age thriller, and *The Quarry Girls* may be her best yet—as dark, twisty, and full of secrets as the tunnels that lurk beneath Pantown's deceptively idyllic streets."

—Chris Holm, Anthony Award–winning author of *The Killing Kind*

PRAISE FOR *BLOODLINE*

Winner of the 2022 Anthony Award for Best Paperback Original

Winner of the 2022 ITW Thriller Award for Best Paperback Original

Short-listed for the 2021 Goodreads Choice Awards

"Fans of *Rosemary's Baby* will relish this."

—*Publishers Weekly*

"Based on a true story, this is a sinister, suspenseful thriller full of creeping horror."

—*Kirkus Reviews*

"Lourey ratchets up the fear in a novel that verges on horror."

—*Library Journal*

"In *Bloodline*, Jess Lourey blends elements of mystery, suspense, and horror to stunning effect."

—*BOLO Books*

"Inspired by a true story, it's a creepy page-turner that has me eager to read more of Ms. Lourey's works, especially if they're all as incisive as this thought-provoking novel."

—Criminal Element

"*Bloodline* by Jess Lourey is a psychological thriller that grabbed me from the beginning and didn't let go."

—*Mystery & Suspense Magazine*

"*Bloodline* blends page-turning storytelling with clever homages to such horror classics as *Rosemary's Baby*, *The Stepford Wives*, and *Harvest Home*."

—*Toronto Star*

"*Bloodline* is a terrific, creepy thriller, and Jess Lourey clearly knows how to get under your skin."

—Bookreporter

"[A] tightly coiled domestic thriller that slowly but persuasively builds the suspense."

—*South Florida Sun Sentinel*

"I should know better than to pick up a new Jess Lourey book thinking I'll just peek at the first few pages and then get back to the book I was reading. Six hours later, it's three in the morning and I'm racing through the last few chapters, unable to sleep until I know how it all ends. Set in an idyllic small town rooted in family history and horrific secrets, *Bloodline* is *Pleasantville* meets *Rosemary's Baby*. A deeply unsettling, darkly unnerving, and utterly compelling novel, this book chilled me to the core, and I loved every bit of it."

—Jennifer Hillier, author of *Little Secrets* and the award-winning *Jar of Hearts*

"Jess Lourey writes small-town Minnesota like Stephen King writes small-town Maine. *Bloodline* is a tremendous book with a heart and a hacksaw . . . and I loved every second of it."

—Rachel Howzell Hall, author of the critically acclaimed novels *And Now She's Gone* and *They All Fall Down*

PRAISE FOR *UNSPEAKABLE THINGS*

Winner of the 2021 Anthony Award for Best Paperback Original

Short-listed for the 2021 Edgar Awards and 2020 Goodreads Choice Awards

"The suspense never wavers in this page-turner."

—*Publishers Weekly*

"The atmospheric suspense novel is haunting because it's narrated from the point of view of a thirteen-year-old, an age that should be more innocent but often isn't. Even more chilling, it's based on real-life incidents. Lourey may be known for comic capers (*March of Crimes*), but this tense novel combines the best of a coming-of-age story with suspense and an unforgettable young narrator."

—*Library Journal* (starred review)

"Part suspense, part coming-of-age, Jess Lourey's *Unspeakable Things* is a story of creeping dread, about childhood when you know the monster under your bed is real. A novel that clings to you long after the last page."

—Lori Rader-Day, Edgar Award–nominated author of
Under a Dark Sky

"A noose of a novel that tightens by inches. The squirming tension comes from every direction—including the ones that are supposed to be safe. I felt complicit as I read, as if at any moment I stopped I would be abandoning Cassie, alone, in the dark, straining to listen and fearing to hear."

—Marcus Sakey, bestselling author of *Brilliance*

"*Unspeakable Things* is an absolutely riveting novel about the poisonous secrets buried deep in towns and families. Jess Lourey has created a story that will chill you to the bone and a main character who will break your heart wide open."

—Lou Berney, Edgar Award–winning author of *November Road*

"Inspired by a true story, *Unspeakable Things* crackles with authenticity, humanity, and humor. The novel reminded me of *To Kill a Mockingbird* and *The Marsh King's Daughter*. Highly recommended."

—Mark Sullivan, bestselling author of *Beneath a Scarlet Sky*

"Jess Lourey does a masterful job building tension and dread, but her greatest asset in *Unspeakable Things* is Cassie—an arresting narrator you identify with, root for, and desperately want to protect. This is a book that will stick with you long after you've torn through it."

—Rob Hart, author of *The Warehouse*

"With *Unspeakable Things*, Jess Lourey has managed the near-impossible, crafting a mystery as harrowing as it is tender, as gut-wrenching as it is lyrical. There is real darkness here, a creeping, inescapable dread that more than once had me looking over my own shoulder. But at its heart beats the irrepressible—and irresistible—spirit of its . . . heroine, a young woman so bright and vital and brave she kept even the fiercest monsters at bay. This is a book that will stay with me for a long time."

—Elizabeth Little, *Los Angeles Times* bestselling author of *Dear Daughter* and *Pretty as a Picture*

PRAISE FOR *SALEM'S CIPHER*

"A fast-paced, sometimes brutal thriller reminiscent of Dan Brown's *The Da Vinci Code*."

—*Booklist* (starred review)

"A hair-raising thrill ride."

—*Library Journal* (starred review)

"The fascinating historical information combined with a storyline ripped from the headlines will hook conspiracy theorists and action addicts alike."

—*Kirkus Reviews*

"Fans of *The Da Vinci Code* are going to love this book . . . One of my favorite reads of 2016."

—*Crimespree Magazine*

"This suspenseful tale has something for absolutely everyone to enjoy."

—*Suspense Magazine*

PRAISE FOR *MERCY'S CHASE*

"An immersive voice, an intriguing story, a wonderful character—highly recommended!"
—Lee Child, #1 *New York Times* bestselling author

"Both a sweeping adventure and race-against-time thriller, *Mercy's Chase* is fascinating, fierce, and brimming with heart—just like its heroine, Salem Wiley."
—Meg Gardiner, author of *Into the Black Nowhere*

"Action-packed, great writing taut with suspense, an appealing main character to root for—who could ask for anything more?"
—Buried Under Books

PRAISE FOR *REWRITE YOUR LIFE: DISCOVER YOUR TRUTH THROUGH THE HEALING POWER OF FICTION*

"Interweaving practical advice with stories and insights garnered in her own writing journey, Jessica Lourey offers a step-by-step guide for writers struggling to create fiction from their life experiences. But this book isn't just about writing. It's also about the power of stories to transform those who write them. I know of no other guide that delivers on its promise with such honesty, simplicity, and beauty."
—William Kent Krueger, *New York Times* bestselling author of the Cork O'Connor series and *Ordinary Grace*

APRIL FOOLS

OTHER TITLES BY JESS LOUREY

MURDER BY MONTH MYSTERIES

May Day

June Bug

Knee High by the Fourth of July

August Moon

September Mourn

October Fest

November Hunt

December Dread

January Thaw

February Fever

March of Crimes

April Fools

STEINBECK AND REED THRILLERS

"Catch Her in a Lie"

The Taken Ones

The Reaping

THRILLERS

The Quarry Girls

Litani

Bloodline

Unspeakable Things

SALEM'S CIPHER THRILLERS

Salem's Cipher

Mercy's Chase

CHILDREN'S BOOKS

Leave My Book Alone! Starring Claudette, a Dragon with Control Issues

YOUNG ADULT

A Whisper of Poison

NONFICTION

Rewrite Your Life: Discover Your Truth Through the Healing Power of Fiction

APRIL
FOOLS

JESS LOUREY

THOMAS & MERCER

Published by Thomas & Mercer, Seattle

www.apub.com

Amazon, the Amazon logo, and Thomas & Mercer are trademarks of Amazon.com, Inc., or its affiliates.

ISBN-13: 9781662519444 (paperback)
ISBN-13: 9781662519451 (digital)

Cover design and illustration by Sarah Horgan

Printed in the United States of America

This book is dedicated to you, the reader.
Thank you for going on this wild, twelve-month ride.

Chapter 1

"I don't like the look of this."

I had to agree with Mrs. Berns. "Maybe it's not as bad as it seems."

She and I stood near the Battle Lake library's front desk, hands on hips, staring down. "I want to poke it with a stick," she added.

I nodded. "That's a good plan. But we don't have a stick."

She reached for a pencil out of the public cup. She waved it in front of my eyes. "You're the one who keeps buying these stupid short pencils. *You* get to poke it. I don't want to get that close. You've watched *The Blob*?"

I had. When I was eight years old. I'd spent the next week sleeping in my parents' bed. I could call up at will the image of the pulsating red lava crawling up the branch and onto the man's hand, absorbing him as he screamed.

"Those are standard-issue library-length pencils," I said.

"Do not get defensive with me," she said. "And only an insecure man would market those as 'standard issue.' Those are itty-bitty pencils." She nudged me. "Now poke it."

I leaned forward and then thought better of it. "Maybe I could tape two pencils together?"

She pinched the soft flesh on the underside of my arm, her hand in and out before I had a chance to swipe at her. For a woman in her early nineties, she was quick. Scratch that—for a *human*, she was quick.

"Ouch!" I yelped, jumping away from her. "What was that for?"

"For being a scaredy-cat."

"You're not poking it, either."

"Not because I'm scared." She fluffed her blue-tinged hair, not taking her eyes off the center of the desk. She was a small woman, five-foot-nothing in heels (not that she'd ever wear them), but she carried herself like she was six feet tall and bulletproof. Her eyes always sparkled, her lipstick was frequently drawn outside the lines, and while she dressed for comfort, it wasn't unheard of for her to strap on a set of cap guns for a little flair.

In short, she was perfect.

"I'm not poking it because I'm smart," she finished.

She wasn't wrong. I thrust my arm as far away from my body as I could, stretching the shaking pencil toward the mystery box. The container had been waiting for us when we'd opened the library, dead center on our front desk. Where we couldn't miss it. After we both checked our keys to make sure they hadn't been stolen, we'd tiptoed over to it. It was a shallow wooden crate, covered in a soft-looking fabric, approximately the dimensions of a small delivery pizza box. We had no idea what was beneath the cloth.

My heart hammered the nearer I got to it, and I couldn't help but notice that Mrs. Berns was keeping a bit behind me.

"I think it's gonna be a box of fingers," she whispered.

"What?" I hissed. "Why fingers?"

I sensed her shrug. "It could be toes."

"It could be a gift," I said, unable to hide the doubt in my voice.

She snorted. "You're awful pie-eyed for a woman who's averaged one dead body a month for the past year. Hey!" She stopped in her tracks and grabbed my arm.

"Ack!" I'd nearly been close enough to lift the covering. "Don't grab me without warning."

"I was just thinking, maybe this is an anniversary present for you? You know, because you've been living in Battle Lake for a whole year? Maybe the chamber of commerce got together and bought you a thank-you gift. They meet at city hall, where a spare set of keys to the library are stored. Probably they snuck it in last night, or early this morning."

"That's a great theory." I jabbed the baby pencil toward the box. "Are you confident enough in it to peek inside first?"

She snorted. "We both know I was just blowing sunshine up your skirt. Probably looks like a toe-finger junk drawer in there."

I threw a glance at the doorway we'd walked through moments before. We could've walked right back out it, but then what? Call the police and tell them that *ohmygosh*, there was a box on the library counter?

What's in it? they'd ask.

Too chicken to peek, we'd say.

No way was I going to sign myself up for that level of embarrassment, especially after what the library and I'd just been through. We'd both only recently reopened for business, the library thanks to generous donations supporting its renovation, and me courtesy of a two-week healing regimen. No, I needed to stand my ground and not let fear run my life. So I stepped nearer, close enough to lift up the corner of the fabric covering the box.

My jaw dropped.

Mrs. Berns couldn't stand the curiosity, and so she scuttled forward, just enough to peer inside.

"What the hell?" she asked.

Chapter 2

The box held four furry green balls, each as large as a plum, nestled in shredded paper.

"Poke one already!" Mrs. Berns commanded, pushing me nearer them.

I had to admit that she was right about the dinky pencils. A full-length one would have been mighty appreciated (cue the that's-what-she-said jokes). This pencil was only as long as my pointer finger. I held the flat end toward the nearest ball and gave it a nudge. It lifted up, revealing a bright-white underbelly.

"Smell that?" she asked.

I sniffed, immediately identifying the odor. "Smells like feet."

She grimaced. "Probably the toes are hidden in the center of the balls?"

"Like secret-center cheese?"

She smiled, lighting up the beautiful wrinkles in her face. "Exactly."

I flipped the pencil so it was sharp end out and pressed the point in deep, spearing the ball. I drew it toward my nose and inhaled. "I think I was right about the cheese part." I squinted. "They're covered in parsley, but they appear to be four cheese balls."

Her chin tucked in. "What the hell kind of sentence is that to utter?"

I held the ball toward her. "Smell for yourself."

She sniffed, circled, poked, and then flicked the other three balls with her finger. "You're right. We've got ourselves a reverse cheese balls bandit on our hands."

I lifted the box, searching for a note. Nothing. "Maybe it really was an anniversary gift for me?"

She took the cheese ball from my hand and tossed it into the box with its three friends. "If it is, someone needs to take a gift-giving class. More likely it's an April Fools' prank."

Of course. While most of the United States put aside only one day to celebrate being an asshat—April 1—Battle Lake celebrated all month long. "Who besides us and city hall has a key to the library?"

"Everybody on the city council. Plus, anyone who knows that moon rock out front that you hide the spare key inside isn't native to Minnesota." She scooped up the cheese box, turning her nose to the side. "I'm gonna store this in the fridge for now. We'll sleuth out these cheese balls after we get the library up and running."

Just another morning in Battle Lake.

I stepped behind the front counter and fired up the computer, preparing for the day ahead now that the mystery of what was in the box had sort of been solved. I glanced outside the window at the gray, cold day, rubbing my eyes before I caught myself. *Curse words.* The spring weather had driven my allergies bonkers. It was caught between ice and heat, white and green, sharp and soft. In that space, my eyes felt like they'd been dipped in poison ivy, my nose was running for office, and I'd sneezed so much that . . . well, that last one wasn't so bad. I liked sneezing.

"You rubbed your eyes, didn't you?" Mrs. Berns asked, returning to the main room.

"No." It's not a lie if no one gets hurt.

"Here," she said, reaching into her pocket. "I stopped by the apothecary last night. Unfortunately, they didn't carry anything to make you a better liar. They did have jumbo-sized anti-allergy eye drops, though."

She tossed me a three-bottle pack, which I'm mighty proud to say I caught. I tore it open, ripped off the first bottle's safety seal, and dropped the cool liquid into each eye. "Ahhh," I moaned.

"Good lord," Mrs. Berns said. "Between that and your sneezing, I think your wiring must be wrong. By the way, those are the real deal—tetrahydrozoline eye drops—so make sure you don't get any in your mouth. As little as a teaspoon will make you so sick you'll wish you were never born."

"How in the *world* would I accidentally get a teaspoon of eye drops in my mouth?"

"How in the *world* do you manage to roll up on one dead body a month?"

She was good.

I'd relocated to Battle Lake a year ago last April and discovered my first corpse in May, laid out in the library, of all places. I'd been dating the guy. June brought me a calcified body near my home; July, a missing twenty-three-foot fiberglass statue with a chunk of head at its base; August, a Bible camp nightmare, complete with a dead cheerleader; September, a state fair run that included a deceased Milkfed Mary, Queen of the Dairy; October, a mysteriously can-kicked political blogger; November, a hunting accident that turned out not to be; December, a serial killer who chased me back to my hometown; January, an iced corpse frozen below the surface of the skating rink; February, a train ride through the Rockies that cost me one of my dearest friends; and March, a coincidental cadaver hidden inside a life-size doll.

"Fair enough," I said, repressing a shudder.

"Thought so." She smacked her hands on the counter. "What's the plan for the day?"

I studied her. Something was off. "You tasted the cheese on your way to put it into the refrigerator, didn't you?"

She wiped a fleck of green off the corner of her mouth. "Why would you say that?"

"Because I know you. Also, you've got some mold-colored stuff between your teeth that wasn't there before."

"I like cheese."

I raised an eyebrow. "Was it good?"

"I've tasted better."

I made a tsking sound. "We still don't know who it's from."

"I'll thank 'em when I find out."

There was no shaming the woman, which was one of a million things I loved about her. She'd taken me under her wing last summer, and she'd grown into my best friend. She was wise and gorgeous, and she grabbed life by the cheese balls.

I glanced over at my to-do list as I logged on to the front computer. "We need to shelve the returned books, rotate the flyers in the foyer, read to the kids, send out confirmation emails to people who've reserved space in the library this month, and of course, help anyone who comes in."

"I'll take that last one," Mrs. Berns said, grabbing the *Battle Lake Recall* off the nearby rack and flopping into the library's recliner tucked in a cozy corner, between the front desk and the bank of computers. It was one of many items that we'd had to replace after last month's fire.

Opposite the recliner was the children's corner, where I read stories to sweet, goobery, fidgety little humans every Monday. The stacks—twelve wall-to-wall shelves, split down the middle and nearly reaching the ceiling—separated the two spaces. The remaining area was taken over by rotating book carousels that held the paperbacks, the newspaper rack Mrs. Berns had just nabbed the *Recall* from, and a handful of reading and laptop desks sprinkled around. While the Battle Lake Public Library was essentially one huge room, we managed to squeeze a lot in here.

There was no reason to argue with Mrs. Berns's unwillingness to do anything but read the paper while she waited for patrons to walk in. She worked for minimum wage, and any money she made, she donated back to the Friends of the Library. She could do as she liked.

I strolled to the front door and flipped the sign to OPEN, leaning over to eyeball the returned books in the bin. A dozen or so hardcovers and three times as many paperbacks stared back at me. "Busy night last night."

"Weekend reads coming back," Mrs. Berns murmured. "This newspaper is crap, by the way."

I bristled. "Are you reading one of mine?"

On top of a column called Mira's Musings and some regular PR articles for the *Recall*, I wrote a weekly bit called Battle Lake Bites, which had started out as a passive-aggressive feature of weird Midwestern meals and had somehow become wildly popular. Who knew so many people liked bland, goopy comfort food with the occasional wild-game recipe?

"Naw," Mrs. Berns said. "I don't want to introduce any questionable food images to my mind until I find out whether that cheese ball's gonna put up a fight. I'm scanning notes from last week's chamber meeting."

"Hard to make that exciting." I wheeled the return bin to the front desk and began the process of checking in the books.

"But this one was."

I could hear the consternation in her voice. "You were there?"

"Yeah. A few of us from the Senior Sunset sometimes go to heckle."

An image of those two *Muppet Show* guys in the balcony seats came into my head.

"Statler and Waldorf," she said, reading my mind, "and you're not far off. Anyhow, we were doing our usual—being engaged citizens while they yakked about zoning and tax breaks and *snore blah de blah*—when they start talking about Battle Lake losing tourism on account of how a slew of dead bodies were discovered here this past year."

Here she paused to bestow me with a pointed stare.

"I didn't kill any of them," I protested.

"That's what I told them when they brought up your name."

"They mentioned me by name?"

"Murdery Mira, they called you."

I choked on my own spit. "What?"

She nodded. "I added the 'Murdery' part. Builds up your mythology in an interesting way, I think. Anyhow, a national tourism board with a lot of pull is sending someone to Battle Lake to decide if they're going to pull our A-plus rating. Apparently, charming businesses, yummy restaurants, and sparkling lakes don't count for much if they're corpsy."

Oh lord. My stomach churned. It was true the death rate had spiked since I'd moved to town, but . . . were people really blaming a decline in business on me? An even worse idea sneaked into my brain. *Maybe it* was *my fault.* My dad had died in a car accident thirteen years earlier. What if that had merely been a warm-up for the devastation that had followed me since I'd taken over house-sitting here for my friend Sunny?

"Did they talk about anything else at the meeting?" I asked weakly.

She snapped the paper closed. "You think the whole world revolves around you? Of course they did. There's an open office next door to the dentist's, Dr. Banks. He owns the building and wants another medical person in there. Also, someone on the chamber suggested the town play up its connection to Barry Janston to erase the stain of your . . . *discoveries.* Maybe a 'Home of State Senator Barry Janston' sign as you drive into town."

Nothing like a billboard to distract from a spike in the death rate. "Who came up with that idea?"

"Karen Kramer. She's the chamber president and as ugly as the first pancake." Mrs. Berns said this without malice, simply stating a fact. "Her best friend is also on the chamber board, plus her ex-brother-in-law, one of my ex-lovers, my second cousin, and Curtis."

The information was coming at me too fast. Curtis Poling, I knew. He was a dashing, wise old coot who lived at the Senior Sunset and fished off the roof in the warmer seasons. There was no lake below, so people in the know would occasionally stick a fish on the end of his line to keep him entertained. "They let Curtis serve on the chamber? And this Karen is related to two of the six chamber members?"

Mrs. Berns shrugged. "It's a small town. She *was* related, by the way. A nasty divorce, so now she's the ex. And yep, they let Curtis out. He has a chaperone to walk him to and from, but the man knows everything about this town and this county, going back more than ninety years. They were smart to include him."

I inhaled deeply. Or at least I tried to. My nose was pretty stuffed up. All the checked-out books from the return bin were now checked-in books. I stacked them back into the bin, grouping them by section, and wheeled it over to the nearest paperback carousel.

"I bet Curtis stood up for me during the commerce meeting," I said.

"I bet he did," Mrs. Berns agreed.

I glanced over at her. She'd reopened the newspaper and was engrossed in another article. "I bet Elvis makes delicious hash browns," I said, keeping my voice level.

"I bet he does."

So she *hadn't* been listening. Well, it didn't matter, because I didn't have anything to say except that it sucked to be considered a bad-luck penny in my adoptive hometown. Not much I could do about it, I supposed, except feel guilty.

Well, sign me up.

Done shelving the romance paperbacks, I pushed the squeaky bin past Jed's altar and toward the mystery paperbacks. I beamed love thoughts at the altar, as I always did when I passed it. I didn't ever want to take it—or my memories of him—for granted. He'd died saving my life in February. We'd been on a train hurtling through the snow-covered Rockies when I found myself getting the breath choked from me outside one of the luggage cars, exposed to the icy elements. Jed had rushed in. He'd rescued me, but my assailant had tossed him out over a deep chasm in the ensuing struggle.

Jed's body had never been found.

I'd never be free of the guilt or the aching, bottomless sense of loss.

The altar was a tiny way to honor him. It'd started out with his photo, all curly brown hair and goofy smile. Then I'd added some of the glass creatures he'd been learning to create. My favorites were the sea-themed ones: an octopus; a puffer fish, complete with tiny glass points extended; a manta ray. His mom had brought the stuffed shark. She said it had been Jed's favorite toy when he was a kid and he'd still kept it on his bed as an adult. Other people in the community had added, too—a photo here, a memento there.

The familiar sadness of contemplating Jed was almost a comfort. I didn't want to look away when the door dinged and in walked our first client. "You're up, Mrs. Berns."

She remained seated. "I don't think that word means what you think it means."

I sighed. Some days she did no work at all. It looked like this would be one of those. I pitched my voice to the foyer. "Welcome to the Battle Lake library! I'm shelving books if you need anything."

I dug into the stack of mysteries, waiting for a response. Nothing, not even a grunt. I peeked my head around the book rack. A man stood right inside the door, dressed in a too-thick-for-April down jacket, a matching hat and scarf, and industrial boots. He was Not from Around Here. He also appeared to be tasting the air.

"Can I help you?" I asked.

Mrs. Berns was making rustling noises behind me, but I didn't have attention to spare. The man hadn't moved, and my hackles were up. I dropped the books from my hands. They fell into the bottom of the bin with a soft *whump*. I walked slowly toward the front. "Sir?"

He swiveled his head, the movement birdlike. The overhead halogens caught his glasses, the reflection hiding his eyes. Something about him set off an alarm bell, and it was more than his Snidely Whiplash mustache. He was a short man, trim, with sandy-colored hair beneath his hat. I stepped closer, which was when I realized what was off. There was something *judgmental* in his stance. People either entered the library comfortably, timidly, or on a mission, never with their nose in the air, as his was.

"Yes, sorry," he said. "I'm new to town."

"You don't say," Mrs. Berns said, appearing beside me.

Topless.

I made an involuntary noise and leaped in front of her, pulling off my own sweater to wrap her in. "Where's your shirt?" I asked her.

She smiled and hooked a thumb behind her. "Draped over the recliner. I grew warm reading."

"You could have rolled up your sleeves."

She looked down at her boobs, her expression dreamy, and flicked one. "Who let the dugs out?"

I pulled my sweater tighter around her, shooting a beseeching look at the man, who appeared appropriately startled. "Are you feeling all right?" I asked Mrs. Berns.

"Pretty relaxed," she murmured. "And hungry. I think I might go for another cheese ball."

The cheese balls. "Let's get your clothes on."

I led her back toward her shirt. She resisted, smiling suggestively over her shoulder at the stranger still standing near the front door. He was pointedly looking away from us, his demeanor gone from judgmental to flustered.

"Welcome to Battle Lake," she hollered at him. "You're really gonna like it here."

"Madam," he said, raising his voice and appearing more offended than concerned, "you should keep yourself covered at all times."

Mrs. Berns smiled. "Will do. Can I borrow your time machine?"

"I'm sorry," I said to the man. "But I've got a situation here. Could you please come back later?"

He huffed and stormed out.

Fine by me. I wrestled Mrs. Berns into her bra, commanding her to lean forward so the girls could land centered. Then I buttoned up her shirt. "Either you're on new medication," I said, "or those cheese balls were spiked. I'm taking you to the doctor."

"No you're not," she said, dropping back into the chair. "I haven't felt this good in years. I'm listening to my body, and it's happy."

"What if you were poisoned?"

"What if you're dumb?" She smiled serenely.

I crossed my arms. "You're not going to go quietly, are you?"

"I don't know why I'd start now." She tapped her chin thoughtfully. "But how about this? You keep an eye on me. If I start going south, you bring me in. Otherwise, let a lady enjoy a free high. Whatever is in that cheese is *good*."

Probably it contained a strain of mold that caused euphoria. I'd read of such a thing. I didn't like it, but I had to admit that other than spontaneously getting top-naked, she *did* seem happy. "Anything else weird, and we go in. Yeah?"

She nodded, flipped open the recliner's leg rest, stretched out, and laced her fingers behind her neck. "Deal!"

I watched her for another minute.

She watched me back. "How's it going with Johnny?" she asked.

I did not want to talk about my sexy, too-good-for-me, kind, recently reunited after he'd thought he lost me in a fire, and did I mention sexy boyfriend—not under normal circumstances and certainly not with a woman who'd recently shed the scant few inhibitions she'd been born with. "I'll be right over here, shelving the nonfiction."

"All right."

I walked backward so I could keep my eyes on her. She was still peering peacefully at nothing when I reached into the rolling return bin for the hardcover copy of *Minnesota's Hidden Treasures*. I might have kept staring at her if the flash of white hadn't caught my attention.

A note had dropped out of the book and was floating like a feather to the ground.

I watched it drop. People leaving bookmarks and such behind was not unusual. Once, I'd come across a photo booth strip of pictures inside a returned novel, two young girls laughing and making funny faces in each frame. Mostly, though, it was laminated scriptures and receipts.

That's what I expected when I leaned forward to pick it up.

It'd landed face down. The back looked like a page ripped out of a waitress pad, lined.

I flipped it over.

It was a note.

Mark James (PV—12)
Lartel McManus (OT—7)
John Guinn (OT—23)
Jefferson Penetal (OT—1)

HELP

The "HELP" was scraggly, written in a different handwriting from the rest of the note, straight out of a horror movie, but that wasn't what caught my attention. Neither was I triggered by the name of Lartel McManus, former Battle Lake head librarian and the man who'd hired me before mysteriously disappearing nearly eleven months ago to the day.

No, I reserved my shock for my dead father's name, written across the top.

Chapter 3

Mark James.

Back when he was alive, he'd looked like most guys named Mark: five-seven with a bit of a beer belly, dark hair, brown eyes, and a mustache and beard covering an unremarkable face. Emotionally, though, he'd been a larger-than-life, destructive man-child, his pain and his drama the eye of our hurricane household.

My mom had dedicated her life to putting out his fires.

She was only one woman, however, and in the end, my dad basically killed himself. He drank enough vodka to drown a Clydesdale, slid behind the wheel of his '75 Chrysler Cordoba, and got into a head-on car crash outside our hometown of Paynesville. He'd died instantly, as had the woman in the other car. Once I'd worked through my sorrow for the innocent, I'd settled on a white-hot rage toward my dad.

Alive, he'd been an exhausting load of work—isolating, moody, lurky. Dead, he was even worse, shackling me with the scarlet *M* for "(daughter of a) Murderer," which was social leprosy in my small hometown. Common wisdom said that anger was an important stage of the grief process, followed or preceded by denial, bargaining, depression, and acceptance. I'd never moved past the anger. And shame.

If you find something that works, *amirite?*

My mom's and my relationship had been shaky before the accident. There was really only room for one child in our house, and it had been Dad. I moved to the Cities as soon as the ink dried on my high school diploma, earned a degree in English, waited tables, made crappy dating decisions, and began nurturing a drinking problem of my own. I might have stayed in that holding pattern if I hadn't stumbled across my then boyfriend, Bad Brad, getting his Yankee Doodle dandied by the next-door apartment sitter.

When my friend Sunny called shortly after to ask if I'd watch her house in Battle Lake, I limped at the chance. Packing up my car, I drove away from Minneapolis, my drinking problem, and Bad Brad. Unfortunately, what awaited me in Battle Lake was a series of interactions with one corpse after another.

You'd almost think I was jinxed.

What I'd realized, though, was that being a corpse magnet came with its perks. First, you found out quick who your friends were. Second, you might discover that you have a knack for solving mysteries. Third, and most surprisingly, you could begin to reconnect with your mom, as I had last year, thanks to a cancer diagnosis and a serial killer on my tail. It helped that I liked her new boyfriend, a man who resembled a senior Tom Selleck and who was an actual adult capable of managing his own emotions.

She and I almost never talked about my dad. Why start now?

I imagined the conversation. *"Hey, Mom, how's it going?"*

"Fine, honey. Spring is on the way! How are you?"

"Good, good. Say, I found some sort of ransom-note-looking thing with Dad's name on it, and I was wondering if he'd ever been kidnapped or kidnapped someone?"

I smacked my forehead, good sense coming home to roost, finally. It *was* my dad's name, but he couldn't have been the only Mark James in the world. The *PV* made me think *Paynesville*, but it didn't necessarily mean that. And the "help"? Sure, the shaky scrawl was unsettling, but it could well be some sort of joke.

"John Guinn lives over by you," Mrs. Berns said over my shoulder, her nearness making me jump.

I breathed deeply. "I need to tie a bell on you."

She pointed at the note. "Where'd you find that?"

I held up *Minnesota's Hidden Treasures*. "One of the books in the return bin today."

"Hmmm," she said, snatching the note out of my hand. Whatever had affected her before had apparently worn off already. "What was your dad's name?"

I didn't want to say it. In fact, I didn't want to know it, smell it, or see it.

She flicked the side of my head. "I know it's Mark, you ding-dong. I was measuring to see how freaked out you are by this. Very, I see."

I grabbed the note back. "There's lotsa Mark Jameses out there."

"How many?"

I risked a glance. Her eyes were owl-focused on me.

"I dunno," I said. "Does it matter?"

She strode toward the front computer. "Let's find out." She began clacking on the keyboard.

"You know," I said, joining her, "for someone who didn't know how to turn on a computer when we first met, you're sure getting fancy."

She remained focused on the screen. "I knew how to turn on a computer before you learned how to braid your hair. I was just using the fish-cleaning rule, and I recommend you do the same."

"The fish-cleaning rule?"

"Yep. If you do not enjoy an activity, never let on that you're good at it." She stopped typing as her eyebrows shot up. "Guess how many Mark Jameses there are in the United States."

"Alive?" I asked.

"No, deep-fried," she said. "Of course alive."

I rubbed my chin. "Forty thousand?"

She swiveled the screen toward me. "1,337."

"That's fewer than I thought." I rubbed the edge of the note. "You said John Guinn is local?"

"Yep. I don't believe I've ever met him. He's a therapist, and he also works with teens. I believe he spearheaded the community center construction. It was built in remembrance of I-don't-know-who."

"Scoot," I said, sliding next to her. "I want to see who checked out this book last."

I wasn't searching for a mystery to solve, I swear.

It took thirty seconds to pull up the name. "Lou Banks," I said. "That's the dentist over on Oak Street, isn't it? The one you said is looking for someone to rent from him?"

"None other," Mrs. Berns said, frowning at the screen. "He's got quite eclectic tastes."

I'd been thinking the same thing. He'd checked out the *Hidden Treasures* volume, a book on building a hovercraft, another on Mesopotamia, two romances, a fantasy novel, and a cookbook, and that was just this week. A search showed that he'd checked out at least ten books a month since I'd been the librarian.

"Do you know what he looks like?" I asked. I must have interacted with him dozens of times and not even noticed.

"Sure. Like I said, he spoke at the chamber of commerce meeting. He's maybe twice your age. Looks like he was homeschooled back in the day. Hair and skin the same color. Mustache."

There's a Mrs. Berns description for you. "Did you check him out?"

"I did not."

"Me neither, not that I remember, and that's impossible considering how many books he's borrowed."

Lord help me, there it was. The whine in the back of my brain, the dusty little squeak that I had to oil, the *need* that drove me to get involved where a normal person would simply move on with her life.

"Your thought bubble tells me you're going to visit the dentist," Mrs. Berns said.

No need to respond. I closed out the search and walked back to where I'd been shelving books when the note fell out. I grabbed *Minnesota's Hidden Treasures* on the way, pausing by Jed's altar. Of course Mrs. Berns was right. I *did* want to visit the dentist right now, this very minute, to find out why he'd checked out this book, and why neither Mrs. Berns nor I remembered ever helping him. But I couldn't leave Mrs. Berns alone, not until I knew what was in that cheese ball.

If only someone could walk through that door and cover for me, I thought, staring at the door and sending my thought rays straight to it. I set the *Treasures* book on Jed's altar so I could focus all my energy on calling in someone to help me.

I was just being goofy. I didn't think it would work, so I suppose I got what I deserved when the last person I wanted to see walked through the door.

In Battle Lake, always be careful what you wish for.

Chapter 4

Kennie Rogers, Battle Lake's mayor, had taken and kept her ex-husband's last name in marriage. Still, she acted like she had been born to it and was forever trying to set herself apart from the famous singer, to prove to the world that she was one of a kind and all woman.

Mission. Accomplished.

It wasn't only that she was a force of nature when it came to city politics, or that she possessed an entrepreneurial drive that had her inventing a new business—sometimes weekly (remind me to tell you about the Minnesota phone-sex line she developed last month). It wasn't that she'd painted her house pink, or that she never took no for an answer. It was all those things, but even more, it was how they came together, spectacularly, horrifyingly, in her wardrobe.

Today was no exception.

Usually I could figure out her theme—sexy cowgirl, sexy secretary, sexy aesthetician—but not today. Today her ensemble was surprisingly staid, her platinum-blonde hair twisted into a victory roll, heavily lined lids behind cat-eye glasses, bright red lipstick, a wispy scarf tied around her neck, a tight sweater beneath a Battle Lake Bulldogs letter jacket, and even tighter cigarette pants—so tight, in fact, that they gave her camel toe a camel toe.

Mrs. Berns popped up next to me. "Going to the sock hop?"

That was it! Kennie, a woman in her late thirties, was dressed like she was living in the '50s.

"We're on the list," Kennie said, blinking her lined eyes.

I'd been so distracted by guessing her outfit that I hadn't noticed the worry lines in her face. "What list?"

"*The* list," she said, demonstrating that enunciating a word makes its meaning not one iota clearer.

Mrs. Berns was still eyeing Kennie's getup. "Surely not the best-dressed list?"

Kennie removed her coat and dropped it dramatically on the front counter, releasing the smell of fresh, crisp air. "The National Travel and Adventure Board releases a list every year of the ten best small towns to visit and the ten *worst* small towns to visit. Or should I say the best small towns to avoid?"

My stomach plopped down to my knees. I had a guess which of the two lists Battle Lake would land on.

"It has come to my attention, as mayor of this great town, that we are about to make the ten worst because"—and here she stopped to hurl an acid stare at me—"of all the dead bodies that keep appearing."

"*About* to?" I asked, hanging on to the sliver of hope. "We're not already on the naughty list?"

Kennie scowled. "The T and A Board"—here Mrs. Berns giggled, and rightfully so, I'd say—"is sending an inspector, as they do to every town being considered for either list. Since being demoted to the ten worst small towns *in the country* is going to tank our economy, they want to make sure they get it right. I imagine you already have your murder victim lined up for April?"

Through force of will, I managed to not glance at the note lying near the computer. For sure it had nothing to do with dead bodies. "I intend to get through April corpse-free," I declared, with more confidence than I felt. After all, like most people, I intended to get through *every* month corpse-free. I just wasn't as good as they were at sticking to this resolution.

Kennie nodded, studying me. "Be on your best behavior. If you cost Battle Lake its tourism industry, you might as well throw a Molotov cocktail through all the storefronts yourself. We can't survive without our summer crowds."

"Is that why you're dressed so conservatively?" Mrs. Berns asked.

Kennie glanced down at her outfit, her expression turning shifty. "Something like that. Did you get the headcheese I left?"

"That was you?" I asked.

"Yes." She preened, acting unduly proud of herself.

I quirked an eyebrow. "I thought headcheese was salty pig jelly." *Note to self: feature headcheese in next* Battle Lake Bites *column.* "Those looked like cheese balls rolled in parsley."

"Did you taste them?"

"Yup," Mrs. Berns said. "I found them delightful. Also, I unshirted."

Kennie nodded as if that were what she'd expected and reached for her coat.

"Not so fast," I said. "What was in those?"

"Part of my latest business plan. That's all I can tell you for now."

"Really?"

"Really. Sorry." She appeared a bit sheepish, which was a look I'd never seen on Kennie. I decided to take advantage of it. "Fine, don't tell us if you don't want to. It means you have to stay here with Mrs. Berns while I run an errand, though." That note was burning a hole in my brain.

Kennie slid into her coat. "No, thank you. I've got important business. Besides," she said, glancing around the library, "there's no one here. Mrs. Berns can handle it."

"She could, if she hadn't eaten a spiked cheese ball."

Mrs. Berns smiled at the memory.

Kennie frowned.

"So," I continued, "you can either tell me what's in those furry mold balls, or you can keep an eye on the Mad Deshirter for a half an hour."

"Fine." Kennie peeled off her coat resentfully. "Though I can't imagine what could go wrong in a public library in thirty minutes."

Chapter 5

Spring in Minnesota meant the Dairy Queen was opening for the season, the birds were high on fermented berries, and the leaf buds thrummed with a green so desperate to bloom that you could almost hear it. Historically, we usually received our last big snowstorm in March, and it buried us. Come April, the sun hinted and teased at the glorious summer to come, melting most of the snow into glassy crystals and slippery ice, shining bright enough some days to tan your cheeks and remind you why you'd put up with winter.

Not this year, though.

We were over halfway through April, and the weather was promising something darker.

I skated up Battle Lake's main street, sliding along the ice. Despite the perilous sidewalks, I was enjoying the sights and sounds of the town I'd moved to unwillingly but come to consider home. Harold, who co-owned the hardware store, waved as I passed. The baking-bread smells of the downtown bakery warmed my nose. The Shoreline up the road served eggs Benedict to die for, soon Stub's Dinner Club would open for the season and I could dig into a plate of fried halibut cheeks, Lionseed Bookstore had something for everyone (including a secret Narnia room for kids to read in), and my friends' Fortune Café served a honey-sweetened café miel that made me swoon.

Battle Lake was a good place to be. It certainly didn't deserve to end up on a ten-worst list. Kennie was right that the town bloomed in the summer, the influx of tourists feeding the economy through the leaner months. I wasn't to blame for all the dead bodies that had sprouted up since I'd moved here—at least, I hadn't *killed* any of them—but it was hard to separate them from me, given my unfortunate proximity to each corpse.

My mood sank the closer I got to the dentist's office. Not for the first time, I wondered if I should move back home, wherever that might be. I'd never return to my childhood home to live, and I didn't really have any friends left in Minneapolis, but if I ditched Battle Lake, at least I'd be shifting my bad luck somewhere else.

I felt that thought like a twist in the back of my throat. I loved Mrs. Berns, I loved this town, and I loved Johnny, even though our relationship had taken an uncomfortable turn. Specifically, it had started to bother me what a pushover Johnny was. I hated to admit that I needed someone to stand up to me on the regular, but *I did*. When he walked away from me in March, I realized he had a backbone, and I'd convinced him to give me one more shot. Thank everything that was holy. I loved Johnny, and it sure didn't hurt that he was as hot as a Greek god. I couldn't imagine moving somewhere he wasn't, but I didn't want to tank Battle Lake, either.

What to do?

I had no answers by the time I reached the dentist, only the knowledge that I hadn't had my teeth cleaned in more than a year. *Blergh.* I tugged the door open, the smell of rubbing alcohol and tooth dust washing over me.

The receptionist glanced up from behind the desk of the small office. "Hello!"

I immediately recognized her as a library regular, which could explain why Dr. Banks had so many books checked out under his name, but we'd never seen him in the library. If the receptionist was using his card, Mrs. Berns or I wouldn't necessarily have checked the name on it, only scanned the number, particularly if she visited often.

I glanced around. Dr. Banks's office was set up like most other small-town medical clinics, the walls a mellow brown paneling with a half dozen chairs rimming the edges. The main difference was here, the two coffee tables were suspiciously empty, not a *Newsweek* or *Highlights* to be seen.

"Hi," I said, depositing a smile on my face. I realized I had no idea what to say next.

She paused for a moment, then filled in the silence. "Do you have an appointment?"

I felt the note in my pocket. "No. My name is Mira James."

I waited for her to say "Murdery Mira?" but thankfully, she didn't. I continued, "I work over at the library?"

Her face lit up. "That's where I recognized you from! I come in all the time, me and the other receptionist. We check out books for the waiting room." She pointed at a basket tucked behind her stacked with books. "These are the latest. Haven't had a chance to put them out yet."

There was one question answered. "You leave the library books out in the waiting room?"

A shadow passed over her heart-shaped face. I put her in her late fifties, fond of home hair-color kits and professional manicures, judging by her brassy red hair and beautifully intricate, bejeweled fingernails. "Is that bad? Dr. Banks likes to encourage people to read while they're here. Plus, he's cheap." She chuckled at this. "Magazines cost money. Library books are free."

My shoulders relaxed for the first time since I'd entered the office. Something about her felt right. I pulled out the note and handed it over. "I found this in one of the books you checked out. It was returned last night or this morning. The book was *Minnesota's Hidden Treasures*. Any idea who put this in there?"

"My goodness." She stared at the note. Then she stared longer.

I read her name tag. "Anne?"

She started. "Sorry. That 'help' looks a bit scary, doesn't it?" She shook herself. "Probably just a doodle. Maybe it was already in the book when we checked it out? You know, half the time no one even opens them when they sit here."

That was a lot of excuses for probably just a doodle. "Do you recognize any of the names on it?"

She bit her lip. "Everyone knows John Guinn. He's a counselor here in town, looks like a rounder Sean Penn, the actor? I think he raised the funding to build the community center, come to think of it. John Guinn, not Sean Penn." She grimaced at her lame joke. "For sure he leads the teen program at the center."

That jibed with what Mrs. Berns had said. It also sent a wicked chill down my spine. I hated the possibility that a teenager may have written that note. "The other three names?"

She shoved the note back at me suddenly, as if it were crawling with bedbugs. "No. Sorry."

"Thank you." She wouldn't meet my eyes. "Is there anything else you want to tell me?"

She took an audible breath and planted a smile on her face. In her best receptionist voice, she finally looked me in the eye and said, "Be sure to floss!"

I backed toward the door. I didn't know whether she was simply quirky or something in the note had set her off, but I suddenly found myself not wanting to turn my back on her.

I gave her a thumbs-up and slipped out the door. If she couldn't tell me about the other names on the note, I knew two people who could.

Chapter 6

A brisk wind had picked up in the short time I'd been in Dr. Banks's office talking to Anne. I shoved my hands deep in my pockets, pausing to glance into the vacant storefront attached to the dentist's office—the one Dr. Banks had brought up in the chamber of commerce meeting, according to Mrs. Berns. The empty space had a FOR RENT sign in the window. I couldn't for the life of me remember what business used to be there, and when I pressed my face against the icy glass, I spotted no hints, only a wide-open room with two doors at the back about two-thirds in, likely one an office and the other a bathroom. The interior was painted a dirty white, or maybe that was the window.

I wiped it with the edge of my mitten and stuck my face back to the glass. Nope, it was a sad paint color. Other than a cardboard box and some papers in the middle of the floor, there was nothing else in view. Well, if Battle Lake got on the naughty list, this wouldn't be the only empty store.

I hung on to that dark thought on the walk to the Senior Sunset, feeling the weather press down much more firmly than it had since I'd left the library. My plan was to visit Curtis Poling. With any luck, I'd catch him during the lunchtime visiting hours. I stepped into the foyer, wriggling my nose. No matter how many times I visited, I'd never get used to that smell: spicy liniment, rubbing alcohol, and cloying dryer sheets. The scent was strong enough to cut through the most stuffed-up noses.

"Here to see Curtis?" asked the attendant behind the desk.

I smiled. Sometimes it was nice to be recognized. "Yeah, is he free?"

The attendant clicked through a computer screen. "Afraid not," he said, staring down his nose and through his bifocals as he read what he saw. "Curtis Poling, physical therapy from eleven to twelve."

My throat tightened. "Is he OK? What happened?" Surely somebody would have told me if Curtis had been hurt. Or maybe they wouldn't. Maybe they would blame me for it.

The attendant threw me a sympathetic look. "No, he's fine. We have a new director, and she's standing firm on the requirement that our clients exercise regularly. They have a choice between exercise class and physical therapy. Most people choose the tai chi, but some . . . some of the stubborn ones go with physical therapy."

I smiled. "Stubborn" would be too generous a word for Curtis. If he made up his mind about something, he sat on it like stone. His feelings about exercise were well known and perfectly summed up in one of his favorite sayings: "If God meant me to lift weights, he'd have made my hands heavier."

"Thank you," I said. "I'll stop back later."

Next stop: the *Battle Lake Recall*.

The paper was the second job I'd landed when I arrived in Battle Lake. They paid below poverty wages. What made it OK was that the owner, Ron Sims, didn't make much more himself, and he was the editor, publisher, printer, and chief reporter. His wife did the marketing—at least, when she wasn't making out with Ron in public like it was a calling. It wouldn't have been cute if they'd been in their teens, but since they were both pushing middle age, it was downright oogie.

Somebody must have talked to them about it, though, because the last few times I'd found myself in their company, they'd refrained from slipping each other the tongue. Fingers crossed they were still exercising some restraint.

The newspaper office was only three blocks from the nursing home. In Battle Lake, everything was a short walk away. I yanked open the door, inhaling the scent of ink and paper. Next to the smell of a library, the newspaper's was my favorite.

"James," Ron grunted by way of greeting.

He must have spotted me walking past the window. I stepped into the all-purpose space, one big room featuring a front counter, Ron's desk behind it, and behind that, a framed map of Battle Lake nailed to the wall. The rest was filing cabinets, stacks of newspapers, and a perennially overflowing trash basket. I wouldn't call it welcoming, but it got the job done.

Sorta like Ron.

"How goes it?" I asked, smiling because I knew it annoyed him.

He was circling something on a proof page. "You should be at work."

"But I also work here."

That warranted me a glare. "You should be at the library."

"Mrs. Berns and Kennie are both watching it. It'll be fine."

He snorted.

I ignored it. "I'm here because I found a note in one of the returned library books, and I want to know if you recognize any of the names on it."

This got his full attention. He loved solving puzzles. I suspected he would be disappointed in this one.

He squinted to read the slip of paper I handed to him. "Well, of course we know Lartel McManus."

We both shuddered. Lartel may have disappeared, but he'd left some disturbing information behind.

"No idea what these numbers represent," Ron continued, "but Guinn is a local guy. He's not in my social circle"—credit me here for not laughing outright, as Ron's social circle was more like a dot—"but I've only heard good things about him. Has his own counseling office, spearheaded the opening of the community center, plus still volunteers at it."

That squared with what I'd learned so far. "The other two?"

29

"I don't know the name Jefferson Penetal, but assuming the *OT* refers to the town of Otter Tail or Otter Tail County, he's from this region. Rhoda's on the microfiche right now, but you can come back later and look them up. As to the fourth name?" He raised an eyebrow, and we locked eyes. "That's your dad."

I felt lightheaded. I'd assumed Ron knew my history. I just hadn't thought he had it so handy. "Maybe."

He tapped the *PV.* "Not many locations have this abbreviation."

"It might not be a location." I knew I was being petulant. I just didn't know how to stop.

He handed back the note. "It might not be. Like I said, you can stop by later and look up the names if you like."

Was that a note of pity in his voice? I preferred the gruff, potbellied, emotion-free man I was used to. Sympathy made me feel things. "Thanks. I might do that."

It was a good idea, and nice of him to offer. I'd take him up on it if I couldn't uncover what I was looking for on TrackerSearch, the online database I'd signed up for when I'd begun pursuing my PI license.

Ron liked goodbyes only a hair more than he liked hellos, so I was halfway out the door when he called me back in.

"Yeah?" I asked. I'd gotten myself mentally prepared to step into the April chill, and now all that work was wasted.

"Where's my recipe column?"

An image of a big, gloopy gray pan of headcheese jiggled across my brain. "Almost ready."

Come to think of it, it was unusual I hadn't run that recipe yet. Items like "Phony Abalone" (chicken soaked in clam juice, which was more expensive than simply buying fish), "Deer Pie" (venison and Velveeta), and "Deep-Fried Skunks" had been my most popular columns. Pig parts suspended in salty gelatin were destined to go gangbusters.

"I want a dessert, too," he said.

I didn't know if he was speaking for himself or for the column. I'd run multi-recipe features around the holidays, but I didn't want him to think he'd be getting free work on the regular. "If you're asking me for two recipes, you need to pay me twice as much."

His eyes narrowed. "I'll pay you twenty-five percent more."

I tried to math it but figured that would be more work than finding some Battle Lake–themed dessert online, swapping out a few ingredients, and slapping on a new name. "OK. Anything else?"

"Matter of fact," he said, turning the sheet he'd been marking up toward me. It was an early draft of an article he'd written, titled "Barry Janston Billboard to Be Built in Battle Lake."

"Alliterate much?"

Ron did not deign to respond. "Senator Janston is a Battle Lake native. The chamber of commerce is trying to improve our image for reasons I do not know." He raised both eyebrows this time, inviting me to fill in the details. If he didn't know about the list, though, and specifically how my involuntary corpse-finding was ruining our national reputation, I wasn't going to tell him.

I kept my eyes innocent and my mouth closed.

He continued, watching me suspiciously the whole while. "Unfortunately, since writing this draft, it's come to my attention that Senator Janston is under investigation by the Minnesota House Ethics Committee."

My ears perked up. Someone else to be the bad guy in town! Plus, what a juicy article that would be. "And you want me to research it and write a piece on it?"

"No." He shook his head. "There's been Bigfoot sightings seven miles northwest of town, near Mosquito Lake. I want you to find out what that's about."

If that didn't sum up my Battle Lake experience, I didn't know what did. "So why'd you tell me about the Janston deal?"

"In case you'd spill why the chamber is so itchy to erect this billboard and slap a new shine on the town. Kennie stomped by the window a half an hour ago. Saw her storm into the library and figured you knew."

Small towns. But just because I knew didn't mean I had to tell. "A two-recipe column, Bigfoot research"—good Christ, that sounded even more foolish spoken aloud—"anything else you need?"

Ron scratched his arm. "Nope. Say hi to Johnny for me."

I tipped my chin. That was the second time today someone had mentioned Johnny. It hadn't been unusual coming from Mrs. Berns, but Ron never spoke about my personal life. "What do you know?"

"Enough to get me in trouble, not enough to make me rich." He'd returned his focus to the article, flipping it back around to face him.

I knew him well enough. Our conversation was over.

I prepped myself for the cold all over again, the uncomfortable breath of a hunch tickling my neck. Johnny was up to something. My birthday was more than a month away, so my best guess was a marriage proposal or an intervention was coming my way, and I didn't know which was worse. We loved each other and had been in a committed relationship for six months, more or less. OK, less, especially taking into account our March blip. I'd always been a flight risk when it came to guys, and I'd probably broken us up more times than months we'd been dating. It was worth it with him, though, because he was so *good*, even if he was missing the bad-boy edge I'd found so damn attractive in past boyfriends.

That probably left an intervention. I'd dumped out all my liquor shortly after moving to town, determined to give myself a fresh start. Then I discovered one dead body, then another. Vodka and Nut Goodies had gotten me through. I pinched my belly through my parka. I'd probably been indulging a bit too much in both, but enough for an intervention?

Pah.

I had real issues to worry about.

Mainly, the note in my pocket was related to my dad. I felt it in my gut. I also suspected that if I kept digging, I wouldn't like what I found.

It might be best to simply return to work and forget about the note.

Johnny and I had a date planned tonight. I could spill all about Mrs. Berns boobing up the library, the note, my visit to the dentist, and Johnny and I could talk it through. At the end, like adults, we'd discuss where our relationship was going.

It was a good plan.

Right?

Chapter 7

"You look beautiful."

Johnny murmuring those sweet words still sent delicious tingles to my shady bits. How could it not? He was a Midwestern Adonis. Eyes so blue I wouldn't have been surprised to see a cloud float across them, shaggy blond hair that curled at his neck in a retro, '70s-style feathered cut. Full lips that curved soft and slow and hid the cleverest tongue . . . I snapped myself back to attention.

"Thank you," I said.

After work, I'd stopped at home long enough to feed Luna, the sweet German shepherd mix I was technically dog-sitting but who felt like family, and Tiger Pop, my asshole cat that I'd throw myself in front of a bus to save. They were happy to see me. I let Luna out after she ate, played with Tiger Pop, swapped out my work blouse for a faded Green Bay Packers T-shirt and my black dress pants for a faded pair of jeans that fit me like a butt-hugging glove, glided on some lip gloss, brushed my hair, and dashed over to Johnny's.

He'd folded me into his arms as I stepped into his house and told me I was beautiful. Did I mention he smelled like vanilla and sandalwood? The guy was a big human man-cookie.

"How was work?" he asked.

Snuggling into his broad, muscled chest, I considered my options:

1. *Good, except I think Mrs. Berns ate Kennie's cheese and got high and showed her boobies to a stranger. Also, I found a note that may connect to my dad—you know, the guy who taught me to not trust anyone? It seemed to be nothing but trouble, so I shoved it into the library junk drawer as soon as I got back from asking Ron what he knew about it. I spent the rest of my day at work day-dreaming about our date, but now that I'm here, I want to have a serious, lengthy talk about our relationship, all right?*
2. *Good, except Mrs. Berns wasn't feeling well—she was back to herself after lunch—and I found out the local dentist stocks his waiting room with library books, and isn't that weird?*
3. *Fine. How was yours?*

Clearly, I had only one real choice.

"Fine. How was yours?"

Honest vulnerability was not my strong suit. Sue me.

Johnny pulled back and studied my face. I thought I'd pitched my voice neutral, but apparently not. At least he knew me well enough not to ask a follow-up question. Was it a pushover move on his part, an avoidance of conflict? Hard to care when his eyes dropped to my mouth like that, ramping up the tingling from my toes to the tippy-top of my head. I tilted my chin for easy access to my lips and welcomed the full-body fireworks when his mouth met mine. We'd never had a bad kiss—no accidental teeth clacking, or one person open-mouthed while the other thought it was going to be a peck, no accidental smacking noises—which was astonishing given that I'd spent the first six months of interaction with him dork-morphing in his presence.

You see, normally guys like Johnny did not end up with women like me. Johnny'd grown up with two parents who loved him deeply. I'm sure they had their flaws, but from what Johnny had shared, they were stable, kind, and affectionate. He'd lost his father last summer, but he and his mom still had the best relationship, joking and sweet, and they both demonstrated the full range of human feelings.

Me, not so much. Growing up in an alcoholic's house meant my homelife always had to be a secret. When I would try to talk to my mom about my dad's out-of-control drinking and general creepiness, she'd tell me I was being dramatic. I soon learned to turn off my feelings, then simply stopped feeling anything on a lower frequency than anger. When I moved to the Cities, I perfected that behavior.

As a result of emotional isolation, my dating life had mostly consisted of being a human garage for guys to park their problems in. I blamed my parents for modeling that particular soul-sucking brand of relationship. Putting my choices on their shoulders worked for the first few years of my adult life. After that, I was old enough to know better and had nobody to blame but myself.

Enter Johnny, openhearted, full of all sorts of healthy emotions and not afraid to express them, sexy as hell, and interested in *me*. To say I didn't know what to do with all that was an understatement. I was like a monkey who'd been gifted a NASA computer. I'd push buttons, tap things, shake it, then jump back, scared and hooting, to watch what happened. Sometimes it was fine. Other times I completely messed things up. Mostly, I just waited for Johnny to realize I was half-feral and dump me. I hoped he wouldn't, of course, even though I wasn't ready to marry him. Or have him lead an intervention against me.

I pulled back. "Smells delicious in here. When's supper?"

He kept his hungry eyes on my mouth. When he'd invited me over for tonight's dinner date, he'd promised homemade Tater Tot hotdish— that's what Minnesota love looks like, folks—with a side of green beans and Caesar salad.

I was starving, but when in Rome . . . I leaped up to wrap my legs around Johnny's hips and let him carry me over to the couch, cupping my bottom. Once we reached the sofa, he laid me on my back and stood over me, yanking off his shirt.

Yum.

The corded veins in his arms and his sculpted chest did something for me, something warm and delectable, every time I was lucky enough to be in their presence. His chest had only a light dusting of hair, and it led down to the beautiful vee of his hip bones, which themselves pointed down to the good stuff, like God had created this perfect man and been thoughtful enough to plant directions right on his body: *go here.*

I might have moaned a little. I wiggled my fingers in a *gimme gimme* gesture, reaching for Johnny as he balanced a knee on the couch next to me. He smiled, mouth tilting, his blue stare walking all over me, teasing me. When he was done ravishing me with his eyes, he placed his strong hand, palm open, on his chest. It was a careless gesture, just the world's most beautiful man touching himself in a casual, achingly masculine way. He knew that drove me crazy.

I for sure moaned this time.

At the same time, my muscles tensed, preparing to launch me off the sofa and onto his body like one of those *Alien* Facehuggers. Not sexy, but sometimes a gal had to do what she had to do. Because all that great surface stuff that was immediately apparent when you first met Johnny? His kindness, patience, sense of humor? It was nothing to how face-meltingly *good* he was behind closed doors.

I had a sense that tonight was going to be even hotter than the usual. Maybe it was the tension of the day needing a release, or the way Johnny was looking at me like I was a T-bone steak and he a starving cartoon lion, or the fact that it had been more than a week since we'd had time for each other, and we were *overdue.*

In any case, my whole body was an inch off the couch, en route to Johnny, when the door pounding began.

I flinched and dropped back onto the couch.

I'm sure my expression shifted from *I'm ready* to *what the hell.*

Chapter 8

Johnny grabbed for his shirt and turned to answer the knock. This was not the sort of banging one ignored. I stood and ran my fingers through my love-tangled hair, my heart thudding sickly in my chest. I should never have let my guard down. If losing Jed had taught me anything, it was that good things didn't last.

Johnny dragged the door open and cold air whooshed in.

There stood Gary Wohnt, Battle Lake police chief, former lover to Kennie Rogers, and my primary nemesis. While it wasn't my fault that dead bodies kept popping up around me, Gary had a different opinion. I had a hunch he'd love to nail me with one of the murders and was biding his time until that glorious (for him) day. It meant I avoided him when I could and was on edge when I couldn't. That uneasiness was made more difficult because Gary had gone from being a greasy-haired, doughy grump with a Carmex addiction to a sleek, ink-eyed hottie.

"What is it?" Johnny asked.

Gary glanced over Johnny's shoulder, his eyes landing on me, his expression cop-inscrutable. "Can I come in?"

My stomach, which had been quivering a couple inches above its usual position, crashed to the floor.

"Tell us why you're here," I demanded. Or, I meant to demand, but it came out as a squeak. Who else could I lose?

Was that a flash of sympathy I caught in Gary's eyes? Unlikely.

"No one's hurt," he said. "There's been an emergency at the library."

My brain screeched to a halt like it had been fleeing the scene before discovering something interesting to hang around for. "Library emergency?" That's one of those phrases that didn't seem to have a place in the world, like "unbiased opinion" and "liquid gas" (though that last one always made Mrs. Berns giggle).

"Yes," Gary said, refusing to elaborate, his stone-cut cheekbones making him appear incredibly serious. "I need you to come with me."

"I'll come, too," Johnny said, reaching for his jacket.

"No," Gary said. One word, a clear command.

Johnny kept his hand outstretched, but everything else about his posture changed. Somehow, without visibly moving, he became strutty. "She's my girlfriend. I'm coming with."

I held my breath. If there was anything I'd change about Johnny—and lord knew I had no right to expect him to alter anything—there it was: I wanted him to be more assertive in moments just like this. Not testosterone-poisoned, not dumb-edgy like Bad Brad, the boyfriend I'd caught cheating in Minneapolis, not *not*-Johnny. Just a little less consistently reasonable. Maybe not following every rule. Possibly instigating a knockdown, drag-out fight for me, sort of like we were in an old-time Western. (This last one implied there would be someone else interested in me, so I got it was a long shot.)

Was this going to be the moment Johnny revealed his edge? If so, that would make him officially perfect. I held my breath, waiting, hoping he would stand up to Gary.

I imagined Gary was waiting, too. The two of them were staging a stare down.

After a few charged seconds, to my great disappointment, Johnny's hand dropped from his coat.

"Take good care of her," he said.

Gary set his jaw by way of answer, sending a ripple up his muscled cheek. His eyes glinted with something uncomfortable, and for the first time since I'd known him, I wished he were wearing his mirrored sunglasses.

I realized I hadn't yet removed my own jacket. Johnny and I had progressed straight from the front door to make-out land. My legs were shaky, all of me feeling discombobulated, but I forced myself toward Gary, pausing to squeeze Johnny's hand. "I'll come back after we're done."

It seemed to take effort for him to meet my eyes. "Sure," he said.

Was he wishing he'd reacted differently, too?

I followed Gary to his car, wondering what the hell had just happened.

Chapter 9

Riding in the car with Gary felt like the drive home after babysitting for a new family. It was always the dad who drove, and it was always, always awkward. You didn't know what kind of person he was, what level of conversation he expected, and if he was going to go full weirdo on you. I bit the inside of my cheek and sat on my hands to distract from the masculine, spicy smell of Gary and to keep myself from filling the chilled air with mindless chatter.

I've never sat in the front seat of a police car before! What happened at the library? Oh hey, and what's up between you and Johnny? Can I drive? Better yet, can I get out of the car and run alongside it?

Thank god it was a short jaunt.

Gary steered his cruiser into the library's dimly lit parking lot, only a sputtering halogen illuminating it. No other police cars—no cars at all—were in the lot. Nothing appeared out of place. My very cells constricted as I turned to Gary. Other than a brief detour to save my life recently, he'd made no secret of how he despised me. Had he driven me here to frame me?

I realized I was white knuckling the inside door handle. "Why did you bring me here?"

He pulled all the way into the lot, facing his headlights at the front door, and pointed.

I'd been staring at his sharp outline. Now, as I moved my focus to the front door, it was clear why he'd brought me. The glass panel running the length of the steel door was shattered. It was tempered, so it had fallen like diamonds onto the ground, glittering in Gary's headlights.

I leaped out of the car, Gary on my heels.

"Let me go first," he said.

I stopped, my breath pluming in the frigid night air. "You haven't gone in yet?"

He'd already stepped in front of me. His shoulders seemed to broaden. "Of course I went in. It was empty. Someone may have returned since I got you."

I had a thought. Gary'd found me at Johnny's, a two-minute drive from the library. Where else had he looked? "Did you go to my house?"

He tugged open the unlocked door. "I saw your car outside of Johnny's on patrol. Same way I saw the library had been broken into."

That set me on my heels. It was a whole side of Gary's life I'd never thought much about. He spent hours cruising around Battle Lake, knowing who was where, doing what. *Huh.* The things he must have seen.

I followed behind, crunching over the glass splinters, snapping on the light when I entered. Gary turned, a scowl on his face, saw I was wearing mittens, and strode to the center of the room. I held back my laugh. Battle Lake's in-house fingerprinting technology hadn't advanced beyond two overhead projectors side by side, each holding a slide of a fingerprint. He could've sent materials off to the county seat, I guessed, but a break-in would not take priority.

"Anything missing?" he asked.

My sassy monologue fell away. Maybe not missing, but *trashed.* My hand went to my mouth to hold back the sob.

"What is it?"

I supposed if you didn't know about Jed's altar, you'd hardly notice it. The shark was still perched on top, but most everything else had been pushed off. His glass sea creatures were on the ground, one of them crushed into powder. "That wasn't like that when I left."

Gary strode toward the altar. He shined his flashlight under the tablecloth laid across it, picked up the now-two-tentacled glass octopus, crouched to study the other detritus. He paused at a photo of Jed. His face tightened. Jed had been a harmless pothead, a small-town handyman with a huge heart. Kids and old people had loved him. Gary, not so much. He hadn't stopped in the library since I'd erected the altar.

"Something to honor Jedediah Heike?"

"Yes." I tensed, waiting for the ridicule.

Gary only sighed and stood. "As far as I can tell, this is the only spot in the library that's been disrupted. Can you confirm?"

I hurried to the back room, peeked into the bathrooms, even opened the break room fridge and pretended to glance at the condiment bottles and cheese-ball box, stalling to make sense of this. Why in the world would someone break into the library to hurt Jed's altar? Not everyone loved him as much as I had, but he hadn't had a true enemy in the world. He was simply too kind.

I walked to the only place I hadn't checked: behind the front desk. That was all clear, too. "Everything else looks good," I said, confusion in my voice.

"Anything worth money on that altar?"

"Trinkets, photos, an old Mickey Mouse watch his mom left. There wasn't anything there that—" My breath caught. I'd been about to say "was worth anything," but that clearly wasn't true. Something on the table had been worth a great deal to someone. I knew because it was no longer there.

Minnesota's Hidden Treasures.

The book in which the note had been hidden.

I'd set it down on Jed's altar and forgotten to reshelve it.

"There wasn't anything there that was what?" Gary asked, his head tilted, eyes sharp.

I was itching like a mad dog to dash to the junk drawer and see if the note was still there, but the last thing I needed was a suspicious Gary

Wohnt. If the note meant something, he'd take it from me. If it meant nothing, I'd look like a fool.

"That you couldn't buy at a dollar store," I said. "It was bits and pieces to remember Jed by, only valuable to those of us who loved him." My voice was defiant at the end, which might have been unfair. As a police officer, Gary wasn't in a position to admire guys who loved to get high every now and again. OK, every now.

Gary's eyebrows drew down over his night-dark eyes. He probably guessed I was lying, or maybe suspicious was his default state. He kept his laser glare focused on me. I fought not to confess. Something about being around law enforcement filled me with the compulsion to share every bad thing I'd ever done . . . and some things I hadn't.

"Anything else you want to tell me?" he asked.

"I don't always wash my hands after I pee." It all came out as a rush, sounding like a single word. *IdontalwayswashmyhandsafterIpee.*

His mouth twitched. "Anything about what might be missing from this table?"

"I think there was a book on it," I said, remembering a hot second too late that the best lie to serve up was always a hot slice of the truth. "It was one of the returns from today. I may have left it on the table and forgotten about it. I'll check the shelves."

I scurried to nonfiction, certain it wouldn't be there, but needing to escape Gary's tractor truth beam before I confessed that I truly liked the taste of Spam and also once had had an R-rated dream featuring Gary, Ronald McDonald, and David Boreanaz from *Buffy the Vampire Slayer.*

"Not here!" I warbled from the back before dashing to the front computer.

Gary was watching me, immobile.

"Let me make sure it wasn't checked out again." I knew it hadn't been, but I couldn't think of another way to reach the front counter. I flicked on the computer and opened the top drawer at the same time. To my great relief, the note was still there.

Mark James (PV—12)
Lartel McManus (OT—7)
John Guinn (OT—23)
Jefferson Penetal (OT—1)

HELP

I sneaked a glance at Gary, who was watching me as implacably as ever. "The computer takes a moment to fire up," I said. "While we're waiting, what's the plan on the window?"

"Glass company is on the way," he said.

Good. The cold air was circulating. "How'd they break the glass?"

Gary stopped staring at me to glance at the window. I used the opportunity to sneak the note out of the drawer and into my back jeans pocket.

"If they're professionals, they had a glass-breaking tool. If it was vandals, a broken spark plug glued to the head of a hammer would have done the trick."

I was impressed. Also, I was surprised that Gary had spoken that many words to me in a row, none of them angry. I typed *Minnesota's Hidden Treasures* into the search screen that had popped up and discovered what I already knew. "The book wasn't checked out again. Somebody must really be dying to read it."

Gary did not return the weak smile I flashed him. "They went through a lot of trouble to get a single book," he said gruffly.

My thoughts exactly, sir. "A single book that I know of. There might be more missing. Mrs. Berns and I'll do a thorough inventory tomorrow morning." I turned off the computer, careful to keep my voice neutral. "I'm beat. Anything else you need me here for?"

He was quiet a moment too long.

"No," he finally said. "I'll give you a ride home."

Home, not Johnny's. An odd word choice, but I suddenly really *was* feeling beat. "No, thanks," I said. "I'll walk back to Johnny's. If you drive me, that leaves the library open and unguarded, and I don't want that."

He didn't argue, and so I walked out.

The part about not wanting to leave the library exposed was true. The part about going directly to Johnny's? A total fib. Now that I knew my instincts had been right about the note meaning something, it was game on.

Chapter 10

Battle Lake at 10:00 p.m. on a Monday was quiet and ice-scented. Johnny's house was a fifteen-minute walk north. Rather than head straight there, I turned east, toward the water tower. The newspaper office was closed, so I couldn't scroll through the microfiche searching for pre-internet mentions of the men named in the note. The library was the only place I had access to a computer and internet, and no way could I hop on TrackerSearch with Gary waiting around for the glass repair people.

That left old-school sleuthing and one really long shot.

The rhythm of sliding along the ice, watching my feet, eased my brain. That's the only explanation for why, as I tried to puzzle out the note's possible meanings, an unwanted thought popped into my head: *Can I spend the rest of my life with a guy with no edges?* I tried to smush that idea back into its dark hole, but it just wouldn't be suppressed. Johnny was a good man, no doubt. In fact, he was *too* good. Damn near perfect. While that sounded great in theory, in reality, it could be a burden. He wasn't messy, emotionally or physically; he was faithful, sexy, thoughtful. Like a damn love robot, almost.

In fact, he'd never even double-tapped me. You know the double-tap. Where a guy does the mean thing, and then gets mad at you because you were hurt by the mean thing?

Tap tap.

Every guy I'd ever dated had done it, as if somehow *they* were the victim of their own crappy behavior. Expert-level gaslighting. The worst part was, usually I fell for it. Bad Brad had been a wizard in that area. I'd tell him he was welcome to take beers out of my fridge, but he needed to write it on the grocery list if he drank the last one. He'd never remember, and when I'd remind him, he'd act all bummed out and tell me he felt criticized.

So, *tap, I drank all your beer and didn't add it to the grocery list,* and *tap, I'm really hurt you're not OK with that.* He was so convincing that I ended up apologizing nearly every time he did something rude. I bet if I'd told him that I'd caught him cheating on me, he'd have acted appalled that I'd invaded his privacy.

Good thing I never did tell him, at least not right away. Instead, I'd removed the wheel screws from his bike.

I'd grown since then. Enough that I couldn't believe I'd been second-guessing Johnny. I smacked my own forehead. *If you find a good person, keep 'em,* Mrs. Berns always told me, and there was no better person than Johnny. So what if he never did anything reckless? What was the big deal if he let Gary act all weird around me? I was irrational enough for the both of us, and I didn't need anyone to fight my fights.

I wiped my mittens together just like they did in the movies, washing my hands of those banana pants thoughts. I was even beginning to smile when a clanging and then a rustling to my right zinged the baby hairs on the back of my neck. I'd been penguin-walking under a streetlamp, nearly at my destination, but I instinctively dived into the winter shrubbery. Nobody honest was out this late on a weeknight, not in the residential area of Battle Lake.

(I'm not honest, so I knew this for a fact.)

My pulse drummed in my ears. The noise had come from behind a dark home on the other side of the street. I squinted to make out the single set of footprints in the crusty snow alongside the house. When my eyesight adjusted, I saw more than footprints. There was a *man*, and he was leaning into a garbage bin!

We didn't have many transient people pass through, especially in winter, but if he was one of them, he needed help. I began to stand, intending to call out to him, when my foot slipped on a patch of ice. I landed smack on my bumper, an involuntary *oof* leaving my lips.

I scrambled to my knees and peered through the bushes. The man had stepped into the light and was peering straight at the shrubbery I hid behind. At least, I hoped they were concealing me, because I immediately recognized him, and I didn't think he was homeless.

Chapter 11

The twirly-mustached man who'd stopped by the library this morning, the one Mrs. Berns had flashed, appeared to be staring right at me. I couldn't make out his expression, but the judgmental stance was gone, replaced by an alert, twitchy posture, like a prairie dog sniffing the air for prey.

I was trying to figure out whether to stand or stay hidden when he made the decision for me and scooted off toward Main Street, glancing over his shoulder once. I watched him go, trying to remember what he'd said that morning. It was difficult to get past the image of Mrs. Berns's serene smile above her boobs and his offended face, but I finally did.

I'm new to town.

That was it. And I didn't think that was his own garbage he'd been digging in. If it had been, he would have kept at it or gone into his house, not fled. I stood, brushing off my knees and my rump. *You can't trust people these days,* I thought, as I stepped out from my hiding place.

Kennie's pink house was just ahead.

It was a long shot stopping by her place, and not only because of the hour, or because it was Kennie. I didn't know if she'd have what I was looking for.

Lartel McManus had originally hired me to work at the library, nearly a year ago. He'd taken off once he'd trained me. While he was away, one of the dark things I discovered in his house included the most epic, skin-crawling shrine to our very own Kennie Rogers. He'd bought hundreds of dolls that looked like a younger version of her back in high school, which was when the two of them had met. He'd been a coach, she a cheerleader.

Then he'd created dioramas featuring the doll-her.

I shuddered, remembering that incident.

The bank that had financed Lartel's mortgage had eventually seized, and then sold, his house. I hadn't thought about it, or its contents, much since then. But Kennie loved anything that centered around her. What if she'd saved some of Lartel's belongings? And what if, among his possessions, I found another note, some scrap of paper, some clue that shed light on the note with his name on it that had fallen out of *Minnesota's Hidden Treasures*?

Like I said, a long shot.

But better than no shot at all.

Kennie's living room light was on. My shoulders relaxed in relief. I didn't know I'd been banking so much on this. I strode up her sidewalk, ignoring the pink flamingos wearing red-and-white-striped scarves lining the walk, just as I ignored the flagrant pink paint of her home.

It was Kennie.

I drew a deep breath on her doorstep. I needed to construct a lie that explained why I was suddenly interested in whether she'd secreted some of Lartel's stuff, a lie that let her know I thought it was fine if she had. I waited three beats. Nothing came to mind. Oh well. Some of my best lies had been born of desperation.

Knock knock.

"Come in!"

My breath caught. I had gravely misjudged the situation, because if I wasn't sorely mistaken, that was Bad Brad's voice coming from the other side of the door.

Chapter 12

I mentioned Brad'd moved to Battle Lake, didn't I?

Came to town to perform with his old band in July and fell in love with the place. He'd since formed a new band, Iron Steel ("twice the metal!"), that hadn't really taken off. Last I'd heard, he'd gone into business with Kennie, both aboveboard business and *monkey business*.

Did I want to open the door?

No, I did not.

Sigh.

But in for a penny.

I twisted the knob and stepped into the light and warmth. "Hi, Brad. I'm here to—sweet Jesus!"

I slammed my eyelids closed, but it was too late. The image was imprinted on the inside of them, upside down and backward: Brad, naked save for a frilly white apron that barely covered Brad Junior, pushing a vintage Hoover upright vacuum. It was not turned on. His expression had been expectant.

What had I walked into?

The door slammed closed behind me. My eyelids flew open.

"Don't let all the heat out," Brad said nonchalantly, as if I couldn't see the outline of his Don Johnson through the apron's thin fabric.

I shielded my eyes. Was I giving off some get-naked vibe? If so, I needed to do a better job choosing my company. "Can you put something on?"

Brad glanced down. "I have something on."

"How about pants? Can you put on pants?" The table behind him was set with two wineglasses, an open bottle of Boone's Farm Strawberry Hill nearby, decanting.

I'd made a horrible, terrible, no-good, lousy decision coming here. I stepped back, grappling for the doorknob. I felt its coolness in my grip just as a knock resonated against the door.

Brad pushed me aside and straightened his hair before pitching his voice high and calling out, "Who is it?"

"Ackley salesman," grunted a deep voice from the other side.

I recognized that voice. I was done for.

I'd walked right into a grown-up game between Bad Brad and Kennie.

It was my turn to push Brad aside. I ripped open the door. Kennie stood on the other side, sure enough, wearing a fedora and a trench coat and holding a scuffed briefcase. Her expression went from surprised to crafty to annoyed.

"Why are you in my house?" she asked.

I didn't even have the patience to lie. "Do you have any of Lartel's things stored here?"

She opened her mouth to protest, but then her eyes snagged on Bad Brad's down below. If I was not mistaken, his worm was stirring. *What is in the water in this town??* I could tell from Kennie's eager expression that she very soon would not have time for me.

I smacked my hands together, drawing their attention to me.

"I need to go through Lartel's stuff. If you point me toward it, I'll get out of your hair."

Ack. Terrible choice of words. Well, there it was.

Kennie nodded toward the rear of her house. "Attic. There's a string that'll release the steps. Light switch is at the top right once you're up there. If the couch is rocking, don't come knocking."

With that, she slammed the door shut behind her and launched herself at Bad Brad.

I stuffed my fingers in my ears and lalalala'd all the way to the back hallway, marveling at the framed photos of her that lined the walls.

Some were graduation pictures—high school and college, by the looks of them—many were glamour shots, others were stills from her beauty queen days, but she was alone in every single one. Probably she didn't want to share the attention, but it still made me a little sad for her.

I'd never been this deep into Kennie's house. I winced again at my choice of words. Why did I have to stop by tonight? More importantly, why had these two decided to hook up? There must have been ten years and a whole set of values between them. Well, at least a pair of values.

Scratch that—they actually made a decent couple, the more I thought about it. What was an age difference between adults? They were both creative. They clearly shared some chemistry. If they wanted their fun, I was in no position to stop them.

I just didn't want to hear it.

I located the attic rope and yanked it to release the stairs.

It was cool, the way they dropped down. Wishing I'd brought a flashlight, I stepped on the first, and then the second step. Where had Kennie said the light switch would be? Top right once I reached the attic level. But right of what?

My head rose above the ceiling. I peered around and could only make out dim, lumpy shapes. The place smelled like old books, with a hint of eucalyptus. A cold weight settled in my stomach at the thought of walking into an unfamiliar dark space. I'd seen a lot I hadn't meant to this past year, and the creepiest had to do with Lartel McManus, whose belongings I was about to paw through. I shuddered, not sure if I should go forward. But then I heard Kennie giggle and Bad Brad bark, and I rushed up the rest of the stairs, felt for the switch, and found it exactly where Kennie had promised.

I flicked it on.

Next to the switch stood a man, staring at me, smiling.

My blood curdled.

My mouth opened in a Valkyrie scream as I launched myself toward him.

Chapter 13

I realized he was a life-size cardboard cutout halfway there.

It took until I was on top of him to realize he was Captain Jean-Luc Picard of the starship *Enterprise*. I didn't know what he was doing in Kennie's attic, but for once, I was on board with her indulgence. Jean-Luc was the best of the captains.

I'd bent him in half on impact, and sturdy as ever, he'd bounced back like a champ.

"Sorry, Captain," I said, patting him as I got my breathing under control. Once calmed, I scanned the attic. It was surprisingly orderly, featuring labeled cardboard boxes and Rubbermaid bins stacked on top of each other in neat rows. There was just enough room to walk on the plywood between them. I took the first row.

I recognized many of the labels as the names of Kennie's failed businesses: COME AGAIN USED MARITAL AIDS, COFFIN TABLES, GUERILLA BIKINI WAXES, MINNESOTA PHONE SEX. That made up the first row. The second was devoted to her past: BABY PICTURES, YEARBOOKS, BEAUTY PAGEANT DRESSES. I tamped down the desire to peek inside and see who Kennie used to be.

I hit pay dirt in the third aisle, where each box featured a man's name. I scanned them until I hit pay dirt: Lartel McManus. I slid the bin to the floor and snapped off the lid, my heart thunking against my rib cage. The top layer was the Kennie dolls I'd discovered on the second floor of Lartel's home. Touching them sent a sick tremor through me. The dolls were intimately connected to the first murder I'd solved back in May.

I stacked all fifteen dolls into a neat pile so I could dig into the reams of paper underneath. Most of them had BATTLE LAKE PUBLIC LIBRARY or CITY OF BATTLE LAKE: OFFICIAL BUSINESS stamped at the top. I was beginning to smell a snipe hunt when I reached the bottom of the bin. A single folder remained, faded light blue with age.

I lifted it out.

Inside, I found the first personal paperwork I'd come across: Lartel's mortgage, receipts and other paid bills, and some loose notes that didn't seem like much.

A bone-deep tiredness overcame me. What in hell's bells was I doing hanging out in Kennie Rogers's attic with Captain Jean-Luc Picard, trying to forge some impossible connection between a note found in a book and my long-dead father? So what if someone had broken into the library and stolen that book? It could've been a coincidence. Or, since I'd shown Anne the receptionist the note only a few hours before the library was broken into, it maybe belonged to her, and she wanted it back for some personal, not criminal, reason. In any case, only an unhinged person would have discovered that note and somehow ended up in Kennie Rogers's attic all in the same day.

April fools, indeed.

I began stacking the paperwork back inside its bin, though I kept the folder out. It made me feel less like I'd wasted my time. I stacked the creepy dolls on top of the paperwork, made sure they were all situated respectfully and comfortably (it's bad luck to be mean to dolls or birds because they are both inherently sinister and will hunt you down if you do them wrong), snapped the lid back on the bin, and hoisted it onto its stack.

Tucking the folder under my arm, I blew Jean-Luc a kiss before flicking off the light and making my way down the steep stairs.

"Kennie," I called out as I shoved the steps back into the ceiling, "I'm taking a folder I found in Lartel's bin. Is that OK?"

I took the muffled *yes* coming from the bedroom as an affirmation and made my way into the chill, lonely night. The sky overhead was starless, a tight weave of clouds obscuring all but the outline of the nearly full moon.

"Mira, you are the biggest idiot," I said, wrapping my arms around myself. The sidewalks were slippery, so I watched my footing as I neared downtown. Sounds of laughter and honky-tonk emanated out of the Rusty Nail. I considered stepping inside for a beer, but the last time I'd been in the Nail, it had been with Jed. A familiar wave of grief and remorse stabbed me. I hadn't been able to push myself through the door since.

I kept on toward Johnny's house. He'd left the living room light on for me. I could slip inside, peel off my sadness along with my clothes, and crawl into bed with him, but none of that sounded like something I deserved.

Instead, I tumbled into my frigid car and pointed it toward home and my animals.

I'd call Johnny when I arrived home so he wouldn't worry.

Chapter 14

Tuesday blew in on a piercing, raw wind, cold threaded with disruptive streams of warmth. A mega storm was brewing, that was a sure deal, but with the way the air smelled, we wouldn't know what would fall from the sky: torrential rain, needles of sleet, or big, whomping buckets of snow. It set my teeth on edge—the intensity, the uncertainty, the clarity that something big was coming but we didn't know what.

Somehow, through it all, my allergies hung on like troupers, mercilessly tickling my eyes and scratching my throat. I'd wanted to drive by Chief Wenonga on my way to work so I could wave to my twenty-three-foot fiberglass crush—he helped to ground me when the rest of my life felt off-kilter—but my allergies had me feeling too itchy. I needed to park at the library as soon as possible so I could douse my googlers with my second wash of allergy drops that morning.

Good thing I was wearing gloves, or I'd be scouring my eyes as I drove. As it was, I was massaging my sockets instead. It was delicious, so close to relieving the itch that was driving me bonknanas. The tickle had been so bad that I didn't even pet Luna or Tiger Pop on my way out the door, scared that touching them would make the itching worse.

The back of my hand rubbed my left eyebrow as I passed through town. I almost didn't catch the clot of people standing outside Ace Hardware, was past them before I could figure out what was going on. I glanced at the dashboard clock. The store shouldn't have even been open at this hour.

This couldn't be good.

I pulled into the head librarian parking spot, turned off my car, and slip-jogged the block back to the hardware store. I had a cool twenty minutes before I needed to open the library.

I noticed the news truck out of the Cities parked in a side street first, Ron Sims on the perimeter second, and the woman being interviewed third. She was none other than Karen Kramer, chamber of commerce president and general control freak. That last quality bothered me because I saw too much of myself in it, always wanting to tell everyone what to do and how to behave. Except I mostly corralled my tendencies. She sprayed hers.

I caught her words floating on that deviling, undecided wind.

". . . guys will be guys. It's not a big deal. Everybody has to be so politically correct these days. It blows everything out of proportion."

I sidled up next to Ron, who was wearing a cap with earflaps and big, fleece-lined mittens.

"What's this about?" I asked, noticing that Karen's teenage daughter, Maisy, was in tow, nodding along to every word her mother said.

"Barry Janston," Ron said.

"The senator from Battle Lake?"

Ron nodded. "He's been accused of sexually harassing an intern."

Oh boy. That sounded about right, given the way Battle Lake's luck had gone since I'd moved to town.

"Not one woman I know hasn't been touched at work," Karen was saying as her daughter leaned in. "You brush it off. It doesn't mean a thing. You certainly don't raise a fuss about it."

That boiled my blood.

Since I had only just learned about the accusations against Janston from Ron yesterday, I had no idea if they were true, but I did know that it was hard enough being a teenager without having your mom tell the world that it was your job to suck up being sexually harassed at work. If Mrs. Berns had been there, she would have called that bullpucky out instantly and loudly.

Watching it made me so angry I wanted to punch a wall, but not brave enough to say something out loud, not with cameras there, and people standing around who might laugh at me if the words came out wrong. The best I could do was decide right then and there to start a Chick Club for high school girls, a place in Battle Lake where they could hang out and learn how to navigate the world and keep their strength and dreams intact. I'd been thinking about it for a few weeks, but overhearing this interview cemented it. Battle Lake girls needed guidance. Maybe Mrs. Berns and Kennie could help me. We'd have three generations of wisdom.

Well, at least we'd have three generations.

"Is Janston going to be fired?" I asked Ron. *It might not be too late to change that billboard.*

"Probably not. Ethics Committee is looking into it."

"You want me to dig around?" I'd already tried that line on him yesterday. Maybe he'd have a different take today.

Ron raised an eyebrow, which was the most emotion I'd ever seen out of him. "I'm writing the Janston story. You're writing the Bigfoot story."

Dangnabbit. I'd hoped he'd forgotten.

"I better get to the library."

Ron didn't respond. He'd already dismissed me.

I slid and shuffled my way back to the library, pushing through the ominous, rattling wind, wondering how the news of Barry Janston had traveled so quickly to Karen Kramer's ears, and who had summoned the news station to Battle Lake.

Chapter 15

Gary was as good as his word. Last night's broken glass had been replaced and any evidence swept away, inside and out. I envisioned some guy in a white van driving around the state, always at the ready to replace glass. *Glasstastic.* That might've been a business idea for Kennie, except if I told her, she'd make it one click off. Like instead of fixing broken glass, her white van would heal broken hearts, willing to drive up and offer supportive conversation and a pint of Ben & Jerry's with only a phone call, at any hour.

Hold the phone . . . that wasn't a half-bad idea.

Heals on Wheels.

I could suddenly understand how Kennie had fallen down the entrepreneurial rabbit hole. There was so much this world needed. Except I was plenty busy with my two jobs plus my PI side hustle. Granted, I hadn't been hired for PI work lately. Minnesota was one of a handful of states that required aspiring private investigators to work under a trained lawyer or licensed PI for six thousand hours before we could earn our own license. Thanks to some odd jobs for a local law firm, I had only 5,899 hours to go.

Sigh.

I flicked on the library lights, assured myself that the inside was cleaned up—it was—and powered on the front computer. My library duties would come first today. If there was time on my lunch break, I'd research and write a double recipe column for Ron, leaving after work to follow up on the ridiculous Bigfoot rumors. I could also use my lunch to scour TrackerSearch to see what I could rustle up on the four men listed in the note, my dad included. In the afternoon, I'd find time to create and advertise the Chick Club. Since we'd be meeting in the library, I could justify using library time to create the marketing materials.

Who was I kidding? At the wages they paid me, I could justify doing anything except selling the books to pay for a vacation. I generally tried to keep my various activities aboveboard, but I never hung on to guilt for working on side projects while here.

The opening of the front door jerked my attention back to the present.

In walked the same curly-mustached man who'd visited yesterday morning, the same one I'd witnessed rummaging in a garbage can last night. This morning he carried himself like he was about to get yelled at. And I just might fulfill that prophecy. I didn't like lurky people.

"Good morning," I said cautiously.

His eyes darted behind his glasses. Probably checking the corners for topless nonagenarians. When he brought his attention back to me, he tilted his head in that odd way that reflected the overhead lights.

"Good morning," he responded.

"Anything I can help you find?"

Like that, he was standing at the front desk, moving his lower body quick, like a blur, while holding his upper body entirely still.

I reeled back.

He didn't seem to notice. Instead, he leaned over the counter, intently. "I spotted a glass repair truck outside, in the middle of the night."

That was quite an opener. "We're considering installing a drive-through window." That's the thing about your lying muscle. You must keep stretching it so it's toned when you need it.

His eyes narrowed. "That's not what I heard. I heard the library was broken into last night."

Hmmm. "Where'd you hear that?"

"Police scanner."

"Yesterday, you mentioned you're new to town."

Now it was his turn to draw back. "Your point?"

"You always listen to a police scanner when you're checking out a new town?"

He giggled at this, a dry noise that was more moving air than mirth.

"What's so funny?" I asked. I liked being laughed at only a little more than I enjoyed guerilla bikini waxes.

"I do," he said, when he'd calmed himself down. "That is to say, I *always* listen to a police scanner when I'm visiting a new town."

The scowl crawled down my forehead and hit my eyebrows, which was how I loaded and cocked my sarcasm gun. I was just about to unload when it hit me. "You're the inspector."

"The what?" he asked, a delighted expression of mock disbelief on his face.

"The person sent here by T and A—"

"We prefer our full name be used," he said, interrupting me.

"By T and A," I continued, "to judge Battle Lake."

"'Judge' is a harsh word."

"Is it an *incorrect* word?" The glare of his glasses was more intense with only a few feet separating us, but when he turned his head, I caught his eye color: light blue, so faded his irises were nearly transparent.

He unzipped his jacket and then removed his glasses to polish them on the front of his shirt. "You have to admit there's been an unusual number of murders here."

Defensiveness rose like a dragon in my throat, but I shoved it down. I couldn't say anything that would hurt Battle Lake's chances. I might not always talk nice about my adopted hometown, but I'd be damned if I'd be the reason it got added to a "worst of" list.

"You're looking at it all wrong," I said, my voice smooth like honey. "We have an incredible record of *catching* murderers. In fact, we've probably got the highest per capita murderer-capturing rate in the country. We're mighty proud of that."

He tipped his chin, obviously confused. Rather than reply, he dug around inside his open parka and pulled out a roll of paper. He peeled a sheet off for me. "Would you mind completing a business survey? We're asking everyone who works in Battle Lake to do so."

I glanced down at the paper.

Thank you for taking the time to answer these survey questions. Your answers will remain anonymous. All the questions pertain to Battle Lake.

1. How likely do you think you are to die here?
2. Do you think you'll know your murderer?

That was as far as I needed to go. "Now hold on here," I said, but before I could get the words out, in strolled Mrs. Berns. She was early for her shift, which was good. Less ideal was the fact that she wore her silver six-shooter cap guns strapped at her waist.

A red began to creep up the inspector's collar, rushing like lava over his tender white skin. I needed to stop it before it reached his hair and melted it.

"Mrs. Berns!" I said, too loudly. "So happy you remembered that I wanted to preview the outfit you'd be wearing at our upcoming citywide costume party!"

The red stopped at nose level. "There's going to be a costume party here?" he asked.

"You betcha," Mrs. Berns said, kicking her heels. I don't think she'd picked up on what I was doing so much as she was living in the moment.

"When?" he asked suspiciously.

For the life of me, I couldn't think of a number. *When in doubt, go on the offensive.* "Are you saying I'm making up that we're having a costume party? That I'm a *liar*?" I demanded.

"No. Well . . . no. I'm sorry. I have to go." He skedaddled out, his eyes on his feet the whole time.

Mrs. Berns watched him leave. "If you removed that wacky mustache, that guy would be the spitting image of vanilla in human form."

Truer words.

"How old do you think he is?" she continued.

I held up the survey he'd left. "Old enough that he learned to type on a typewriter." I jabbed a finger at the two spaces after periods. "You could park a whale in here."

Mrs. Berns glanced at it. "You noticed that?"

"With computers, you're only supposed to hit the space bar once after any kind of punctuation," I said, unable to reel in my inner geek fast enough. "They do the rest."

"You're weird," she said, unholstering a gun and popping off a cap in my general direction. "I'm gonna start a pot of coffee."

Shaking my head and smiling, I made my way to the drop box attached to the front door on the opposite side of the glass that had been shattered and replaced. *A drive-through wouldn't be a bad idea,* I thought as I discovered the one area the glass repair people had missed. The bottom of the book-return bin contained four books bedazzled with bright pebbles of broken glass. I gave the bin a shake and retrieved the books, tapping each on the side to make sure it was clear.

After a moment of thought, I also held each by the spine and shook. No notes.

I trailed the bin behind me to the front counter, set down the books, and then brought out a trash can to empty the bin into. It was unwieldy, but I managed to shake the remaining glass cubes loose.

The activity shook a thought free.

I really should call my mom.

I'd last spoken with her in March, when I'd called to wish her a happy birthday. The conversation had been short and superficial. Had it really been a month ago? A pang of shame shot through my chest. I could do a better job. Except . . . my mom and I didn't have much in common. She'd ask me about my job and animals, I'd check in with how her boyfriend was and what her church group was up to.

That was it.

The one thing I did want to talk to her about—my dad—was the untouchable subject. If I told her about the note, it would only upset her. What possible information could she provide, thirteen years after his death? Would she remember Dad mentioning the names of one of the men on the note? Unlikely. My best bet would be to drive out to her house one of these days and riffle through Dad's stuff.

But for what? The same pile of nothing I'd found in Kennie's Lartel box, a file of basic info, which I'd stored in the back room of the library? I breathed an exasperated sigh. *How about I stick to what I know and create a double-header recipe column for Ron, as requested.*

I set my bumper in the captain's chair and googled "headcheese recipes."

(Don't try this at home, kids. Same thing with "holiday nuts." You think it's going to be all right, but it's not.)

The first recipe that appeared required "one pig's head" as the initial ingredient, like that was a thing you picked up between the snack mix and red apples. Well, I'd have to trust that the good people of Battle Lake could land their own porkers. I read through a dozen recipes and took the easiest bits from each.

Face it, there's nothing better than headcheese if you're looking for a low-carb snack! You can buy it at the grocery store, but nothing beats fresh. Follow the recipe below for a can't-miss treat.

Crock-Pot Headcheese

Ingredients
    1 pig's head
    1 onion, diced
    6 cloves garlic, minced
    2 tablespoons salt
    1 teaspoon nutmeg
    1 teaspoon ground pepper
    ½ cup white vinegar
    Enough water to cover the head

Add all ingredients to an extra-large Crock-Pot. Simmer on low for 24 hours. Allow to cool, then pull out the head. Remove skin, including from the tongue. Dispose of it along with the skull bones, and shred the remaining meat. Arrange in a shallow pan and salt and pepper to taste. Pour the Crock-Pot liquid into a stockpot and boil until reduced and slightly thick. Pour over meat until covered. Refrigerate until the mixture is cool and the texture of gelatin. Slice and serve!

I was ashamed that I was salivating while typing up the recipe, considering it was one that included "skull bones." It was just that my grandma used to make headcheese every Christmas, and I'd devour that jiggly jelly, loving how it slid in and out of my teeth and how its tartness delighted my tongue. I hadn't known what it was made of, and once I found out, it was too late to stop loving it.

I wondered if I could pay someone to make it for me. Food for thought.

My next task was to hunt down a dessert recipe. I figured the headcheese was so time intensive that I should go easy on the sweet stuff. I searched "no-bake cookies," and voilà! Up popped moose farts. Some graham cracker crumbs, chocolate chips, and coconut all rolled together like sweet, chunky air, and you were good to go.

This being for Battle Lake Bites, though, I needed to give it a Minnesota twist.

Deer fart bars are sweet and easy treats the whole family will enjoy.

Deer Fart Bars

Ingredients

¼ cup unsalted butter, melted

1 14 oz. can sweetened condensed milk

1½ teaspoons vanilla extract

2 cups graham cracker crumbs

1½ cups dried, unsweetened coconut flakes

1 cup semisweet chocolate chips

½ cup peanuts, chopped

Pour the melted butter into a bowl with the sweetened condensed milk and vanilla. Stir until the mixture is a creamy beige color. Set aside ¼ cup of the graham cracker crumbs, then mix the remaining crumbs, coconut, chocolate chips, and peanuts with the liquid. Stir until well combined. Pour the mixture into a buttered 8-inch-by-8-inch pan, dust with the reserved graham cracker crumbs, and refrigerate for at least an hour. Cut into squares and serve!

I ran spell-check and emailed both recipes to Ron. *Job well done.* The satisfied smile was still on my face when Johnny walked through the front door. My grin widened until I noted his tight expression.

"Hey!" I said, my tone bright despite the sudden uneasiness. "I didn't expect to see you this morning."

He returned my grin, but the line between his eyebrows didn't ease. "I thought you'd be back over last night."

My smile dropped to the countertop with a splat. "I was too tired," I said, defensively. "I left a message on your machine when I got home."

He nodded and glanced around the library. I felt my blood begin to freeze from the outside in. He was here to tell me something. That was never good.

"How's your day going?" I asked, pushing off the inevitable. Was he going to tell me he was mad at me? Break up with me? I wouldn't blame him if he did. I'd begged him for one more chance, and I was already blowing it.

Instead of answering my question, he offered me one of his own, his deep-blue gaze intense. "What did Gary show you last night?"

That's when Mrs. Berns appeared from the back room. She held a steaming cup of coffee in one hand and spun a pistol, Old West–style, with the other. "Hot dog, Johnny Leeson is here!" She popped a cap. A thin plume of smoke drifted out the end of her pistol, followed by the smell of sulfur. (When I'd asked her why she sometimes wore the guns, she declared that there was no reason kids should have all the fun.)

"Hi," Johnny said, smiling his first true smile since he'd walked in. "I like the outfit."

She ogled him head to toe. "And I like the body."

He chuckled, deep and warm. "Thank you."

She cocked her head. "You do look a little tense, though. It's Mira, isn't it?"

If my eyes could have smacked her, they would have. "Gary picked me up from Johnny's last night," I said.

Mrs. Berns's eyebrows shot up.

"Because someone smashed in the library window," I said, before she got any ideas. "They stole a book, I think, but nothing else was missing. Gary stayed to get the window fixed, and I went home. I'm really sorry, Johnny. I should have stopped by to tell you rather than just called."

"That *Minnesota's Hidden Treasures* book?" Mrs. Berns asked.

I could see the gears turning in her head. "Yeah," I said, hopefully. "Don't suppose you took it home with you last night?"

"Don't suppose I did." Mrs. Berns walked right up to Johnny. "You should fight Gary for Mira's favors," she said, as if she were recommending he check out a new TV show. "Ladies like that testosterone hooey."

My cheeks blazed. "I don't want that!"

Johnny's eyes shot to me, then to the floor. "I better get to work," he said.

He tossed me a last glance on his way out the door. I couldn't read it. Sad? Embarrassed? Regretting every decision he'd made that had brought him to this point?

"Keep April twenty-seventh free," he said, before stepping outside.

I turned to Mrs. Berns, indignant. "What was that about?"

"I dunno. An anniversary?"

"Not the 'April twenty-seventh' thing. The 'fight Gary' thing."

She shook her head. "Don't pretend for a second that you don't notice that both of them are on your scent, and that it wouldn't give you a big old girl boner to have them fight over you." She set her coffee on the counter and walked off toward the stacks, still talking. "I'd want Johnny to win, of course, but I wouldn't mind if Gary broke a sweat, maybe had to take his shirt off."

My mouth was opening and closing. I didn't have enough wherewithal to even sputter.

The only good news was that my expression went perfectly with the person walking through the library door, barely closed since Johnny had walked out.

Chapter 16

I might not have stayed in regular contact with my own mother, but I'd visited Sal Heike, Jed's mom, at least once a week since mid-February. It was the only way I could stay ahead of the guilt I felt over her son's death. He never would have been traveling on the Valentine Train to Portland, Oregon, if not for me, and he certainly would never have been thrown out of it if he hadn't been trying to save my life.

I'd yet to grow comfortable with the gut punch I felt every time I laid eyes on Sal's lined face. It had aged a decade since she'd found out her son was dead, with not even a body to mourn. The police and a search and rescue team had scoured the area as well as they could along the base of the railroad bridge straddling the gaping chasm in the Colorado Rockies, but the area was thickly wooded, the sides of the valley impassably steep in places.

Jed was gone, in more ways than one.

I swallowed past the ugly sludge of remorse. "Hi, Sal. Nice to see you." Before Jed's death, she'd been a handsome woman, her hair always pulled in a neat bun, her clothes tidy and wrinkle-free. Since February, her hair was rarely washed, let alone combed, and she always seemed to be wearing the same loose jeans and black sweater. It hurt to look at her.

"Morning, Sal!" Mrs. Berns called from the stacks. I wondered what she was doing back there. Probably best I didn't know.

Sal smiled wanly and made her way to Jed's altar. "You changed it."

My breath caught. I didn't want to tell her it'd been disturbed. I also didn't want to lie to her. "Someone broke into the library last night."

She turned, her mouth a small O.

"Only a book is missing," I said quickly. "It was on the edge of the table. Some of the items got knocked off, too."

I watched to see how she'd take the news. She seemed not to care, and why would she? She'd lost her only child. What did some disrupted trinkets matter in the face of that?

"I found a bracelet that was his," Sal said, digging in her pocket and coming out with a brass ID chain. "He begged me to buy it for him in eighth grade. All the kids were wearing them back then."

My eyes grew misty at the thought of curly-headed, bright-eyed fourteen-year-old goofball Jed wearing a cheap bracelet because that's what everyone else was doing. He'd grown up to follow his own path for the short time he'd been allowed, but I guess everyone went through a conformist phase.

"Are you going to leave it on the altar?" I asked. "It'd be nice to have a new addition."

"If it's OK?"

"Of course." I walked around the counter to join her. "It's better than OK."

She held the bracelet by the clasp, dangling it over the spot where the book had rested yesterday. "I think I see him sometimes," she said, so quietly that I had to lean in to catch the words.

My heart *ba-thumped*. "Jed?"

"It's silly, I know." She dropped the chain on the table. "Out of the corner of my eye, sometimes, when I'm working outside at the resort, I think I spot him. It's a glimpse of his hair, or the set of his shoulders, off in the woods. I'll look, sometimes I even call out his name, but it's never him. Of course it's not."

I rested my arm on her shoulder, and she fell into me. I held her while she wept softly, her body shaking. It took no more than a minute before she collected herself and pulled away.

"It's not your fault," she said, her eyes beseeching. "You know that, right, Mira?"

It was how she ended every one of our visits, and it touched me deeply every time. "Thanks, Sal." It wasn't true, of course. It *was* my fault. But I wouldn't reject her kindness. "You'll let me know if you need anything?"

She nodded. "Bye, Mrs. Berns!" she called out.

"Later, Sal!"

I still didn't know what Mrs. Berns was doing in the back. It certainly wasn't reading. Maybe she was organizing, making sure the books had been shelved correctly? A person could hope. Before I had time to confirm, though, in walked Kennie. We were a regular community central today. Hm. Actually, as a library, that's exactly what we were.

"I have two business propositions!" Kennie proclaimed as she entered, again dressed conservatively, and alarmingly so. She balanced an unmarked cardboard box in her hands, the same size that a ream of printer paper came in but unmarked.

Mrs. Berns appeared immediately. "I'm in," she said.

"You don't even know what it is!" I protested.

"It's got to be better than this boring job." She hooked a thumb toward the children's section. "I'm forced to glue googly eyes onto the books just to stay awake."

My head dropped into my hands. "Why would you . . . fine . . . what is it?" I said, turning to Kennie. "What is the business?"

"You might want to change that attitude," Kennie said, nose in the air. "You should be delighted I'm sharing with the two of you first."

Mrs. Berns, clearly doing this right, rubbed her hands in anticipation. "Let's hear it!"

Kennie smiled. "That's more like it. Gather round."

She set her box on the nearest reading table. When the door donged open and a middle-aged couple walked in, she leaned over it protectively. The couple made their way to the bank of public computers against the far wall, oblivious.

"As I said," Kennie whispered, "I have two possible propositions. Here's the first."

With a flourish, she snaked her hand into the container and came out with a blue velvet jewelry box.

My interest immediately perked up.

She opened the lid. Inside, nestled in plump silk, lay an ornate silver ring with a gumball-size container on its top.

"Poison rings?" I asked. I'd been introduced to them at a little West Bank import shop when I lived in Minneapolis. The space under the bezel was intended to smuggle poison to use on your enemies—or on yourself to evade capture or torture. They were big in the sixteenth century, and then again with hippies in the twentieth.

Kennie snapped the lid shut. "*Flavor* rings. They hold salt or pepper, or a mixture of both. You can discreetly tap it over your food when you've been invited to a church dinner."

"That's a brilliant idea," I said before I could stop myself. Kennie and I had a complicated relationship, but you don't deny genius when you're in its presence. While I loved the hot, soothing gloppiness of church-basement cuisine, the food was usually beige, both in color and flavor. I might even be able to smuggle some hot-pepper flakes in one of those rings, and no one would be the wiser.

"How much?" I asked.

She handed me the box and took out another for Mrs. Berns. "They're free to affiliates. You have to sell five of them for thirty dollars each in the next month or give it back."

I leaned down for my purse. A salesperson I was not. It felt too manipulative. "Or, here's thirty dollars."

"Suit yourself," she said.

Mrs. Berns shook Kennie's box. "What else you got in there?"

Kennie craned her neck to eyeball the people working at the library computers. "We better go to the back room for this."

That set my curiosity aflame. I told the patrons I'd return in a moment and then followed Mrs. Berns and Kennie into the back.

Kennie kept her voice low, even in the protected space. "Here they are," she said, removing a smaller box from the larger one. She lifted its lid. Nestled inside were two of the same cheese balls she'd left yesterday. I swatted Mrs. Berns's hand away as she reached for them. "We already know about these. Remember? You left four here yesterday."

Kennie nodded. "It's only a misdemeanor if I'm caught with two. Three or more is a felony."

My eyes darted to the refrigerator and then to Mrs. Berns, whose gaze was locked on those furry balls. "What's in them?"

"Marijuana."

I slapped my forehead. "You left us with four balls of pot—"

"One," Mrs. Berns interrupted me. "She only left one."

I turned on her. "You ate the other three, didn't you?"

Mrs. Berns shrugged. "Kennie's fault. She didn't provide instructions."

Kennie didn't seem to mind that Mrs. Berns had eaten the product. "If you'd asked me ten years ago if I'd be engaging in illegal activity," she said, "I'd have said no."

Mrs. Berns and I hooted simultaneously. Kennie had made a career out of skirting the law.

She ignored us and continued. "But marijuana is the future. It's going to be legal in Minnesota one of these days, and I don't want to be caught unprepared. I've landed a supplier straight out of Colorado. He said he can sell me medical-grade marijuana, which I transform into party food. I'm envisioning a mail-order club. Mary & Jane's—we deliver to people in the know."

"I'll be Jane!" Mrs. Berns said, snapping up one of the balls and popping it in her piehole before Kennie or I could protest. It was so big that she had to cover her mouth with her hand to keep all the cheese in.

"And I lied," she mumbled around her stuffed gob. "I ate all four of the other ones." She rubbed her belly. "Good eating."

"I refuse to get involved in drug dealing," I said.

"Drug *catering*," Kennie said. "Not drug dealing. And we'll only put out feelers so we're ready when it's legal."

"Count me in," Mrs. Berns said.

"No way," I said. "Not me. I don't want anything to do with—" But then I stopped. I did need both Kennie's and Mrs. Berns's help on something. Besides, marijuana was as harmless a drug as they came, as long as it was in low, controlled doses. "Anything but the recipe end of it. I'd be happy to help you research party food to disguise it in."

"If?" Kennie said, her eyebrow raised. She had my number.

"If you both help me start a club for the preteen and teenage girls in town. I want somewhere for them to come free of society's influences, where they can learn to be empowered. Taught how to be entrepreneurial, even," I said, sweeping my hand over the last cheese ball.

Kennie appeared thoughtful. "How're you going to get them interested?"

An excellent question I hadn't thought of.

"Invite preteen and teenage boys?" Mrs. Berns offered.

"You are being a big point-misser," I said.

"Make the first night a Pretty in Ink party," Kennie said, sounding wise.

"Say what now?"

She pulled up her right sleeve, displaying a vibrant, black-ink tattoo of a dandelion fluff on her inner wrist. "Pretty in Ink. They're semipermanent, professional-looking tattoos. Last nearly a month. Every girl in the county is clamoring for them. How have you not heard of this?"

"How have *you*?" I asked.

She rolled her sleeve back down. "I bought a couple traveling kits when I saw how popular they are." Her expression grew crafty. "I can see a definite market developing right in front of my face."

The woman was always looking for an angle. I had to respect her hustle. "So, if I let you lead a, what's it called, a Pretty in Ink party at the first meeting, you'd get behind me starting a Chick Club here in town?"

"Not only would I throw my support *emotionally and financially* behind it, but if you start tomorrow, you can use the community room in the city council offices. The Adult Children of Passive-Aggressives requested to book it but haven't confirmed."

"Thanks, but I'll hold it here," I said, thinking through all my options. "I do like the idea of starting tomorrow, though."

"I'll come!" Kennie said. "I was supposed to lead the ACPA meeting, but I'd rather be here."

"Are you going to tell those whiners?" Mrs. Berns asked.

"No," Kennie said. "I don't like any of them."

"That's the way," Mrs. Berns said, giving her the thumbs-up. "Anyone want that last cheese ball?"

Chapter 17

The day was getting away from me, and I'd done hardly any library work. I spent the next hour helping patrons, but when there was a lull, rather than leave for lunch, I fired up my TrackerSearch database, ignoring the rumblings in my tummy. With Mrs. Berns watching the front, I removed the note from my pocket, smoothed it on the countertop, and studied it.

Mark James (PV—12)
Lartel McManus (OT—7)
John Guinn (OT—23)
Jefferson Penetal (OT—1)

HELP

Was there something in these few words worth breaking into the library for? I was still assuming "Mark James" referred to my dad and *PV* to Paynesville. Lartel and Guinn were from Otter Tail, and so I figured that's what the *OT* stood for, and that was where Penetal hailed from, too. The more information I inputted, the better the database worked, so I started on that last guess, typing in "Jefferson Penetal, Otter Tail County."

I'd gambled that the unique nature of his name would winnow the hits, and I was right. Only four came back, which was about average for a person who wasn't a criminal: his mortgage, his birth certificate, a marriage license, and a death certificate.

Jefferson had been born in Fergus Falls, the Otter Tail County Seat, in 1944. He married a Maureen Oldham in 1968, they bought land outside Battle Lake in 1972, and he'd died last year. I left the database to peek at the last time someone had checked out *Minnesota's Hidden Treasures*: January, and then again in November. No way had Jefferson stuck the note in there.

Next up was John Guinn. There were a surprising number of people with that name in the database, but when I added "Otter Tail County," it narrowed to a single man, and all of it was squeaky clean. His birth certificate showed he was born a year after Jefferson, never married, also owned land outside Battle Lake (only a couple miles from where I was living, I saw), and was still alive.

I exited the database to google Guinn, using "Battle Lake" in the search box. Up came a single press release from the *Battle Lake Recall*, the article written almost a year ago to the day. Ron Sims had penned it, and it was solid and to the point, just like him.

Local Businessman Raising Funds for Perham Community Center

John Guinn, LMFT, PhD, is spearheading a fundraising effort to build a community center in downtown Perham, Minn. Guinn was instrumental in raising money to build the Albert Eltek Community Center in Battle Lake in honor of one of the town's founding fathers. He has adopted a more supportive role in the proposed Perham community center fundraising, forming the board and taking charge of locating matching funds. As a practicing therapist, Dr. Guinn believes "a gathering space for citizens, particularly school-aged boys and girls, is vital to the health of a community."

The Perham Community Center fundraiser aims to raise $500,000 before June 1. That amount will be matched by an anonymous donor. Those interested in donating should contact him directly at 218.864.7472.

One milquetoast man (Jefferson Penetal), one man who was a saint (John Guinn), and my dad and Lartel. Well, I knew which side of the balance Lartel fell on, even before TrackerSearch pulled up a rash of information stemming from all the coverage he'd received back when I'd discovered my first corpse. The articles underscored what I knew, including the fact that Lartel had simply vanished after the murder.

None of the Lartel articles shed light on the note. I'd need to take Ron up on the offer to peruse the archives. The old newspaper microfiche might contain information that wasn't database-worthy, or that the database hadn't been able to access.

I realized I was putting off a search on my dad. Who wanted to find out nasty or possibly criminal information about their parent, especially when the parent in question was dead, and what I already knew about him wasn't great? But if I took this note seriously, if whoever had scrawled "help" truly needed rescuing, I couldn't leave any stone unturned.

My fingers were poised to type "Mark James" when Mrs. Berns's cough drew my attention to the front door. People had been streaming in and out steadily all day, checking out books, reading the newspaper, using the public computers. But when I looked up and saw Karen Kramer stomping in, I knew she wasn't there for regular library business.

"Not much to do around here, is there?" she said with a fake smile, glancing around the library. She'd caught us in the first lull of the day.

I held my tongue, not sure how much control she had over the library budget.

"At my church," she said, strolling toward the front counter, "all the staff are volunteers. Only the pastor is paid, and he takes just enough to live off. What a wonderful man."

Minnesota Nice, we called what she was doing. Amazing that people who were not from around here thought it referred to legitimate kindness.

"Would you like some cheese?" Mrs. Berns asked her.

I scrambled off my stool and inserted myself between Mrs. Berns and Karen. "What can we do for you?"

Karen's smile was brittle. She must've been around Kennie's age, except she usually dressed professionally, wearing suit coats or nicely cut sweaters and kitten heels nearly every time I'd had the poor luck to encounter her. "It's what you can stop doing for Battle Lake," she said.

My brows knit. "Excuse me?"

"You may have heard, but thanks to you, we have an inspector from the Travel and Adventure Board in town. It's his job to either take away or affirm our five-star rating. If he writes us a bad review, this town shuts down, plain and simple. The Fortune Café won't have the summer rush that carries them through the winter, Stub's won't have enough customers to sustain their staff, and we certainly won't need a library. Some dusty old bookmobile will do."

Her words knifed through me. "It's not my fault," I said quietly.

She harrumphed and turned away, leaning over to dig in her purse. Her short jacket and sweater rode up, revealing a *Last Supper* tramp stamp. She was upright and facing me before I could process that.

She slapped a stack of newspapers on the countertop. They were from all over the state, and each featured a headline with some version of Tiny, Bucolic Battle Lake Becomes Minnesota's Murder Capital.

I tried to swallow but didn't have enough spit. "I didn't kill anyone."

Karen bent over the counter. She smelled like a cheap, fruity perfume, the scent at odds with the high-end look she tried to cultivate.

"If you could refrain from discovering dead bodies, that would be great," she said, really slow, like I was dumb.

"If you could refrain from being a bully," Mrs. Berns said, inserting herself into the conversation, "that would also be bang-up."

Karen shot her a withering glance, but before she could get in a word edgewise, Mrs. Berns said, "By the way, we have a church group meeting here Wednesday nights. Tomorrow's the first night. It's girls only. You know, to keep it pure. Any chance Maisy is free?"

Delight and suspicion rolled across Karen's face like vinegar and oil. "She could stop over after her religion class."

"Thought so," Mrs. Berns said. "Have her spread the word to her friends. Starts at seven. We'll provide the snacks and the chaperones. Now, if you don't mind, we have work to do."

Karen stood there for a full thirty seconds, unused to being dismissed, before she finally turned to leave.

"How'd you know I had her girl in mind for the Chick Club?" I asked.

Mrs. Berns raised her eyebrows. "Lucky guess. Women who are squeezed so tight their ass picks up the chair when they stand up usually don't do their daughters any favors."

I smiled, not realizing until then that I'd been grinding my teeth. "Thanks."

Rubbing my hands over my face, I returned my focus to the TrackerSearch home screen. I typed in "Mark James, Paynesville," and held my breath.

When the first hit appeared, the shock of it about pushed me off my chair.

Chapter 18

My father had been a private investigator.

There it was, for all the world to see, his license from the Minnesota Board of Private Detective and Protective Agent Services.

The same license I'd been struggling to obtain for months.

What the holy heck?

My whole life, my dad had worked in finance. Or so I'd thought. He'd leave for work in the morning, come back at five, and start drinking his vodka waters. Eventually, the drinking took more of his time than his job did, and he spent his days holding down a recliner in front of the television, drawing a military pension while Mom did seamstress and secretarial work to try to make ends meet.

Had my mom known? Had anyone?

I peered at the dates. He'd earned his license in 1968, the same year my mom became pregnant with me. He'd kept it up to date until the year before his fatal car accident. That meant he'd completed the annually required six hours of continuing education and, for the love of Betsy, the additional six hours of weapons training required of any armed PI.

My dad had carried a weapon.

Except that he had served in Vietnam, and because of that, he'd been clear that there would be no guns in our house. Or had I made all that up?

Who *was* my dad?

A cold, creeping paranoia drove a flurry of searching.

My dad *had* served in Vietnam. That much, at least, was true.

He'd gotten three DUIs. No surprise there.

His birth date and death date were accurate with what I'd been told, as was his wedding date to my mom.

"Are you OK?" Mrs. Berns asked.

The concern in her voice rescued me from the wormhole I was falling into. "I don't think so."

Her eyes flicked from the computer to my face. "TrackerSearch telling you something you don't want to see?"

"It's that obvious?"

"Your face is the color of my ass. In case you didn't know, my ass is real pale."

I swallowed and nodded. "I think I need some fresh air."

Mrs. Berns pointed at the clock. "Only an hour to close. Why don't you leave, and I'll shut things down tonight? I can even make an updated poster for that girls' club you want to form."

"Chick Club," I said, gratefully, "and you're the best."

"That I am. Now get out of here." She made a shooing motion. "Your erpy expression is making me seasick, and I want to hang on to the last of my cheese buzz."

I exited my search and was about to grab my jacket from the back room when I decided to make two copies of the note. One I stashed in the library drawer, one I tucked into my purse, and the original I slipped in my back jeans pocket.

"See you at the gym tonight?" I asked Mrs. Berns on my way out. We'd been taking a Tae Kwon Do class on and off for months but had vowed to get serious about it now that my burns from the library fire were mostly healed. *If life gives you lemons*, Mrs. Berns was fond of saying, *you learn how to kick 'em in the seeds.*

"Yup," she said, waving me out. "Be off with you."

She didn't have to tell me twice.

The outside air smelled fresh, like iced watermelon. I sucked in the scent of impending green, ignoring the itchy just-about-to-storm vibe that was right below it. Winter and spring were fighting it out, and we'd find out in the next week which was going to win.

Since it promised to be either the rainstorm or the blizzard of the century, might as well search for Battle Lake's Bigfoot before it hit.

Chapter 19

Ron had given me precious little to go on when he'd assigned the story. Rumors were circulating that a gigantic, hair-covered creature that resembled an ape but walked like a man was terrorizing the Battle Lake countryside. The story had burned through all the local bars until no one was certain where the myth had started, but it seemed every citizen had either a theory or a personal sighting story.

That left me no one and everyone to interview.

But really, if I found a person who truly believed that they'd spotted a Bigfoot, what would I ask them? *How'd he smell?* Actually, that was something I'd like to know. My time was limited, though, until I figured out what that note was all about. My best bet was to visit the region where Bigfoot had been most frequently spotted, search for evidence, find none, and write a short piece exposing it for the folktale it clearly was.

The only good news was the area Bigfoot had most recently been spotted in overlapped with the hundred acres of property I was house-sitting northwest of Battle Lake. With any luck, I could scout a nice chunk of land without encountering any No Trespassing signs, discover nothing—or better yet, find some evidence of a big animal, like a moose or a bear, in the area and take a few photos of its den—and lay this story to rest.

When I pulled into my driveway, I was still debating whether to take Luna along on the scouting mission. She loved long walks with me, but if there was a large, wild animal out there, I didn't want her to scrap with it. Same if I had to peek on some land that might not be clearly marked as private property. I didn't like to involve those I loved in criminal activity.

"Sorry, girl," I said to her, when she waggled all over me inside the door. "You can stretch your legs while I get you and Tiger Pop fresh water and gear up, but this walk is me alone."

Her tail *thwap thwapped.* I swear she smiled at me, so I scritched her behind the ears before opening the door to release her into the charged spring air. She seemed to sense the weather weirdness, stopping to cock her head before bounding off to chase some early returning ducks. I let the door lightly close, my heart filling at the picture she made. Luna was 100 percent Sunny's dog. Sunny had found her abandoned on the side of the road when Luna was no more than a floofball puppy. She'd raised her and adored her so much that the thought of leaving her behind almost kept her from heading to Alaska with her monobrowed paramour.

Then I'd moved in, kicking and screaming against Fate, and found that I loved so much here, Luna included.

"Hey, sweetheart," I said, as Tiger Pop rubbed against my leg. It was unusual for my calico kitty to show affection. Fine by me. I liked my cats aloof. When I reached down to pet the base of her spine where it met her tail, she rolled over on her back and swatted at my hands, her claws sheathed.

"Such a good kitten," I murmured.

That pushed her over the edge. Too much affection. She charged off into my bedroom and sprawled across my quilt, her favorite spot. I swapped out her and Luna's water bowls for clean ones, filling them with filtered water. Both animals would probably be fine with the orange, mineral-laden water that came from the well, but I wanted the best for them.

I'd feed them when I returned.

I grabbed a slice of cheddar cheese and an apple out of the fridge, wolfing them both down as I struggled into my snow pants and winter boots. Most of the snow had compressed from melting and refreezing into a few inches of sharp crust, but I didn't know what I'd find in the woods, where the sun didn't directly shine. I zipped my winter parka on over the snow pants, nestled the digital camera in a pocket, tugged on a hat, and called Luna back inside.

She dashed through the door, bringing the clean scent of winter-spring in on her fur.

"What do you think, honey?" I asked her. "Snow or rain coming our way?"

She whined.

"I agree," I said. "I'm ready for winter to leave."

I tossed a longing glance over at my seedlings. I'd started them earlier than was prudent, as was my habit. Johnny had helped me to build the four shelves that sat in front of the window, draped in plastic to retain as much of the sun's heat as they could.

Lifting the front of the plastic, I took a big inhale to remind me of the good stuff: basil, thyme, peppery tomato, pulpy green and earth brown with their own special warmth and life. It soothed my heart.

"I'm going to find Bigfoot," I told both the animals as I headed outdoors. "Send help if I'm not back before the sun sets."

Chapter 20

The crunch of my footsteps was oddly soothing, and the late-afternoon sun sparkled off the crystals, lighting up the ground like a field of diamonds. The edges left by my footprints were just as sharp.

I kept Whiskey Lake to my left, forging my own path southeast through the snow crust. In most places, the snow came only to my ankles when I broke through, but a few spots caught me off guard, sinking me nearly to my thigh. The third time it happened, I recalled that Sunny had an old-fashioned pair of snowshoes decorating her living room wall, animal sinew binding white ash. Would they have been useful in this type of snow? I thought not. I pushed on, appreciating the physical exertion, the way it heated my chest and warmed my cheeks.

The only unusual object I'd found on this edge of Sunny's land was a deer stand I'd never seen before. It was old, the wood rotting, deer scat below thumbing its nose at past and future hunters.

I poop in your general direction.

The No Trespassing signs facing outward told me I was crossing from Sunny's land to the public access, the only spot where people who didn't own lake property could launch their boats to access the crystalline waters of Whiskey Lake. I stumbled across some kicked-around, charred wood plus crushed Hamm's cans. Unless Bigfoot was a fan of 3.2 beer, it was evidence of a late-night party held by some hearty Minnesotan teens with nowhere else to go, not a sign of a transplanted Himalayan monster. I snapped photos, already writing the headline in my mind (Bigfoot? Try Lightweight), and then stuffed the cans in my coat pocket to recycle later.

Another hour of tramping through the quiet woods turned up nothing unusual, just snow, trees, and some deer rut and rabbit turds. The cold lemon sun was beginning to drop below the horizon, and my legs were starting to burn from lifting them so high to release myself from the cutting snow. I probably had enough evidence to close this X-File. The one swath of public land that I hadn't searched was a five-minute walk ahead, in the deepest area of the woods, the spot where the sun for sure didn't shine.

I sighed.

No one would know if I'd failed to check it out.

To be honest, I didn't even know if I was still on public land. Weatherworn signs were nailed to some of the trees, their original wording faded beyond recognition. Were they warning me away? If they weren't, the dipping sun certainly was. In twenty minutes, it'd drop like an egg yolk below the horizon.

I sighed again.

I really should go home.

Except . . . curiosity was a cruel taskmistress and the only one I entertained regularly.

Twenty more minutes, and I can call this a wrap.

I trudged onward, scratching at the tickle in the back of my neck. While most of this area was hardwoods, this particular forested area consisted of tight jack pines and spruce, their healthy, woodsy scent calming my hackles.

Wait, why do my hackles need calming?

I felt in my pocket for my trusty Z-Force, the zapping gun I usually carried when I investigated. My heart plunged. I hadn't brought him along. And why would I? A stun gun would be as effective as a mosquito against a real Bigfoot, and anything else in these woods would run away from me.

I patted my cheek, the scratchiness of my mitten grounding me. No way did I think I was going to stumble across a knuckle-dragging Sasquatch in my backyard, grunting and generally hanging out.

Except, was that a rustic hut twenty feet in front of me, built into the base of a tall, sticky spruce? My feet drew me toward it. It was definitely an intentional structure, the outer walls shaped like a cone, pine boughs woven between rough-hewn branches.

I stepped forward, cautiously, scaring up a flock of crows that had blended with the shadows. "Gah!" I yelled, flailing my arms.

The birds shrieked and flapped, their startling noise and movement stopping my heart. As they took to the sky like a black calamity cloud, I leaned against a nearby tree trunk to steady myself. Birds had always freaked me out. A whole murder of them? That couldn't be good.

Once my heart had resumed beating, I was able to make out the corn sprinkled near the makeshift lean-to. Someone had been feeding the flying lizards, which explained why they'd gathered at dusk. The ground around the structure was trampled, the footprints human, but not quite. I didn't have the courage to peek inside it, not yet, not with the fright of the crows still so recent. But I could take photos of the outside.

I saw my hand pulling out my camera before I was aware I was doing it, my pulse clap-thudding at my wrists.

I drew the camera to my eye, my mouth dry.

I snapped four photos, one right after another, before he grabbed me.

Chapter 21

"I wouldn't get too close to that," he said, his arm circled around my waist.

I spun and pushed against the body, not recognizing the voice. I drove my knee into the tender flesh of his groin, powering my leg with the force of unspent adrenaline.

"*Urk,*" he said, dropping to the ground.

That was the only noise he could make. I'd kicked the breath out of him, and that was about what he deserved. Who grabbed a woman around the waist from behind? But I could see exactly who. I recognized his broad face and the over-dyed black hair peeking under his cap from the news. I gave him a full minute to gather himself, and for my rage-fear to settle down to a manageable boil.

"Senator Janston?" It was more of a "what are you doing here?" than a "is it really you?" He was wearing a Realtree camouflage jumper, his cheeks swathed with black greasepaint. Most times of year you could go all in with the animal slaughter, but I didn't know of any creature that was fair game in early April. I searched for evidence that he'd carried a rifle but didn't see one nearby.

I offered him a hand. He took it, using my counterweight to hoist himself to his feet.

"That's quite a handshake you've got," he managed.

"Why'd you grab me?"

He pointed at the makeshift hut. "It might be dangerous in there."

"It might be, but you're not answering the question."

Finally able to stand, he drew himself to his full height. He was a big guy, maybe six-four, with green eyes that sparkled even in the fading light, smile crinkles at the corners telling me he spent a fair amount of time at least acting easygoing. Something about him set me off, though, and it wasn't only that he'd thought it appropriate to lay his hands on me before we'd even met. Maybe it was because he reminded me of every other guy who thought he knew what was best for me. In any case, I suspected the Ethics Committee had their work cut out for them with this one.

He held up his hands. "Look, I'm sorry. I messed up. I checked out that hut earlier, and it looks like someone is living in there. I didn't know if he'd returned, and I wanted to save you from a nasty surprise. Likely an indigent."

Or a Bigfoot.

"What are you doing in the woods?" I asked.

He made a sweeping motion with his arm. "Scouting for an upcoming turkey hunt."

"You're aware you're on public land?"

He raised an eyebrow and grinned. "You're aware you're on my friend's private land?"

Curse words. I was afraid of something like that. He wasn't worth the trouble of coming up with a lie. The truth was so outrageous he might believe I was fibbing anyhow, so I went for it. "I've heard there's been Bigfoot sightings in this area. I'm researching it for a newspaper article I'm writing. If you don't mind, I'll finish snapping photos of this structure and leave."

"Be my guest."

He was so self-assured now that he could breathe again, so overconfident, that I feinted to the right, as if maybe I were coming for his balls again. He instinctively hunched forward, his hands rocketing out to shield his weakness. It was hugely satisfying. The angry expression that settled on his face immediately after, less so, but I couldn't imagine a future where I'd need to be on the good side of state senator Barry Janston.

Good thing it wasn't hunting season on dummies, or I wouldn't have made it out of those woods with my life.

"I'll be going," the senator said, his voice tight. "I suggest you do the same as soon as you're done here. Nice to meet you."

He turned and walked southeast, his Realtree camo blending into the shadowed woods almost immediately. I felt the cold finger of regret trace down my spine as I rethought my decision to embarrass him. It had been my experience that men who ran things hated nothing more than feeling powerless. Ah, well, as Mrs. Berns would say, *Let me borrow your time machine.*

I snapped some more photos of the structure, inside and out, including the animal fur, bones, and other evidence suggesting something wild had taken up residence inside this human structure. Satisfied that I'd done what I could, I tucked the camera into my jacket.

I shivered as I made my way back home. The temperature had plummeted with the sun, turning the woods into an icy moonscape, but that wasn't it. It also wasn't the way last fall's popple leaves clung to the trees, scraping and waving. It wasn't even the way I kept spotting small movements out of the corner of my eyes, like rabbits dashing home before complete dark.

No, something completely different was giving me the willies.

It was the sense that someone, some*thing*, was watching me, and it wasn't Janston.

Chapter 22

The unsettling, goose bump–y feeling of being watched hung with me back at the house, even though I tried petting therapy with Luna and Tiger Pop to shake it. It prickled my skin as I drove to Battle Lake, parked my car, and walked the short distance to the Tae Kwon Do gym, which was housed in the basement of a CPA's office. I was so sure that something was going to jump out at me that it was almost a relief when I ran into Gary Wohnt coming around the corner.

My head collided with his chest. I was pleasantly surprised that he smelled clean, and then I was so flustered by that thought that I shoved him to create distance between us.

"Hey," I said.

"You shouldn't be walking alone at night," he said, brusquely. He looked as uncomfortable as I felt.

"Chief Wohnt!" Mrs. Berns said, appearing behind me. "You really shouldn't be walking alone at night."

His eyebrows drew into a confused vee.

"There," Mrs. Berns said, her voice satisfied. "Now you hear how stupid it sounds. Our legs don't stop working when the sun goes down. Nor does our need to get things done. Now, if you'll excuse me and Mira, we've got some Toe Can Do to apply."

I'd tried correcting Mrs. Berns's pronunciation, but eventually given up. I threw my arm around her shoulders.

"What's that for?" she asked.

"It's been a long day," I said.

"Time to kick some butt, then. See you later, Chief."

We walked around Gary and into the separate entrance for Master Andrea's gym, removing our coats and shoes at the door. Mrs. Berns and I'd both achieved the rank of yellow belts, and we arrived in full uniform rather than changing in the cramped restrooms. The smells of old sweat and gym mats coupled with the sounds of people warming up were strangely soothing. I'd come to look forward to the practice, to dropping into my body and punching and kicking, even if it was only imaginary demons I was fighting.

"I'm taking a side job as a driver," Mrs. Berns said, struggling to remove her winter boot.

I studied her dubiously. "Do you even have a driver's license?"

She fished around her jacket pocket and came out with the most recent issue of the *Fargo Forum*. "I don't think they require it. They're looking for co-drivers, not behind-the-wheel drivers. The only requirement is that they need people with a sense of humor. Funnies, they call 'em."

I unfolded the newspaper she handed me and read the circled ad. I shook my head. "They're looking for *cos*-drivers, and they want *furries*."

"Say what now?"

I held the paper out to her. "Drivers who wear costumes. Specifically, animal costumes with human characteristics. Like mascots?"

"Nice," she said. "That sounds even more fun!"

She finally had the boot off. I shook the paper for her to take it, and a section fell out, landing face up. The headline read, Perham Girl Disappears.

I reached for the section and scanned the article. "A teenager has disappeared from Perham. Anita Juarez. The paper said she's a sophomore at the local high school, that her family moved here from Mexico when she was young. She's been missing for two days."

Mrs. Berns and I were both quiet. I was imagining how frantic her parents must be, and I bet Mrs. Berns was, too.

"She might be a runaway," a middle-aged green belt said, coming up behind us. I couldn't remember his name, just knew that I avoided him when it was time to pick workout partners.

I finished the article. "Says she's a good student, and that she worked at the turkey plant. Sounds pretty responsible."

He made the *you never know* gesture. "They left their country. They're leaving kind of people. Probably went back to her real home."

"You should be a leaving type of person," Mrs. Berns said, giving him the stink eye.

"Whatever," he said, walking past us to the restrooms.

"That poor girl," Mrs. Berns said. "She sure doesn't sound like a leaver to me. Maybe we should head to Perham to get to the bottom of it?"

Mrs. Berns had long imagined herself Robin to my Batman. A more apt description would be a Laurel to my Hardy. Perham was only a half-an-hour drive, though, a small town even though it was four times the size of Battle Lake, its economy built around the turkey-processing plant. I'd driven through a few times and been charmed by the downtown area, sprinkled with family-owned stores and a few great coffee shops, but I didn't know the area well.

"I can see your mind working," she said. "Is there something else you have to do in Perham? To justify the trip?"

I thought back to what I'd discovered on John Guinn this morning. "One of the guys on the note is trying to raise funding to build a community center there. I'd like to check it out," I admitted.

"You haven't talked to him yet? You've had that note for a full twenty-four hours and you have not reached out to the *one* person we know is still alive and lives nearby?"

I held up my hands. "What if it's nothing?"

"Tell him you want to interview him for the paper. Feel it out. If there's more there, your gut'll let you know."

It wasn't a half-bad idea.

She pinched my arm. Again. "Call him right now. Use Master Andrea's phone. You'll be stewing all night if you don't."

"You're right."

I got permission, found John Guinn in the phone book Master Andrea kept underneath her phone, and let it ring, my pulse rapid firing. Then I reminded myself that my cover story was perfectly legit. In fact, I could *actually* write an article on him and the community center. Ron might even pay me for it.

Guinn's answering machine clicked on. I waited for the beep.

"Hi, it's Mira James, a reporter for the *Battle Lake Recall*? We'd like to run a full story on your proposed Perham community center." I chose not to offer my phone number. I hated talking on the phone. "I'll stop by tomorrow morning, eight o'clock? Hopefully I'll catch you then."

I hung up, my finger tracing from his name in the phone book to his address. There was something about it . . .

My breath caught.

John Guinn owned the land I'd run into Barry Janston on. I knew he and I were neighbors from the TrackerSearch, but hadn't made the connection until I'd seen the address in print just now.

What had Janston said when I'd asked him what he was doing in the woods? That he was out turkey hunting. Then I'd called him out for being on public land. And he'd corrected me.

You're aware you're on my friend's private land?

I had no idea what it meant, Janston and Guinn being friends, but the knowledge settled like a cold stone in my stomach.

Chapter 23

Later that night, I gave Luna a proper walk, even though it was after nine and as dark as a grave when I finally returned home, blissfully sore from Tae Kwon Do sparring. She and I took off down the driveway and then veered right, toward Shangri-La Resort. The resort had been a gorgeous mansion with servants' quarters in the 1930s, transformed into a family-friendly getaway a decade or so ago. Perched on a peninsula, the only way on or off it was to travel down Sunny's driveway, past her little private beach, and across a narrow strip of land.

The gravel road was icy in patches, so I picked my way carefully, barely glancing at the tract of forested land where I'd almost been killed last June. Luna walked contentedly alongside, nuzzling my hand every now and again.

"I'm OK, girl," I said.

Except I wasn't, and I couldn't lie to myself any longer. The note had resurrected unresolved pain about my dad. His name was on a list with one very bad man and two apparently good men. He'd been a private investigator, which could go either way in how it reflected on a person's integrity. The fact that he had lied about it suggested it did not lean positive.

I paused. But maybe he hadn't lied about it? Maybe Mom knew, and they'd decided it was best not to tell me? But that thought woke up a whole new level of pain brought on by reminders of my mom's distance. We'd never been particularly close. Maybe it would have been the same if Dad hadn't been in our lives through to his bitter end, if Mom had ditched him when he'd sunk into alcoholism and hadn't cared to find a way out, but I didn't think so. She'd *liked* taking care of him. Based on how she'd allocated her time and attention, managing my father had given her life meaning. More, apparently, than she would have gotten from nurturing a close relationship with me.

Still, could I straight-out ask my mom if she knew Dad had been a licensed private investigator? Seemed an easy thing to do, but just thinking it poked at long-buried misery.

Luna whined, and I started walking again. The air felt thick and cold, the impending weather hanging over us like a guillotine, spurring electric shivers underneath my skin. The heavy night clouds obscured all but the brightest stars.

I recalled that eerie feeling of being watched in the pine woods and my skin started feeling seriously crawly.

"Luna, I think we should head back."

She wagged her tail in agreement.

Tiger Pop was happy to see us return so soon. Not so happy that she'd demonstrate it, but I could tell she was experiencing internal fireworks. I scratched her until she purred and rolled on her back, kidney beaning her head to her tail.

"You're such a good kitty," I said, meaning it. "Want to go look through photo albums with me?"

I didn't know where that had come from, but it felt right as soon as I uttered it. I'd carried two photo albums with me from apartment to apartment after I'd moved out of my childhood home. They now resided in Sunny's spare bedroom, along with my old mixtapes (never knew when they'd come back in style), watercolor paintings from my tortured-artist phase, and clothes that would fit me again once I reined in my Nut Goodie habit.

I retrieved the albums, plopping down in the doorway of the spare bedroom to page through, Luna at my back and Tiger Pop watching me from a few inches away. Her beautiful marble eyes were suspicious. (Or caring. I should give her the benefit of the doubt more.)

"Haven't peeped through these in a while," I told them both. Luna's tail thumped.

My mom had made the albums, offering them to me as a high school graduation gift. I'd paged through them back then, believing them more of a burden—an anchor to the memories I was trying to leave behind—than the gesture of love she'd meant them to be. They were too precious to discard, though, and I'd hauled them around even though I hadn't had a reason to open them in the past decade or so. The first album's plastic was stiff, making an irritable creaking noise when I opened it.

The introductory photo was a sucker punch, my dad holding newborn me in a hospital room, my mom a faded outline in the bed behind. Dad wore a white T-shirt, his hair a military buzz cut, his expression a messy, raw laser beam of protectiveness and surprise, like he couldn't imagine a world where such a tiny thing could survive.

I slammed the album shut. I felt hollowed out, cold. I tucked my hands into my armpits to warm them. Tiger Pop hopped away, and Luna whined.

I'd seen the photo before, sure, when I'd first received the album. What had I thought back then? That my dad was a creep, a killer, someone who couldn't process or even rein in his own demons, who refused to get any sort of real help, and so destroyed other people's lives rather than fixing his own.

I'd been right about that, but it hadn't been the whole picture, no pun intended. There'd also been love there, a human, a man who'd done some good things for me and my mom. That was a lot to make room for.

I heard Mrs. Berns's voice, as I often did when I was being an idiot. *It's not brain surgery. People aren't black and white. Pick that album back up, look at every picture, feel the pain, accept the love. And watch for clues that explain the note, you dumb bunny.*

She was right. Or, the imaginary her was. And she knew whereof she spoke. For all her assertiveness now, she'd spent most of her life married to an abusive husband. People didn't get divorced back then, she'd told me. She followed that immediately by cautioning me to not fall for crock-of-shit lines like that in my own life, because while they might be mostly true, it didn't matter. A person needed to do what was right for her, not for the rest of the world.

I sat straighter, conscious of my breath, steeled myself, and reopened the album. Seeing the photo of my dad holding me didn't shock nearly as much the second time. I could appreciate the fuzzy quality of the old picture, notice how everything appeared surrounded by a hazy orange fog, and wonder who'd snapped the picture. A nurse? An acquaintance of my parents'? Friends had mostly fallen away as my dad's drinking progressed, but I remembered the names of people who used to show up. Richard and Monica. Dave and Doreen. Had one of them been there to support my parents when their only child was born, my dad newly out of the military?

A bittersweet ache crept in as I leafed through the photos. Me staring at a chocolate cake with a fat "1" candle burning in its center, a birthday hat tilted over my wispy brown hair. Mom helping me to open a Christmas present, both our mouths wide in laughter. Dad and me sticking our faces through cutouts of long-bearded elves on some family road trip.

Something in me began to melt. The rigid concept of my dad as a creepy drunk began to fade, an image of him as a family man replacing it. I shook my head. But that wasn't right. These photos were capturing the best times, the moments when someone thought to bring a camera, paid for film to be developed, when everyone was on their best behavior.

I tamped down the warmth that had been flooding my limbs. I needed to examine these pictures like a private detective, searching for evidence that my dad had visited Otter Tail County, that he'd been a PI, that he knew Lartel McManus, John Guinn, or Jefferson Penetal.

My logical mind took over. *Uff da.* That felt better. Emotions had been clouding my judgment. I studied the remaining photos, noticing from a distance that my dad was in fewer and fewer of them, and then it was just me, my mom snapping the picture because my dad hadn't wanted to come along, or wasn't able to leave the house much by the time I got to high school.

None of the photographs featured any recognizable Battle Lake landmarks that would prove my dad had visited this area. The pictures showing him alongside men I didn't know didn't contain any names on the backs, only dates. I committed them to memory anyhow, in case interviewing John Guinn tomorrow shook something loose. I would track down a photo of Jefferson Penetal and do the same.

Feeling an unsettling mix of empty and off-balance, I returned both albums to their box. It was near ten. I should have gone to bed, but I didn't want to carry this emotional weight into dreamland, so I flicked on the television and began watering my seedlings, checking each tender shoot for brown leaves or signs of blight.

The local news was beginning in the background. The weather was the top-of-the-hour story, and that fact was troubling in a state where a temperature range of forty degrees in a twenty-four-hour period was considered no big thang.

"... a potential thundersnow coming our way, due to the complex synoptic weather bearing down on north central Minnesota."

I'd been bending toward my seedlings. At the word "thundersnow," I bolted upright.

What the ever-loving heck?

"We expect the system to break in the next five days, bringing with it a blizzard the likes of which we haven't seen since Halloween of 1991."

Those were fighting words in the Midwest. Everyone had their Halloween of 1991 story. I'd been in my early twenties, excited to wear my handmade California Raisin costume to a friend's party. Instead, I spent the night watching a blizzard fall as thick as a lead apron over the state. By morning, the snow was waist-high. As a fairly new adult tucked into her apartment, it had been thrilling. No work or school, perfect fort-building conditions.

As an adult living in the country, with two animals to care for? The thought was unsettling. At least the incoming system explained the weird air pressure I'd been feeling. I'd need to stock up on food and water and carry in enough wood for the potbellied stove Sunny had installed as backup heat in her living room. I'd yet to use it, but I'd be damned if I'd welcome *thundersnow* unprepared.

Sigh. April in Minnesota.

There was nothing more I could do about that tonight, so I returned to my seedlings, delighting at the way the crumbly black dirt thirstily drank the teaspoons of water I poured, scaring up the rich scent of wet earth. My teensy basil sprouts were on the top shelf, their leaves already dark green and bossy. Next to them, timid, prim thyme grew nicely alongside some goofy dill and cilantro. That pan was my favorite, but don't tell the fuzzy tomato sproutlings directly below.

My indoor greenhouse also nurtured bell and jalapeño peppers, eggplants, zucchini, cucumber, and ground cherries. I didn't like the flavor of the latter—they were to vegetables what raisins were to cookies—but I loved the surprise of them, a perfect orange globe nestled in a Chinese lantern.

I was humming happily when Barry Janston's mug appeared on the screen. It was the same official photo I'd seen earlier. In it he looked very senatorial despite the jarring, too-black color of his hair, not at all like the grabby hunter I'd run across a few short hours earlier.

A female news anchor spoke. "It's troubling news for Minnesota state senator Barry Janston, who was under investigation for a single sexual harassment case coming from a woman who volunteered on his most recent reelection campaign. Three more women have come forward today, all with the same attorney. They are accusing Senator Janston of sexual assault."

My stomach gurgled. Four women. One would have been more than enough, but four? That pointed to predation. Before I could sit with that, Karen Kramer's grim face appeared on the screen. It was the interview I'd seen her give earlier this morning. Had the press known about the most recent allegations when they'd come to town? Unlikely. Ron would have told me.

"I don't like making such a fuss about some harmless groping," Karen was saying into the camera. "Let's face that guys will be guys. It's not a big deal. Everybody has to be so politically correct these days."

Maisy stared at her mom as if she were hearing gospel, nodding along. I dearly hoped Mrs. Berns had followed through and created flyers for tomorrow's Chick Club meeting. These girls needed to know that "harmless" and "groping" didn't belong in a sentence together.

When the story switched over to an uptick in sex trafficking in north central Minnesota, I clicked off the television. I'd had enough for one day. Besides, I needed my rest so I was ready to interview John Guinn bright and early tomorrow.

Chapter 24

John Guinn was my country neighbor since our lands abutted, but because of the way the county was platted, it was still a seven-minute drive to reach his home. I had to travel down my nearly mile-long driveway, turn left on the gravel, then left on the blacktop, passing the driveway of a man I'd gotten to know a little too well last November, when I was investigating that questionable hunting accident. Another half mile past Clive's place, and I spotted the fire number marking Mr. Guinn's driveway, which was shorter than mine but no quick hike, curving as it did back toward the frozen lake.

His house was neat and compact, a modern build rather than the retrofitted farmhouses most people occupied around here. I didn't know my architecture well, but the cozy front porch featuring an enormous bay window and dormered second-floor windows gave the home an inviting feel.

I parked my car and crunched up the walk to his front door. I was hopeful he'd received last night's phone message. As it was, I ran the risk of waking him up, which was never the best way to conduct a first meeting.

I saw a doorbell to the right of his door. *Huh.* Most of us around here didn't have those newfangled contraptions. We preferred a good honest knock. I pushed the button anyway.

While I waited for the sound of footsteps, I stepped off the porch to eyeball the outbuildings. Two of the three looked like they'd stood there for decades: a decrepit, faded red barn near to falling over and, next to it, what appeared to be an old chicken coop that hadn't housed fowl (at least intentionally) in years.

Near the rear of the property, though, on the edge of the tree line of jack pine and spruce, stood what appeared to be a new garage-slash-workshop built to match the house. That meant Guinn had enough money to tear down the original farmhouse that must have stood here and rebuild on top of it.

No surprise if he was a successful therapist.

The front door opened, catching me off guard. I dropped my snooping face and dug around for my journalist expression. I didn't think I'd slapped it on in time, judging by how his eyes narrowed.

"Hello," I said, holding out my hand as I covered the space between us. "I'm Mira James. From the *Battle Lake Recall*? I hope you received my phone message last night."

His face relaxed. He accepted my handshake. "Of course," he said. "I didn't expect you to arrive so early."

"I'm sorry," I said. "I'm on my way to Battle Lake to open up the library. My weekday mornings have a bright and shiny start."

"It's no trouble at all." He ran his hand through a haircut that could be best described as preppy. Anne had been correct that Guinn resembled a beefy Sean Penn, though Guinn's lips were fuller and his nose sharper. "I'd forgotten you're the town librarian. What important work."

He stepped aside and held out his hand in a *come inside* gesture. "Can I pour you a cup of coffee?"

The delicious, dark smell of freshly ground coffee beans filled my nose. My mouth watered, Pavlovian-style, but I didn't want to grow too comfortable. I had a long day ahead of me. "No, thanks. I just have a few quick questions." I rustled in my coat pocket and came out with a notepad. "Do you mind if I take notes?"

"Not at all," he said. "Let's move this into the living room."

I followed him, removing my jacket as we went.

His house was masculine and clean, but not compulsively so. There were no dead-animal heads hung on the walls, but there were cobwebs in one corner of the hallway, and either he had a robot vacuum cleaner or was not a great sweeper, because little dust bunnies had gathered along the edges of the floor trim. The decorations were neutral and soothing, including a runner over the hardwood floor in wine and dark jewel tones that were picked up by abstract paintings on the wall. All in all, this was a bachelor pad that would look more in place in a trendy Minneapolis neighborhood than the Otter Tail County countryside.

"Your house is lovely," I said, truthfully.

"Thanks!" He dropped into a cozy-looking, overstuffed chair that he'd obviously been sitting in when I rang the bell. A steaming cup of coffee sat on the nearby table, and a large book was propped open near it. I leaned in, trying to catch the title, when I saw that it wasn't a book at all, but a shiny laptop concealed in a carrying case designed to resemble a book. It was über cool, and I vowed to get myself one of those as soon as I could afford a laptop to put inside it.

I settled on the corner of the leather couch across from him. "We're neighbors, you know. I'm house-sitting for Sunny Waters." I hitched my thumb behind me in what I hoped was the direction of my home and forced a smile.

"That's right! I feel awful that I've been a bad neighbor this whole time." He pursed his Sean Penn–ish lips and ran his hand through his dark hair again. There was something unsettling about the gesture, but I couldn't put my finger on it. "I should have stopped by to welcome you a long time ago. You've been there since this past summer?"

"A year, actually. But don't worry. I'm not a great neighbor, either." A thought struck me. Like, it literally hit me with an open palm, bringing with it that familiar buzzy feeling telling me that I should probably keep the idea to myself.

I was terrible at listening to that feeling.

"Speaking of not being a great neighbor," I started hesitantly, "I think I may have accidentally trespassed on your place yesterday."

He chose that moment to take a sip of coffee, so I couldn't read his expression. When he looked up again, his face was smooth. "I may have heard something about that. You ran into a friend of mine?"

"If we're talking about Barry Janston, then yes. I was looking for evidence of a Bigfoot for a story my editor assigned. Imagine my surprise at finding a senator instead."

John threw back his head and laughed, full-throated. His show of good humor seemed out of place for the situation, but maybe he was one of those people with an awkward wit.

"I've heard those Bigfoot rumors," he said. "Didn't put much stock in them. So does the gossip say they're living in our backyards now?"

"Something like that," I said, thinking about the evidence I'd discovered in that rudimentary hut. "Janston really a friend of yours?"

There was no mistaking the change in his expression now. His mouth grew tight. "He is. We go way back. Went to high school together."

I barreled through my second warning flag of the conversation. "Any comment on his current situation?"

My words hung in the air between us for an uncomfortable few seconds. I thought I'd worded it as neutrally as humanly possible, but the disapproval in Guinn's voice when he finally responded indicated there was no good way to ask that question.

"I won't speak against a friend," Guinn said, his tone less genial now. "Ever."

He said it like a challenge, but it was a principle I understood.

"Fair enough," I said. "Can we talk instead about the community center you're raising money for in Perham? What's the motivation behind that, especially since you've already overseen the building of a center here in Battle Lake?"

Guinn's shoulders immediately relaxed, and he leaned forward, his elbows on his knees. "While I'm less involved in getting the Perham center up and running than I was ours, it's still something I'm passionate about. Kids simply need a place to hang out," he said, "and the ones who depend upon the center most are too young to drive from one town to another. If we don't create community at a young age, particularly for the immigrant children in our area, it's almost impossible to instill a sense of belonging later on."

He brushed his hand through his hair before continuing. "I think every kid deserves a chance to feel safe. Don't you?"

I thought back to my childhood. I agreed with him. Still, his abrupt mood switches and his overloud laugh from earlier had me on edge. Either he was a flighty guy, or something about my presence made him prickly. I sniffed the air. I could only smell the coffee, and maybe evidence of fried eggs for breakfast. I flicked my glance to the edges of the room. Nothing was out of place. Plus, Guinn was currently relaxed and leaning toward me. Why was my intuition yelling at me that something was not as it seemed?

"I do think that, and I also think it's very kind of you," I said, realizing I'd been quiet for too long. "A lot of people don't necessarily take on other people's problems."

He spread his hands, palms up. "We all rise together, that's what I think. Comes with the job. I have a clinic in town. I specialize in counseling teens, but I also work on relationship counseling and anything else people need."

Here he locked eyes with me for an unnervingly long time, saying nothing. He wanted me to fill that space, maybe confess that I needed therapy. Well, I sure as heck did, but not from him. I might not know what was off with this guy, but something was rotten. My instincts didn't lie. I faked checking my notes.

"When's the Perham community center slated for completion?"

He smiled, moving smoothly from therapy to straight business. "If we get our funding, we'll break ground this summer, and the center will open to the public next year. Barry is doing some good work and helping me to raise money, by the way."

I wasn't going to touch that one. I'd found that some people thought two rights fixed a wrong. That'd never been my experience. The only things that could fix a wrong were a sincere apology and amends, for starters. I switched the topic, pretending to jot in my notebook to set him at ease while I spoke. "Have you heard about the girl disappearing from Perham?"

The squeak of the chair made me glance up. Guinn made as if he were about to stand, poised on the edge of his seat. I got the distinct impression he was fighting the urge to kick me out. Well, that was interesting. I reviewed the question. Had I asked it in a callous manner?

"I'm sorry if that upset you," I said. "I was asking as a journalist. My thought was that mentioning the girl's situation in the article might help your cause. We certainly don't have to talk about it."

He did stand now. "If you don't mind, I should get ready for work." He glanced at the doorway. He wanted me to walk through it.

I rose. What else could I do? Not come out and ask him about the note. I'd already accidentally cheesed him off plenty for one day. Besides, I didn't want to reveal the note to him until I figured out what about him was setting off my radar.

I let him guide me to the front door, where he seemed to have something of a change of heart.

"Look," he said, turning to face me. This close, the Sean Penn resemblance was startling. Guinn could be his body double, easy. He ran his hand through his hair for the fourth time since I'd arrived. "Sorry about being so abrupt. You hit on a sore spot, is all. I'm upset that I can't move faster. I feel like I could help girls in Perham, maybe not the one who disappeared, but other ones who might get the idea to follow her, if only I could get that community center built more quickly."

I hardly heard what he was saying over the alarm bells dinging because there it was, plain as day, what had been setting me off. Most people, but especially con men, have a unique way they carry themselves when they're lying: a quirk to their lips, a shifting of the eyes, a breathlessness to their voice. It's called a tell. Card players, cops, private eyes, and world-class liars were always on the lookout for tells.

And I'd just witnessed Guinn's for the fourth time. It was so blatant that I couldn't believe I hadn't spotted it before.

When he lied, he ran his fingers through his hair.

"I'm so sorry," I said, feigning an uncomfortable realization, "but can I use your bathroom?"

I saw him weighing his options. Since he was at his front door while I was still in his hallway, balanced on that jewel-toned runner, he had none short of being rude. For some reason I could not yet fathom, he did not want to do that.

"Of course," he said, releasing the doorknob and making that welcoming gesture again. "The first door on your left. You passed it earlier."

"Thanks," I said. "Shouldn't be more than a minute."

The door revealed a half bathroom roughly the size of a small utility closet. It contained a narrow door likely leading to linen storage, a toilet, and a sink with a cabinet under it and a mirror above it. I lifted the lid on the toilet and turned on the cold water in the sink to cover my snooping sounds.

The linen closet contained only bathroom supplies: towels, disinfectant, rags, a toilet brush. Same with the mirrored medicine cabinet, which housed an old toothbrush, some toothpaste, and a half-full bottle of eye drops. Everything looked normal.

I closed the cabinet and flushed the toilet, turning off the faucet while the toilet swirled. When it was done, I switched the water back on, as if I were washing my hands. I was running out of time. I had no idea what I was looking for. I'd dashed in here as an impulse, my only logical opportunity to discover a clue to I-didn't-know-what before Guinn kicked me out of his house for good.

With the water running down the drain, I knelt. I opened the cupboard under the sink. I pushed aside spare rolls of toilet paper and boxes of tissue.

My chest constricted. In the far back, I finally spotted what I was looking for, even though I hadn't known what it would be until I laid eyes on it: a Pretty in Ink kit, the hottest item among teenage girls, and a half-used box of maxi pads.

I didn't know if Guinn had a client, or a niece, or even a daughter who stayed with him. Any of those possibilities would justify these items.

But that wouldn't explain why my skin was crawling and every baby hair on my neck was standing at attention.

Chapter 25

My thoughts settled like cold, congealing concrete as I drove to work. The leaden gray sky perfectly reflected my mood. The sense that a dam was about to break and unleash some epic ice and snow grew stronger by the moment. I held so many pieces but wasn't even sure there was a puzzle to be solved.

My dad's name headlined the note. He could have been listed as a private investigator, or his name could have been added for some other reason. Had all four men been in a gang? Unlikely, given where we lived, and who my dad had been. Some sort of betting ring? Possible, but also doubtful. Lartel McManus had been a bad guy beyond any doubt, but he'd been tight with his money.

Jefferson Penetal was dead and couldn't speak for himself, but his paper trail said he'd shown up in the world as an ordinary citizen, not so much as a parking ticket to his name. John Guinn also appeared virtuous on paper, but in person he was as slippery as a greased tapeworm. Maybe the same would have been true of Penetal had I gotten a chance to meet him.

And the word "help"? Who'd scribbled that on the note? Had it been a joke? Or a desperate, last-ditch plea stuffed into a book in the hopes that it would land in the hands of somebody just like me? Who knew about it being placed in the book besides Mrs. Berns, Anne the receptionist, and me? Whoever it was wanted it back bad enough to break into the library.

I stabbed the radio dial, craving a diversion. I was hoping for some of the '80s arena rock so popular in this area but was instead greeted by the news.

"Anita Juarez of Perham is still missing, last seen in a white '94 Pontiac Firebird. Please keep your eyes peeled and call . . ."

I turned off the radio, my attempt at distraction ending up with the opposite result. Hearing about that poor girl chilled me. If her family didn't believe she'd run away, then I didn't think she'd run away, either. Who'd taken her?

When I reached the first Battle Lake stop sign, rather than turning right toward the library, I steered left toward the cop shop. It was a bad habit, this inability to sit with discomfort and unknowns. I'd been born needing to act.

But now that I found myself parked outside Gary's work, I didn't know exactly what my next step might be. I sat in my idling car, studying the squat, ugly Battle Lake Police Department building under the ominous sky. I normally tried to *avoid* going in there. On the occasions when I did find myself inside, not one time had it worked to my benefit.

I couldn't stop thinking about that missing girl, though.

Before I lost my courage, I turned off my car, stepped outside, and stomped toward the station. The metallic sky seemed to bear down on me as I went, its judgment cold and heavy.

Gary, seated behind the main desk and writing on a yellow legal pad, did not glance up when I walked in. "What do you need, James?"

He must have spotted me through the window. My cheeks flamed. Probably I'd looked like a big old dork out there, trying to talk myself into entering.

"I need you to tell me something," I said, too loud.

His jaw clenched. He paused for a moment, pen raised, but then returned to loud scribbling, the ballpoint's nib scraping viciously across the paper.

"What I'm wondering," I continued, when it was clear he wasn't going to speak, "is if we can talk about that Perham girl who disappeared.

Anita Juarez. I want to know if you have any theories about what happened to her."

I realized I'd been holding my breath. It hurt to ask Gary for information like that, to open myself up to the rejection that was sure to come.

This time he set his pen down. He slowly dragged his eyes to me, his cheekbones poured steel, his hair jet-black and slicked away from his face. I noticed his hands for the first time. They were large and strong looking, like they could keep you safe. Not knowing where that thought came from, I returned my focus to his stare. His eyes were two inky abysses into nothing and forever.

I held my tongue. I'd been about to confess that I'd stolen Mindy Johnson's Twinkies back in second grade (after stealing John Fuch's snack cakes in first grade—call me a regular old Hostess hijacker) cuz my parents wouldn't buy me any sugary food.

Gary finally spoke, and *oh*, I found myself wishing he hadn't.

"I think she's been sex trafficked," he said, his voice even, speaking plainly for the first time since I'd met him. "Anything else you want to know?"

My guts twisted. I was surprised he'd answered me, but I'd sensed deep down that if he did, that was exactly what he was going to say. I knew from a newspaper article I'd written a couple months ago that Minnesota had the third-highest sex trafficking rate in the country. Something to do with the way major highways converged. It was a terrible truth, one I hadn't wanted to dwell on when I was researching for the article but was forced to consider now.

I hated how meek I sounded when I finally found my voice. "Any leads on her disappearance?"

He ran his hands across his face, the gesture of somebody who'd worked many late nights. The rasping sound drew my attention to a five-o'clock-going-on-midnight shadow that hadn't quite registered before. If Anita Juarez's disappearance wasn't weighing heavily on Gary, something else sure was.

"Not a single one," he said. "Nothing other than the white Firebird bit you likely heard on the radio, which caused you to storm into my office demanding answers about something that has absolutely nothing to do with you."

I was unexpectedly pitched into deep humiliation, shrinking into the cold, lost feeling of having made a terrible mistake. Gary was right. I'd come here throwing a tantrum because I didn't have all the information I wanted while he was trying to get important work done.

"Sorry," I said, stumbling backward toward the door. The knob turned before I reached it.

I was startled to see my sweet, gorgeous Johnny Leeson appear in the doorway. His cheeks were flushed from the brisk air. He must have walked here. His eyes were bright as ever, his thick, dirty-blond hair mostly hidden under a winter cap.

"Johnny!" I said, warm relief replacing the shame.

I'd expected a hug, but Johnny's eyes shot from me to Gary and back to me again, blazing.

"What are you doing here?" he asked.

I looked over my shoulder. Gary, impassive as ever, was giving us his full attention.

I swallowed past my suddenly dry mouth. "I was asking about the girl missing from Perham."

"Why?" Johnny asked. "Are you on the case?"

His tone was sarcastic, something I'd never heard from him before, and I didn't like it, not one bit. My skin grew clammy as I felt myself tumbling back into humiliation, but this time I fought it, inviting anger instead. This was another new emotion between Johnny and me.

"No," I said, my teeth gritted. I shouldn't have jumped so quickly to anger, but it was more comfortable than the shame. "I'm a concerned citizen. What are *you* doing here?"

Johnny shoved his hands into his pockets and glared at his feet. "I have something I need to talk to Gary about."

My mouth had gone from dry to dirt. Johnny and I were having our first fight, at least our first two-way one, and it was happening in front of Gary. I wanted to yell, *What could you possibly talk to Gary about that you wouldn't have mentioned to me already?* They weren't exactly enemies, but neither did they much like each other. But I wasn't going to make myself any more vulnerable than I already had, not in front of both men. I would not let Gary know that I had no idea why my boyfriend was here, and I refused to let Johnny see how hurt I was.

"He's all yours," I said, pushing past my sandalwood-scented hunk and into the freezing air.

I was thankful for the temperature. It cold-cauterized my tears before they fell. Sliding into my car, I told myself I needed to get more sleep and eat better. I was clearly stretched too thin if I grew so emotional about small things, like Johnny acting weird.

But as I fired up my car, I found my feelings sliding back into anger, as they were wont to do. What was Johnny up to behind my back? Why was he acting so strange lately? My best guess was that he wanted to break up with me.

Well, that might be just fine. Once and for all.

On impulse, I steered into the parking lot of Dr. Lou Banks, DDS. I had seven minutes before I needed to unlock the library door. Fortunately, Dr. Banks's office opened an hour before we did. I peeked again into the empty storefront next door. I didn't spot anything new inside. Such prime real estate. I was surprised it was still unclaimed. I made my way into the dentist's office.

"He's booked solid until noon," Anne said by way of greeting.

Did I have a "read my mind and tell me bad things" note scribbled on my forehead today? Because if so, I would need to scrub it off with some steel wool.

"Maybe I could stop by over lunch hour?"

"Maybe, if you want a cleaning."

I mentally checked in with my bank account. "How much would that cost?"

"What kind of insurance do you have?"

"Whatever the city gives."

"Then a cleaning is free." She clicked her computer keyboard. "Dr. Banks's next opening is May twenty-sixth."

I reeled back. "I thought it was noon today."

She smiled serenely. "Sorry. I've got him blocked out for lunch."

Dang, she'd played me. "What if I can't wait that long? What if my teeth need an emergency cleaning?"

"Do they?"

Ah, the Kryptonite to my lying superpower: an unexpectedly direct question. "No," I said humbly. I'd need to take some master playa classes from this woman. "Put me down for the twenty-sixth."

Her smile widened. "You got it."

She continued entering my appointment as she spoke, multitasking with the expert air of someone whose hands can work independent of their mouth. "And you know, I bet Dr. Banks doesn't know anything about that note. He's a hard worker, a family man, and he keeps his nose clean. The biggest drama in his life right now is trying to rent that place next door."

"You didn't tell him about the note?"

"Oh no," she said, eyes wide. "I didn't want to bother him."

Interesting. If she was the one who'd broken into the library, she'd just cut her alibi pool by one. "Did you tell *anyone*?"

She shrugged. "No. Should I have?"

"No," I said. "I bet it's nothing."

If she was telling the truth, and it felt like she was, that meant that either the library break-in was a coincidence in no way tied to the book or the note, or, much worse, that someone with bad intentions had found out about the note independently from me talking to Anne and was willing to commit a crime to get it back.

I accepted the appointment reminder she handed me and was turning to leave when I had a hunch.

"Hey," I said, swiveling back to face her. "Remember how John Guinn's name was on the note? Do you know anything about him and Senator Barry Janston being friends?"

She made a face like she'd discovered old cabbage rotting in the back of her refrigerator. "I don't know a thing about their relationship, but I know more than enough about Janston," she said. "Used to be a regular here, until a hygienist got him blacklisted for getting a little too handsy."

I mirrored her grimace. "I hope he didn't pull any of that on you?"

"Not me," she said, reaching for a Louisville Slugger from behind her desk. "I keep myself prepared."

I couldn't fight the smile. Before it got too comfortable on my face, though, she leaned in and hooked her finger at me like she had a secret to tell. I moved closer.

"If you want to know what Janston is really like," she whispered, even though we were alone in the waiting room, "you should ask Karen. The things that woman put up with."

"Karen Kramer?" I asked, remembering her interview in front of the hardware store defending Janston.

Anne sat back, satisfied. "That's the one. They dated after her marriage ended. It was serious, until he cheated on her."

Chapter 26

Mrs. Berns was sitting at the main computer, typing, when I yanked open the door. She'd beaten me to the library, thank goodness, as the stop at Dr. Banks's meant I was running late.

I started filling her in on my morning without waiting for a "hi how are ya."

"I went to Guinn's house. It was nice, neat, but not too neat. Looked like a relatively new build. Nothing super-weird on the inside, no heads in bags or anything like that." I began removing my parka as I strode toward the front counter. "He looks like a pudgy, shifty Sean Penn," I continued. "Plus, he had bathroom supplies that were out of place in a single man's home."

"I do think we should order new bathroom supplies!" Mrs. Berns said, without looking up from her typing. Her voice was loud and chirpy and her face was pinched.

"What?" I stopped halfway between the front door and her, my jacket half-off. "I was talking about the community center guy? John Guinn? I got the worst vibes at his place. The note, and then the Janston thing in the woods, they both have me jumpy." I did an all-over body shake, like a dog trying to ditch a flea. "I'm probably seeing creeps everywhere. Overreacting."

"I will check if we have books on flea circuses and mental health," she said, her voice still too loud. "You say it must have 'try not to over-react' in the title?"

She bugged her eyes out and twitched her head toward the stacks. For the second time in a single short week, I contemplated whether Mrs. Berns was stroking. "I *don't* need a book on overreacting. I need you to listen to—"

A movement near the stacks startled me. I'd assumed Mrs. Berns and I were alone in the library this early. I yanked my coat back over my shoulders as the mustachioed inspector walked out with a book in his hand. I immediately understood what Mrs. Berns had been doing.

"Good morning!" I said to him. "I'm so glad that you're using our beautiful library today." I rushed over to his side, accidentally knocking the shark off Jed's altar. I jumped over it to reach the inspector's side. "What are you reading?"

I realized I was being overly effusive and committing the number-one librarian no-no of expressing interest in a specific book someone was reading. As librarians, we had to behave like doctors or therapists and treat all books as equal. No judgment. We wanted our patrons to feel like they could read whatever they wanted to. Sure, we made some fun behind their backs, but that's life.

I was desperate to connect with this trim, milquetoast Snidely Whiplash of a man, though, and to make him think for a moment that maybe Battle Lake wasn't Dangertown. The image of that empty storefront next to the dentist's office was haunting me. There might be all sorts of other businesses in that same situation if the inspector didn't see that this was an amazing town, despite the corpse problem.

The inspector studied me suspiciously, but he held up the book: *Food Is Medicine: Meals to Heal Any Condition.*

"Are you a chef?" I asked.

His cheeks bloomed. "I like to do some cooking on the side."

I led him back to the front desk, returning Jed's shark to the altar and fully removing my jacket on the way. "I'll get you set up for a temporary card. A permanent one takes about two weeks to process from our central office in Fergus Falls, if you want to apply now? I hope you'll think of returning to our lovely town once your work is done."

His smile melted. "Please do not try to bribe me. I'm here to do a job, and I will conduct myself ethically no matter your feeble attempts at influencing me."

"Understood," I said, simultaneously trying to figure out another way to bribe him. While entering his information into the computer—his name was Robert Hartman, not Snidely Whiplash—I asked him what his plans were for the rest of the day.

"I prefer not to say," he said, sniffing.

If getting to the bottom of the note, and Bigfoot, and setting up for tonight's inaugural Chick Club meeting were not eating all my time, I would have followed him. As it was, I could only scan his book and return it to him.

"I hope you have a wonderful day," I said. "And if you have allergies like me—they're terrible this time of year—I can recommend some fantastic eye drops they sell at the apothecary down the street."

He clutched the book close to his chest and scuttled out the door.

Mrs. Berns had pulled up a chair near the front counter and already had her legs crossed, chin in hand, leaning forward. "Now tell me that whole story about that creep whose house you just left," she said. "And if you doubt your instincts at any point, I will come over there and hug you until you cave."

I shuddered. She knew I was afraid of open displays of love. "It was normal looking on the whole," I said, recapping what I'd been telling her when I'd walked in. "Other than maxi pads and a girls' tattoo kit under the bathroom sink. But Guinn works with kids. It makes sense that teenagers in trouble would stay with him sometimes, or that he would have supplies or gifts for them."

She lunged at me with her arms open, and I drew back.

"Did his place look like it regularly hosted teenagers?" Mrs. Berns asked. "Did you spot supplies for boys, too?"

I mentally scanned his bottom floor, the only rooms I'd seen. It had appeared every bit the bachelor pad except for what I'd discovered in the bathroom. "No."

I expected Mrs. Berns to scold me again. She dropped her hands and drew in a ragged sigh instead. "Do you remember the Mayfair girl?"

I shook my head.

"I wouldn't expect so. It was before you came to Battle Lake. About twenty-five years ago, actually. The Mayfair family lived south of town, driving toward Ashby. Churchgoing, successful farmers as much as you could be back in those days, three kids who weren't trouble to anybody."

Her face had gotten loose in the telling, but it suddenly tightened up.

"I found myself in the grocery store with the middle Mayfair girl," she continued. "Daphne. She was maybe fifteen at the time. Had my own problems back then, trying to figure out if I needed to spring myself outta my problematic marriage, getting my kids to do their homework, that sort of stuff. Daphne and I found ourselves at the butcher counter at the same time. I knew who she was because it's a small town and was smaller back then, but I didn't pay her much attention. Said hi to her, she said hi back, and then I placed my order."

Mrs. Berns's eyes fell shut, and she drew in a ragged sigh. "But then something made me look back at her, so I did. That's when I saw it."

"What?" I asked. The library suddenly felt like someone had left the door open on the tundra.

"Nothing that would hold up in court, nothing that I could call out specifically, but I knew instantly that she was getting hurt at home." When her eyes opened, they were laser bright. "When you see a girl carrying that particular shame, you recognize it. Instantly."

My stomach grew hollow. "What did you do?"

"I did what people do. I asked her if she was OK. I still remember how she looked back at me. That naked-bone expression that I'd caught when she thought no one was looking? It fled, and she slapped her church smile back on. Said she was fine. My gut heard her real language. It heard her crying out for help. But I didn't listen. I accepted my cut of beef from the butcher. I drove home. I cooked that pot roast for my family. And when a few weeks later I heard through the phone tree that

Daphne's father had killed her and then taken his own life, I knew it was my fault." A tear trickled down Mrs. Berns's cheek.

I opened my mouth to argue her assertion, but she held up her hand.

"It wasn't my fault like it was *his* fault, I understand that. He'd been hurting her for years, and then that same evil drove him to strangle his own child with his bare hands. But when God put me in her path, it was my job to hear what her eyes were telling me. Those insights are precious." Mrs. Berns shrugged. "It couldn't have been any louder, and I looked away. When you ignore what your God-given instinct is telling you, you become party to whatever happens next. Including unspeakable tragedies."

I dropped into the nearest chair. All sorts of rational arguments were crowding into my head, but I knew Mrs. Berns was right. My intuition told me something was terribly off-kilter at Guinn's. If I was wrong, the worst thing was that I would look foolish. If I wasn't overreacting, though, and I ignored my instincts, somebody could die. It sounded dramatic because it was.

John Guinn was a bad man, and he was up to something criminal.

Except I had no evidence.

I needed to get some, and quick.

Mrs. Berns yanked me out of my reverie. "I swore to myself that if I ever got a chance at helping somebody like that again, nothing would stop me from doing it. And if I come across a man who hurts girls? I'll rewrite his story with a Chicago Typewriter. You know," she said, miming holding a tommy gun. *"Ratatatatat."*

"Seems like a solid plan." She may have been watching too much Turner Classics, but she wasn't wrong. "Also, you're right that I need to trust my gut. It's telling me to head back to Guinn's and search for more evidence. Something I can take to the police."

I swallowed saliva that felt like thick paste. Mrs. Berns's confession was drawing one out of me, too. "But here's the thing: I think I've been looking the other way about this whole note and its implications because I don't want to find out that my father was involved in sex trafficking."

It came out as one long word: *butheresthethingIthink . . .*

My heart was beating so loud it was causing tremors, because that terrible notion had been nagging at me since I'd first read the note, but I hadn't let it form a coherent thought in my brain. I was too afraid that thinking it would make it real.

But there it was. I'd said it out loud, and I couldn't take it back. It was a black, sticky, evil thought. My father and the other three men had been sex traffickers, and John Guinn still was, and the "help" had been a cry from some poor girl trying to escape their ring.

It was what my gut was telling me.

All my cells were poised for Mrs. Berns to pronounce judgment on my father and on me.

She did turn on me, coming at me like a rocket, but it was a swoop to hug me. "Our parents' crimes are not our own."

Then, lest I think her soft, she gave a quick twist to my tenders. I'd need to start wearing padding.

"Anyone ever tell you that you're not supposed to pinch your friends?" I asked, rubbing the sore spot with one hand and swiping away tears with the other.

"Nobody who didn't want to get their other arm pinched. Besides, I did that for you so you wouldn't feel things were getting too mushy. Now hop on that computer and start researching. I can see that you're dying to."

I smiled through the tears. There is a certain kind of joy in somebody knowing you well and still loving you. I was a research nerd. While I could and often did uncover important information in the field, I preferred to get all my ducks in a row before I went out. Actually, who was I kidding? I mostly ran by the seat of my pants, but if the computer was available, I really enjoyed digging in.

The first online stop was to see if there was any new information out on Minnesota sex trafficking since I'd written the article about it.

A quick scan revealed that if anything, the problem had intensified. Minnesota still was the third-biggest state. Sex trafficking spiked when there were large conferences or sporting events in the area, but it was an insidious, horrible crime consistently operating throughout the United States, and law enforcement couldn't seem to get a handle on it despite their best efforts.

The image of the missing girl from Perham came into my head, unbidden. I shook it out. I would keep her in my heart, but I needed my brain clear to get to the bottom of this. Still, it wouldn't hurt to confirm what Gary had told me.

My research immediately proved that he'd been telling the truth. There were no new leads in the Anita Juarez disappearance except the mention of the Firebird, and that was a slim one. Someone had spotted the white Pontiac in the neighborhood the same time the girl disappeared. They hadn't gotten a license plate. The car could belong to anybody, and not be connected at all.

I glanced over the top of my computer. Mrs. Berns was rearranging Jed's altar. I quickly typed in "Daphne Mayfair Battle Lake." The story appeared immediately and was even more heartbreaking than Mrs. Berns had said. The father had been abusing Daphne for years. Police believed she had been planning to run away the night that he killed her.

My heart ached for the family, and for Mrs. Berns.

The front door donged, startling me. New patrons came filing in. Well, how about that, we were a working library. I didn't want to leave my computer, but I had to do my job.

Mrs. Berns and I stayed busy throughout the day. I suspected the impending weather was the cause. People felt it bearing down, their pioneer genes whispering to store up on food and entertainment because we were all about to be trapped in our houses. It became an assembly line to check them out, with the only breaks those I took to blow my nose and squeeze in eye drops every hour or so.

In the few blissful moments where no one needed my help, I quickly researched inspector Robert Hartman. I had his address from his temporary library card application. Made it easy. I was surprised to discover that he'd earned a bachelor of science degree in nutrition, had studied cooking in France, and yet was now working for the tourism board. Seemed like a waste of passion, but I knew from the outside that happiness didn't always come wrapped like we thought it should.

Digging deeper, I came across Mr. Hartman's online dating ad on Littlepond Bigfish. Like a complete doofus, he'd included his real name. The ad read:

> Accomplished chef and well-traveled Renaissance man looking for companionship. No expectations except friendship. My name is Robert (Bob) Hartman, and geography is not a barrier.

I'd seen worse. In fact, the guy was growing on me. His job wasn't great from where I was sitting, but it wasn't his fault he was here to determine if he should blacklist Battle Lake. I owned at least half of that. With that in mind, I found I genuinely wanted to do something nice for him, not only to bribe him, but because I was beginning to suspect he was a good guy despite his odd manner and the fact I'd seen him digging through someone's garbage.

I pulled up WorldCat.org to search for the book I had in mind. I discovered it at a southeastern Minnesota library. I ordered it overnighted on interlibrary loan, hitting the submit button just as someone appeared at the front counter asking for help locating "that book about the people who travel and one of them's a plumber?"

Before I knew it, it was almost closing time.

"What a day!" I said.

Mrs. Berns could only nod, swiping the back of her hand across her forehead in the universal *I'm beat!* gesture. You wouldn't think library work would be so demanding. You would be wrong. It combines the best as well as the most challenging aspects of retail, counseling, conflict resolution, detective work, and party planning. Speaking of, the first teenage girls were filing in, peering around the library tentatively.

"Mrs. Berns!" I couldn't hide my gratitude. "You handed out the flyers!"

"What, am I trying to form a garage band? No, I did not hand out flyers. I jogged over to the high school and asked the principal to announce what was going on tonight. He said he would, and not only that, he'd award community service points to any girls who attended."

I smiled broadly. "You're a genius."

"It is the ant who thinks the grasshopper a giant," she said, cackling.

I lunged for her underarms.

"Don't even think about it," she said. "That level of bodywork is not for the uninitiated."

I shook my head. "Do you know if Kennie is coming by? I don't have a curriculum plan for tonight."

Mrs. Berns pointed at the door by way of answer.

My jaw dropped.

Chapter 27

Kennie sashayed into the library dressed like a high school sophomore.

That is, if it were 1993, we were about to get saved by the bell, and she was gunning for a date with Screech. Her hair was crimped and piled high on her head, held in place with a scrunchie. In lieu of a warm coat, she wore a lime-colored, double-breasted men's smoking jacket with generously padded shoulders. A long pearl necklace hung nearly to her knees. Her bottom half was covered with gloriously puffy mom jeans, their faux rips mended with cheetah-pattern fabric.

Kennie clapped her hands to grab everybody's attention, as if that were necessary. "Who's ready for a girl party!"

The dozen or so teenage girls who'd assembled rolled their eyes.

Kennie tipped her smile. "I've got a full Pretty in Ink kit in my car."

Their faces lit up, and they rushed her, every one of them talking at once.

"I want the dandelion fluff one."

"Do you have any of the little silver stars?"

"I want a rose with thorns! It is so symbolic of who I am, internally."

Mrs. Berns inserted her pinkies on each side of her mouth and whistled so loud that she nearly ruptured my eardrums.

"While Kennie runs out to her car to get this ridiculous tattoo kit all of you think is the second coming of Christ," she said once everyone was staring at her, "I'm going to give you young ladies a lecture on what it really means to be a woman. Now gather around, girls, or there will be no tattoos."

Kennie pouted. She was no longer the center of the universe. Likely realizing there was only one way to fix that, she skedaddled out to her car. Mrs. Berns wasted no time.

"Take notes, because here's the thing: This world is going to try to tell you how to look, what to say, and worst of all, how you should feel when somebody treats you poorly. But I'm going to let you in on a secret. It's everything I've learned in ninety-plus years on this planet, boiled down to two words. The *only* two words, really, the ones you'll need to not only survive but to make your mark, walk proud, and live the glorious life you deserve."

She tilted forward.

All the girls did the same.

"Fuck 'em," Mrs. Berns said, hooting. "Fuck 'em all!"

Eyebrows shot up. A few of the girls gasped, and then nervous giggles broke out as they exchanged surprised glances.

"No," Mrs. Berns said, "I mean it. You find a good group of friends, you surround yourself with them, and you live this life like it's the only one you've got. Say nuts to anyone who wants to judge you or hold you back or tell you who you are. But remember to also check in with yourself because you don't want a big head. If your gut and your heart tell you that you're doing the right thing, though, you listen, no matter what."

Some of the girls were writing this down. I didn't blame them. It was a continuation of my earlier conversation with Mrs. Berns, and it was pure gold.

"Another thing," she said. "When someone warns you not to cause trouble, to keep your mouth shut and not make a fuss? Those people are what we call 'asshats.' Don't listen to them."

Believe it or not, my eyes started misting over. If I'd known Mrs. Berns at the age these girls were, I could have saved myself a whole

131

mess of heartache. I started to relax, thinking that maybe she could run tonight's show.

"Now," Mrs. Berns said, disappearing behind the library counter and returning with a cardboard box, "I brought you each a hand mirror. We're each gonna take a peek at our own gorgeous cooters and—"

"Hold up!" I jerked to attention, inserting myself into the conversation. "Mrs. Berns has given us a lot to ponder. How about we spend the rest of the time in conversation, hearing more from all of you while you give each other tattoos?"

The front door opened, letting in an icy wash of air scented with green. I was expecting Kennie to stride in, but Gary appeared instead. He held himself as if he were even more disgruntled than usual, which was to say that he'd gone full Archie Bunker.

"What is it?" I asked around the sudden chalk in my mouth.

Gary lasered every single girl in that room with his stare. I didn't doubt he knew them all by name. Some of them grabbed on to each other, sensing his mood.

"Is Maisy Kramer here?" he asked. His voice was a deep growl.

I skimmed the girls. I knew Karen Kramer's daughter hadn't shown up, but I didn't want to face the pit that his question had opened up beneath me.

"No," a cherry-lipped brunette in the front row said. "She left school during lunch and didn't come back."

Gary seemed to grow larger and angrier. I was afraid he was going to pop, and we'd be cleaning Gary out of our hair for weeks.

"Did she leave with someone?" he asked.

The girls exchanged wary glances, all of them doing some version of a shrug.

"I only know she left because she texted me that she had errands to run," the brunette said, handing Gary her phone.

He took it. He read the text. He nodded brusquely. "If any of you hear anything from or about Maisy, and I mean *anything*"—he paused to make eye contact with each girl as well as Mrs. Berns and me, his gaze so intense that it left a scar—"you contact the police department immediately. Do you understand?"

We all did.

Gary left without another word.

The girls began whispering among themselves, a tense, heated sound. Mrs. Berns and I exchanged a troubled look.

"I have to head back to Guinn's tonight," I said, pitching my voice low. Mrs. Berns nodded.

"I don't recommend it," a blonde wearing her hair in a ponytail said matter-of-factly.

I needed to get name tags for these ladies. "Why not?"

The brunette who'd shown Gary her phone spoke. "Guinnie is a real creeper. We don't hang out with him unless we're in pairs."

Anger and ice gurgled in my stomach. Anger that at this young age, these girls already knew they had to stay in pairs to keep safe, ice that they were corroborating my worst fears about John Guinn.

"He's in Perham tonight," piped up a girl from the back. "Spends a lot of time there. He says it's to set up the community center. Just like he did here."

At that last bit, all the girls in the room exchanged an ominous glance.

"Has he tried anything with you girls at the community center here?" Mrs. Berns asked. I'd never before heard that tone of voice from her. It was soulful, deep, and tired, but also fierce. Her face had gone pale, her eyes ablaze.

"Nothing, yet," the blonde said, her ponytail swishing as she shook her head. "It's just the way he looks at us, little comments he makes, the way he always wants to tell us where he'll be at night, like we care."

"I'm heading to his place right now," I said, halfway to my jacket.

"He could return at any time," the brunette said, as if she were a seasoned cop.

"What's your name?" Mrs. Berns asked.

"Peaches," she said.

Mrs. Berns tucked in her chin. "Your parents want you to be a stripper when you grow up?"

I gave her an elbow.

Peaches had probably heard all the jokes, because she continued in stride. "If you're gonna case his place, you want to make sure you're not caught. You won't help anyone if you are."

Dang, now teenagers were smarter than me? "What're you recommending?" I asked.

The girls studied each other, all thirteen of them making eye contact and sharing some unspoken language before Peaches spoke up again. "We'll go to the Battle Lake community center right now, all of us. We have Guinnie's number. We'll text him to let him know. He'll for sure want to hang with us. We'll keep him busy. Even better, we'll let you know if he leaves."

"No way," I said. "I'm not putting any of you in the path of danger."

"Welcome to our life," Peaches said, rolling her eyes. "We deal with this every day. But don't worry. We're good at sticking together and taking care of each other."

"And I'll go with them," Mrs. Berns said.

I wanted to argue, but their logic was unassailable. Plus, I couldn't tamp down the warm feeling of having a whole brilliant girl gang on my team, as long as they were safe.

"It's just a community center," Mrs. Bern said. "Brightly lit. Kids go there all the time."

That decided it. I was driving out to John Guinn's house to search for more evidence, leaving behind a powerhouse troupe of girls running cover for me, chaperoned by my favorite nonagenarian of all time.

I didn't even have time to relish Kennie's confused face as I rushed past her, her arms full of tattoo gear.

Chapter 28

I estimated I had between one and two hours to snoop around Guinn's place, given that it was a thirty-minute drive back from Perham, and the girls and Mrs. Berns would reasonably be able to keep him occupied for at least an hour. Then Guinn would have another ten-minute drive back to his place. That gave me plenty of time to explore his three outbuildings and look for any sign of a struggle, a kidnapping, or unexpectedly high traffic passing through, things I simply hadn't been on the lookout for when I'd dropped by this morning.

Breaking into somebody's house, or at least trespassing to spy on them, was serious business. If I was caught, I could lose any chance of earning a PI license, but I was more worried about the possibility of being shot since a lot of people around Battle Lake were gun owners. I glanced at my dashboard clock to see if there was time for a stop. Any domestic violence history, a gun license, or evidence of Guinn being a ninja would change how I approached his house tonight.

I had time.

Ron was not happy about me dragging him out of his house three blocks up the street to unlock the *Recall's* office after hours, though. He told me I should have come in earlier to check out the stuff. He was right, but here we were. I didn't fill him in completely on what was up because I didn't want him to talk me out of it, but I explained that the note might be connected to the missing girl in Perham and I needed to find out more about John Guinn.

He grumbled and glared, but he let me in.

After promising I'd lock up on my way out, I dashed to the back room and powered on one of the two microfiche machines. I knew John Guinn had been born in 1945, so I began my search looking ten years before and ten years after. Nothing. In fact, it wasn't until I expanded another ten years on either side that I came across his name in the local paper. It was his 1963 high school graduation photo. I stopped the fleeting view of words to stare at his picture. It was grainy. He didn't wear glasses now, and he hadn't worn them then.

A man who resembled Barry Janston stood behind John Guinn in the photo, and he did wear the heavy-framed glasses of the period. Reading the caption confirmed that they were in the same Battle Lake High School graduating class.

I started another whirring search. Four years flew by before I found another hit. This time, it was Guinn's college graduation announcement. He'd earned his BS in psychology from the University of Minnesota and, four years later, his PhD from Bethel University in Michigan.

Guinn showed up in only a few other mentions after that, most of them for conferences around the Midwest where he was the keynote speaker. Apparently, he was very good at what he did as a therapist and a community organizer. *Dang.* What if I was completely wrong about him? That lecture from Mrs. Berns was still rattling around my skull, though, reminding me to follow my gut. It helped that the girls had confirmed my suspicions about Guinn.

The most recent articles about him were also sparse, and unfailingly positive. They mentioned the Battle Lake community center and how it was working with local organizations to create a safe haven for teens. If this guy was also involved in sex trafficking, it was one of the most gruesome things I'd ever run across in my life, and in the past year I'd seen a thing or three.

I shut down the machine and returned the microfiche to its file. Guinn had no violent record, or even any evidence of owning a hunting weapon. There was nothing more for me to learn here.

Locking the door behind me, I patted the pockets of my parka. I'd had the foresight to charge and bring Z-Force along, so I wouldn't be alone. Still, my heart knocked in my chest as I pulled into the light, early-evening traffic and steered toward Guinn's, and it was downright shuddering when I pulled up his driveway for the second time that day. I worried about making fresh tracks alerting him he'd had a visitor, but his gravel road was almost prim with the firmness of its frozen dirt. The skies pressed down with the weight of an icy, unshed warning. The air smelled charged, and I wondered if the storm would break tonight.

I hoped not.

When Guinn's homestead came into view, I was relieved to find the house washed in shadows and darkness. Only his yard light shone on the empty driveway. I turned my car around to prep for a fast get-away and parked outside the farthest edge of the cold circle of light. If anybody pulled up, they'd spot my car if they were looking for it, but it wouldn't be immediately obvious.

Gripping the Z-Force in one hand and a penlight I kept stashed in my glove box in the other, I exited my car, closing the door gently. Cocking my head, I listened. An uneasy breeze scuttled through the occasional dried leaves still clinging to burr oak branches, and I heard a far-off crack, either the resonance of lake ice shifting or a gunshot. I sniffed. The ionic scent of incoming storm was stronger out here, urgent, cleaner in its own way.

No putting this off any longer.

I gingerly slid across the ice toward Guinn's house. I stepped onto his porch. I glanced in the large bay window, cupping my face so I could peer in without shadow. There was the bathroom I had visited earlier that morning. In the gloom, it gave me chills. It was eerie peeking into an unfamiliar house at night. I was acutely aware that a stranger's face could slap itself on the other side of the glass, screaming like a nightmare clown, demanding to know what I was doing here.

But that didn't happen. Everything appeared as it had this morning. I pressed my ear against the cold glass. No sounds coming from inside.

I did the same to every window I could reach. Toward the rear of the house, there was still crusty snow left where no one had walked. I fell through once, the jagged edges of the ice cutting into my ankle. I covered up the hole as best I could, flattening the snow all around so it wasn't identifiable as a footprint.

Staring off toward the forest, I considered calling out to see if anybody would answer. Except I didn't know if I wanted to hear a response. Plus, the ghostly quiet of the night woods demanded the same. I studied the barn, chicken coop, and workshop. If Guinn had Maisy tied up in any of the three, it would make the most sense to keep her in the newest building. It was probably heated, and soundproofed.

That was, if he was keeping her alive.

But I needed to check all three buildings, so I began with the nearest. I stepped toward the faded barn, its creaking frame sloping toward the evergreen forest. Crossing the open expanse, I felt more exposed than I had since I'd arrived. When I fell through the snow crust a couple more times, I didn't bother hiding my footprints. My lizard brain had taken over, no finesse. I was all flight-or-fight, waiting for the cue to fulfill either. My heartbeat was rat-a-tatting and loud, and my cold nose and the tips of my ears reminded me how mortal I was.

As I walked, I swept the snow with my penlight. Somebody else had recently walked to and from the barn, and the chicken coop, and the new outbuilding. Maybe more than one somebody, given the number of snow crust punctures.

I reached the barn. Its door swung open enough for me to slide through. The inside smelled like dusty, moldy hay. Once my eyes adjusted, I saw the animal cubicles were all empty.

"Hello?" I said softly.

No response. I paused to let my eyesight adjust to the interior, feeling the hairs on my arms rise.

Slivers of moonshine broke through the pregnant storm clouds and filtered through the dusty window above the haymow. I rushed up the ladder toward the weak light before I lost my last drop of plummeting courage. The moon-splattered haymow was empty except for old straw and a blanket laid flat, the type you could pick up at any tourist trap along the Mexican border. I yanked at it, scaring up acrid dust.

From this vantage point, it was clear the rest of the barn was empty, too. Just a pile of old machinery in the back corner, some rotting bridles, and a stack of heavy, unfamiliar metal. I let myself down and out into the frigid evening air, making my way to the chicken coop. I found it in a state similar to the ancient barn's. The coop had once been functioning but was now little more than a museum of old-school husbandry.

I let myself out of that low-roofed building and peered toward the only outbuilding I hadn't yet explored: the new garage/workshop.

It stared back at me, the moon reflecting balefully off the two top windows. My heightened imagination felt their glance as unfeeling as long as I left now, but hateful if provoked. My car sat about forty yards away. I knew from my high school track days that I could cover that distance in five seconds if I needed to.

A branch cracked in the woods, and I jumped, my neck prickling. Was I being watched? I waited, my breath huffing. There was no follow-up sound. I stared back at the house. No one watched me from the windows. I sucked in a deep breath and told myself this was about to be over, one way or another. I *had* to explore the last building. If there was any chance there was a girl in it, I couldn't live with myself if I walked away.

Just as Mrs. Berns had said.

My senses were on high alert. I was a mouse listening for an owl as I scurried across the snowscape to the workshop's front door. There was always the chance that it would be locked. I did not have a plan in that case.

Fortunately, as I turned the front knob, I discovered that Guinn was a regular Minnesotan in one way: he didn't lock his outbuildings.

Relief washed over me. I was going to peek inside, verify everything was normal, and head back to the community center to let the girls and Mrs. Berns know, no harm, no foul. I had been overreacting this whole time. Nothing new about that scenario. There were a hundred good reasons for Guinn to store maxi pads and a girls' tattoo kit in his bathroom, another hundred why he'd kept running his hand through his hair.

I opened the door, prepared for the standard layout—a workshop on one side and a single-stall garage on the other—given how the outside of the building appeared. One quick sweep each direction with my flashlight, and I could leave satisfied.

What I wasn't ready for were the tennis-shoe-clad feet I spotted in the workshop side of the building.

I also was unprepared for my flashlight to travel up a shivering body tied to a chair.

But it was the terrified, beseeching eyes of Maisy Kramer staring back at me, a gag in her mouth, that completely knocked me on my heels.

Chapter 29

"I don't know," Maisy said. Repeatedly.

I don't know.

It was the same answer she'd given me on the drive to the Battle Lake Police Department, trembling in the passenger seat even as my heater blasted and I kept reaching over and patting her arm. She'd left school at lunch because she was bored. She had been walking home. She took a shortcut through an alleyway. Somebody conked her over the head, and when she woke up, she was in a building, tied to a chair, suffering from a headache and terrified. She swore she didn't know who grabbed her, or even where she was hidden until I told her it was Guinn's place.

She'd gone ashen at hearing that, but she stuck to her story.

I don't know who took me.

Other than the involuntary shock-shudders, she'd kept her cool as I navigated the roads to the police department. I was so grateful to see Gary when I led her into the station that my knees buckled, even though he shot me a sharp, unreadable glare that almost made me pee my pants. He got us comfortable and then made a number of calls before coming over to take Maisy's official statement.

The girl kept her cool, but when her mom showed up a few minutes later, wild-eyed, and hugged her close, she started sobbing, joining her mother's tears. I couldn't blame Maisy one bit. She'd been through a horrible ordeal. I suspected she'd left out the real reason she'd ducked out of school and who she'd left with, but the lump on her head and the fear in her eyes told me that she truly had no idea who'd abducted her, though all signs pointed to Guinn.

An EMT showed up. She gently checked out Maisy with her mother hovering nearby, then said that she might have a concussion, but didn't need to go to the hospital. Her mother could take her home as soon as Gary was done asking her the same questions I'd asked on the ride over.

Shivering in a blanket and cupping a mug of hot chocolate, between fits of sobbing, Maisy gave him the same answers she'd given me. Fortunately, Gary had not yet taken me aside to ask what I had been doing out at Guinn's place. His focus was completely on Maisy. It was only a matter of time. While it was probably in my best interest to slip out before Gary turned the cop-questions on me, I couldn't leave Maisy until I knew she was completely safe.

And that wouldn't happen until Guinn showed up.

I kept one eye on the door and the other on Maisy, who wept in her mother's arms while Gary wrapped up his questions. On my suggestion, Gary had sent a deputy to the nearby community center to find Guinn. My plan was to launch myself at the predator as soon as he walked in, kicking him in his shady spots while screaming questions at him. Probably I could get away with a good ten seconds of that before Gary peeled me off.

The police station door opened.

All of us in that room held our breath.

In walked the devil.

John Guinn, his potato-y Sean Penn face a perfect mask of surprise and innocence.

I sprang, but before I reached him, he ran toward Maisy, his expression stricken.

"Oh my god, what happened?"

Confusion held me in place. Karen mirrored my expression. Gary's face grew stern. He glanced over Guinn's shoulder, his face relaxing when his deputy walked in and gave Gary a small nod.

The deputy had brought Guinn. So why was Guinn pretending to be clueless? That was stupid. The deputy could clear this up with a comment. Unless he hadn't told Guinn why he was bringing him here, and Guinn really was . . . innocent?

At the signal from his deputy, Gary stalked toward Guinn, seeming to grow larger as he neared. The fierceness in his eyes was intimidating. I was grateful that for once I was not on the business end of it.

Guinn, who'd made it halfway to Maisy, had the brains to back away from Gary. He held his hands up, palms out. "Please, what's going on here?"

"You tell me," Gary said.

From my vantage point, I could study both their faces. Guinn's appeared legitimately blank.

When he didn't respond, Gary said, "We found this girl in your shed."

Gary's mouth twitched. I could tell he wanted to look my way and curse me out for being on Guinn's property. That would come.

In the meantime, Guinn was either putting on an Oscar-worthy performance or truly had no idea what Gary was talking about. In one fluid movement, he crumpled to the floor, landing on his knees with a crack. That would definitely hurt in the morning. His face fell into his hands, his voice coming out a broken sob. "I swear to heaven I don't know anything about that. I was at my clinic all day. I drove straight to Perham afterward, and then back to the community center here in Battle Lake. I haven't been home since early this morning."

That information did not sway Gary, nor did he show surprise at Guinn's dramatic denial. "You have witnesses to your whereabouts?"

Maisy's broken weeping continued in the background.

"Oh my god," Guinn choked into his hands. "Maisy."

I didn't like the way that he kept saying her name, as if they knew each other well. I had my bullshit meter checking all over him, hunting for a crack in his behavior. I was upset I couldn't find it. He appeared to be telling the truth. Or at least *he* believed he was.

The door opened, interrupting the tense scene. Mrs. Berns rushed in along with some of the girls from the center. The girls hurried over to Maisy before Gary could stop them. They were all trying to hug her at once, asking questions one on top of another.

What happened? Are you OK? Who did this to you?

I kept my eyes fastened on Guinn. He seemed to grow paler when the girls showed up, but I could have misread it. The police station lighting was not great.

Mrs. Berns walked over to me. "You found her."

I tipped my head toward Guinn, pitching my voice so only she could hear. "Bound in his freaking shed. He says he has no idea how she got there."

Mrs. Berns harrumphed, not bothering to lower her voice, her sharp eyes taking in a broken-looking Maisy. "Pretty hard to have somebody accidentally tied up in your shed. In fact, I've managed to go my whole life without that happening."

I nodded, keeping my expression neutral.

"I just want to go home," Maisy wailed above the din. "Can I please just go home?"

A muscle in Gary's jaw was doing gymnastics. He stepped back so he could peer from Guinn to Maisy. He did not like what was happening, that was clear from his expression, but he needed to usher these girls out of his station.

He signaled for his deputy to confer with him. They spoke in hushed tones before Gary returned to Maisy's side. He offered his hand to help her stand. "If you're feeling physically up for it, and it's all right with your mom, you can go home," he said gently. "We'll station an officer outside your house."

He seemed to be directing this last bit to Guinn. I willed my muscles to relax, relieved that Gary was going to make sure Maisy was safe tonight, and that he wasn't fully buying Guinn's innocent act. While I hadn't been able to punch a hole in it, it seemed too pat, too perfect. Unless I'd completely misjudged the man?

Gary turned his full attention to Guinn. "You will stay and answer questions." It wasn't a question, but Guinn treated it like it was.

"Of course," he said.

Mrs. Berns and I tried to blend into the background while Karen Kramer and Gary led Maisy out of the police department, the crowd of girls filing behind. I noticed Guinn was attempting the same trick as me and Mrs. Berns, making small movements, trying to disappear into the space, except he was watching those girls, watching every one of them.

And I scrutinized him, which was why I had eyes dead on his face when he turned to leer at me. The look he flashed was so quick, so coldly evil, that I couldn't believe he'd chanced it in the police department.

How'm I doing? the look said.

My pulse froze. He'd given me a lightning-quick, cat-who-caught-the-mouse smirk. Hadn't he? Had I misread that, too?

"Bastard," Mrs. Berns said, lunging toward him.

I held her back. I hadn't misjudged Guinn's expression. Mrs. Berns had witnessed it, too. What arrogance, what belief that he would get away with it, to risk such open-faced audacity, no matter how brief it'd been.

"Just like the Mayfair girl," Mrs. Berns muttered.

The stress of the night made it so it took me a moment to remember the story. "No," I said firmly. "It's not. Guinn is *here*, in the police department. Gary is not going to let him go. There's no reason for you to get involved."

"If he's hurting girls and he gets away, there sure as hell is," Mrs. Berns said.

She strolled over to him before I could restrain her. On her tiptoes she leaned her nose up close to his ear and whispered something. Guinn grew as pale as snow. Before I could intervene, Mrs. Berns was out the door.

Gary returned, towering over Guinn. "You're all right if we go search your place?" Gary asked.

"Certainly," Guinn said, all evidence of that smirk erased from his face. He was the picture of contrition. "Would you like me to go with?"

"No," Gary said. "I would like you to spend the evening in a cell."

I choked back my relief. Gary wanted to lock him up. I knew he couldn't, not legally, not without pressing charges. Was he going to take that step?

Guinn made it so he didn't have to. "I'm happy to stay here," he said. "I'll willingly check myself into jail. The sooner we get to the bottom of this, the happier I'll feel. I just want Maisy safe. *Then* I want my name cleared. Someone with a real sick sense of humor is trying to frame me." He ran his hands through his hair.

Man, he was good. I might have fallen for it if not for that look earlier, and his characteristic tell letting me know that he was lying.

Gary locked him up in the back and then returned to the main room, his face dark and furrowed.

"I'm going with you," I said.

Gary didn't even bother with a response. In fact, he acted like I was invisible. He took a call on his radio telling him that a second deputy was a minute away, so almost able to take over at the station, and then he pulled on his fleece-lined parka.

"Gary," I said more insistently. "I found her. I want to go back. I could help you."

He turned on me even more quickly than he'd come at Guinn. "You. Will. Not. Go. Back," he said, his voice low and dangerous. "You're lucky I don't put you in the cell next to Guinn. You were trespassing, and if I catch you doing it again, I will lock you up so fast you won't even have time to say goodbye to your pets."

A surge of boiling anger rose so powerfully within me that it almost bowled me over. "If I hadn't been *trespassing*, who knows what would've happened to Maisy?"

Gary was so close that I could smell the mint on his lips, his warm breath caressing mine. He lifted his hand and then paused, leaving it floating in the air between us. For one bizarre moment, I thought he was going to touch me—soft or hard, I couldn't tell.

"If the person who snatched her had been around," he said, his voice deeper than I'd ever heard it, "who knows what would have happened to *you*?"

Before I could respond, he spun on his heel and strode for the door, slapping the wall on the way out. The noise made me jump.

What *the hell* had just happened?

More to the point, how could I reach Guinn's place and spy on Gary without him knowing?

Chapter 30

A seven-minute drive, and I reached my place. Another nine minutes, and I was crouching in the woods on the perimeter of Guinn's house, watching Gary search inside. He must have gotten the keys from Guinn when he'd locked him up.

I didn't expect Gary to find anything, honestly. Guinn wouldn't have handed over the keys if he thought it would endanger him. He was too canny for that. In fact, I was beginning to realize he was shrewder than I'd imagined. I'd severely underestimated him.

Gary was thorough, I'd give him that. He searched the whole house, flipping on lights as he entered room after room, then moving to examine the whole barn before striding to the shed, where he snapped photos. As I watched him work, I realized how late it was, and how cold I'd become. I gave my arms a vigorous rub, then leaned my head against a fir tree, not caring if my cap stuck to the sap. The stress of the night combined with the adrenaline letdown and the late hour found me exhausted. My head was bobbing. I couldn't imagine what else there was for Gary to search for.

I might have given in to the urge to sleep, if not for a sound coming from the edge of the forest, about twenty feet north of where I was hiding.

My flesh bristled with fear. It'd sounded like breathing. Had I grown so still that an animal had mistaken me for a tree? My heartbeat pounded in my chest. I turned my head slowly toward the out-of-place noise, trying not to draw attention.

Please please please be an animal.

It wasn't, though.

It was a man, watching Gary as I watched him.

Every nerve in my body jumped through my skin.

The man was in profile, tall, wearing some sort of thick fur coat. Did Guinn have an accomplice?

Gary's flashlight bobbed as he made his way from the shed to his car. He was done searching. He was heading out, leaving me alone with this stranger in the woods.

A fresh burst of adrenaline surged, and I took off toward the guy. I thought of calling for help from Gary, but the roar of his car told me I was on my own. There wasn't time to think or time to be afraid; I had to act. I charged across the snow crust, toward him. I made it only ten feet before I fell to my knees, the rough snow bruising my palms through my mittens.

When I stood, the man had ghosted away.

I drew in a ragged breath, trying to see everywhere at once.

There was no one.

Had there ever been someone standing there?

I was so tired I might have been hallucinating.

I stood, yanking my flashlight from my pocket and playing it across the woods as I walked toward the spot where I thought I'd seen him standing. There was little snow in this section, and so no footprints. I'd just about given up when a glint of light caught my eye. I moved toward it, deeper into the forest.

I knelt when I reached it.

It was an empty can of beans tucked into the base of an oak tree.

I removed my mittens and wiped the inside with my finger. The residue was not yet frozen. Somebody had eaten this recently. Somebody who had either abducted Maisy, or who may have seen who had.

The weight of lives and of powerlessness settled on my shoulders.

There was nothing more I could do with this information tonight. Suddenly, I was so tired that I wanted to nestle down in the forest and fall asleep. I managed to drag myself home, listening for the mystery man the whole time. When I reached my double-wide, I trudged inside, locked the door, stacked cans against it so I'd be woken up if anybody tried to sneak in, and dropped my coat to the floor.

Tiger Pop and Luna followed me into bed, snuggling on each side. Sometimes they were psychic like that.

Chapter 31

I woke up craving cheese and chocolate and itching to pick a fight with someone, anyone.

That's how I knew I was pretty stressed.

The note I'd discovered three days and forever ago was surely connected to what had happened to Anita Juarez and, presumably, to Maisy. It couldn't have been a coincidence that two girls had been nabbed since I'd discovered that slip of paper.

Of course, I had no proof.

My only consolation was that hopefully Gary somehow linked Guinn to Maisy's abduction beyond the obvious fact that I'd found her on his property. Later today, I'd make time to comb the woods again, looking for clues as to who'd been watching Gary search Guinn's property last night. I'd already decided it was likely the same person who'd built the hut in the woods, the one I'd been snapping photos of for the Bigfoot article when Janston grabbed me. It hadn't been Bigfoot, surely, but someone camping out, somebody who might have seen something that could definitively pin Guinn to Maisy's kidnapping.

I chewed on all the possibilities on the drive to work and came up with no satisfying conclusions. I opened the library on my own, itching for Mrs. Berns to show up early so we could talk. When she finally arrived an hour late, it turned out there wasn't much to say.

"Do you know if they've made an arrest?" she asked. She looked tired and wild, her hair uncombed, deep bags under her eyes, her clothes rumpled. I'd never seen her like this before.

I swallowed past a knot of worry at her appearance. "No, but they had Guinn locked up when I left last night, and I'm hoping they make formal charges today. The circumstantial evidence is overwhelming."

Mrs. Berns's mouth was set in a hard line. "Sometimes the system doesn't work."

She was thinking of the Mayfair girl, still. "Sometimes it doesn't, but it usually does."

She gave her head an angry toss before turning away. There was nothing left to do but dig into my work with vigor. I noticed Mrs. Berns acted odd the whole morning, snapping at patrons, leaving books lying around. It finally became too much.

"Hey, Mrs. Berns," I said after she'd yelled at a preschool-age child for sneezing. "Maybe you should head home after lunch? I can handle it alone today."

She scowled at me, but before she could argue, Peaches walked in. Her face was stiff with worry.

"Hey, how's Maisy doing today?" I asked. I hoped the girl was somehow recovering from her horrifying abduction with the resilience of youth.

Peaches scanned the library. Nearly a dozen patrons were milling around or examining books, but none within earshot. "That's why I'm here," she whispered. "Maisy is fine. Or mostly fine. I visited her this morning. While I was there, though, Mrs. Kramer got a call. The police had to let Mr. Guinn go."

I gasped. Mrs. Berns went deathly still.

"I guess enough people testified that he was at work all day yesterday, including Senator Janston, who had lunch with him. But the police don't know everything." Peaches swallowed. "I didn't want to tell Mrs. Kramer this, I don't want to tell anybody, but . . . the girls voted me as the person to come to you."

I didn't like how ashen she'd grown. "What is it?"

"Do you promise not to tell anybody?"

I couldn't do that. Not if I needed to go to the police to protect the girls. Fortunately, Peaches didn't wait for me to respond.

"It's just that . . . me and some of the girls, we make videos."

A loud buzzing filled my ears, but it sounded far away. I recognized it for the stress response it was.

"What kind of videos?" Mrs. Berns asked, shooting me a worried glance.

As I fought to ground myself, I realized I already knew.

"Well, they were for our boyfriends," Peaches said, a blush crawling up her freckled cheeks as she confirmed my darkest fears. "But Mr. Guinn got a hold of one of our cameras. He downloaded some of them. He said that unless we did whatever he asked, he would show them to our parents."

My blood began simmering. Mrs. Berns looked like a cartoon character about to blow her top. I sent her a warning look and kept my voice even. "What has he asked you to do?"

"That's just it," Peaches said. "It's kind of weird because he never cashed in those videos. We all sort of forgot about it. I mean, we knew he was creepy, but he wasn't actively hurting us until Maisy disappeared and was found at his place."

"Was she going to meet him when she left school yesterday?" I asked.

Peaches shook her head so vigorously that hair fell into her eyes. "No, I swear. She was going to meet her boyfriend."

"What's his name?" I asked.

"I can't tell you. It's a secret. He's a good guy, though. He isn't involved in any of this."

I didn't know about that. It was clear she'd already revealed all she intended to, though. I steered the conversation back to what had brought her here. "If the police know that Mr. Guinn is keeping those videos, they might be able to put him in jail."

Peaches rolled her eyes. "No way does he have them just lying around, and if he does, he can say he confiscated them because he's trying to protect us or something. It'd be his word against ours, and who believes teenagers over a therapist who opens community centers?"

My chest ached. She might've been right, but if there was anything we could do to lock up Guinn, we had to do it. "Thanks, Peaches. Can I have your number? I can call if there's any new information, and you can do the same for me. I'll give you my home number plus the library number."

As soon as she left, I rang the police station to tell Gary about Guinn and the girls' videos. I didn't feel good about sharing something Peaches didn't want me to, but I technically hadn't promised not to, and her safety—and the safety of the other girls—was more important than them liking me.

I got the answering machine. I left a message for Gary to call me back. When I looked for Mrs. Berns, she and her coat were gone. She must have taken me up on my offer to leave early.

The library slowed down after lunch, so I used my time waiting for Gary to return my call to dig deeper into Guinn. I fired up TrackerSearch, using Guinn's first and middle initials as well as his full name. When that didn't turn up anything new, I added "Barry Janston," trying his full name as well as his first initial and every combination I could think of.

It was that last one where I got a hit. Both L. Guinn and B. Janston had attended a conference at Mosquito Bay Lodge, a nearby conference center, fourteen years earlier. Guinn had been the keynote speaker, and the senator was one of many public officials in attendance. The topic was Teen Mental Health.

My dad would have been alive that year. Nearly incapacitated by his alcoholism, but alive.

I printed out the article and went back in for more. I was so buried in my search that I barely registered the police cars screaming past. *Must be quite a speeder out on the highway.* Twenty minutes later, I was about ready to give up on uncovering any new information on Guinn when Kennie rushed in, her eyes as big as dinner plates.

"You have to come to the police station. They've arrested Mrs. Berns for murder!"

Chapter 32

I dashed past her before the words fully left her mouth, not even pausing to grab my jacket. I charged down the sidewalk, elbowing through townspeople, the fraught winterspring air heavy in my lungs. I slipped once, slamming onto the pavement and scraping my hands raw. I propelled myself back up and kept running. I must have looked like a wild animal when I finally erupted through the door of the Battle Lake Police Department.

Gary sat at his desk. His deputy stood near the radio in the far corner.

"Where is she?" I demanded.

Gary rose slowly to his feet. He appeared different. I couldn't put my finger on why.

"Who?" he asked.

"You know!" I screamed, finally figuring out what looked off about Gary. He seemed *old*, like he'd aged ten years since I'd last seen him. Before I could put that idea in its place, I heard Mrs. Berns holler from the holding cells.

"I'm back here!" she yelled.

I ran to the rear of the police station. Mrs. Berns was in the same cell Guinn had probably spent last night in, and now that monster was free, and my best friend was locked up.

"What the hell!" I choked on my own words as I scanned her through the bars. "Are you OK?"

She appeared all of her ninety years, frail and vulnerable, her eyes watery and her mouth heavy. She worked up a crooked smile nonetheless. "I've been better."

I spun on Gary, who was striding up behind me. At first, I didn't recognize the expression in his eyes. He looked almost . . . gentle.

"You know Mrs. Berns didn't kill anyone," I said, my voice verging on a shriek. "What do you have her in here for?"

Gary spoke plainly, telling me things he did not have to, another five years landing on his shoulders as he spoke. "She shot Guinn through his bay window."

Gary's words did not initially fit in my ears. Once they got through, though, I had to grab the bars of the jail cell for support. "What?"

"I was hunting," Mrs. Berns declared defiantly.

I'll say. "For what?"

"Light goose."

God, I hoped that was a real thing.

"See?" I said to Gary, struggling to gain control of my emotions. "She was hunting. It was an accident. If you let that kidnapper go for 'mistakenly' having a girl tied up on his property, you can certainly release Mrs. Berns. Do you know that Guinn has compromising videos of Battle Lake High School girls?"

Gary's eyebrows knit together. "How do you know that?"

"One of the girls just told me. Guinn is an awful man."

"I've got work to do," Gary said. He turned and strode back to his desk, pausing to growl over his shoulder, "You have five minutes, and then I'm kicking you out of here."

My gut was heavy when I turned back to Mrs. Berns. All her fake bravado vanished in an instant. She collapsed onto the cot like a puppet that had been discarded. I reached through the bars for her, but she was too far away to touch.

"He wouldn't have stopped," she said in a low moan. "Once they start, they don't stop."

Chapter 33

Johnny showed up as I walked out of the police station. There was tension between us, taut and sharp like electricity, but I didn't have it in me to address it just now. Judging by how he held himself, he felt the same way.

"I heard about Mrs. Berns." He wasn't offering me an embrace.

"She's inside," I said, also not hugging him. "She didn't do it."

"I know," he said. He still hadn't put his arms around me.

I guessed I hadn't put mine around him, either. But that wasn't my biggest problem right now. What was really eating at me was the fact that Mrs. Berns *had* shot Guinn. I knew she had. I'd seen it in her eyes. Even worse, I knew she'd been planning it from the moment she'd whispered in Guinn's ear in the cop shop last night. It didn't matter why she'd done it—she wasn't going to let another girl be a Daphne Mayfair, or a Maisy Kramer—and it also didn't matter that I knew in my heart that Guinn was a monster. She'd killed him to save others, but it still meant she'd spend the short rest of her life in jail.

I couldn't go there.

"I'm going to visit my mom," I told Johnny. I hadn't known it until I uttered it, but I had no choice. The note with my dad's name was the only clue I had. I needed to get to the bottom of this mystery so I could prove that Guinn had been a demon. Justifiable homicide carried a lesser sentence. Didn't it?

Johnny's shoulders tensed, but he didn't ask me questions. "I'll stay here with Mrs. Berns," he said. "Gary probably won't let me see her, but I'll wait anyways, just in case."

The love I felt for him washed over me, hot and unnerving. I couldn't reach out to him, though. It would make me seem too exposed at a time where I was already feeling skinned alive.

"Thanks," I said instead. I shuffled off to the library before he had a chance to respond. I had no idea what he would have said.

Chapter 34

After ensuring that Kennie had the library under control, I made the two-hour drive to Paynesville. Mostly, Mom spent her time volunteering, attending church, and playing cards with her bridge group. That had changed last year, when she'd started dating a salt-and-pepper-haired Tom Selleck look-alike. As much as I enjoyed his company, I hoped he wouldn't be at her place when I pulled up.

I didn't spot his car in the driveway when I crested the rise. Small bit of luck. I turned off the car at the same time my mom stepped out of the front door, an open-mouthed expression of shock on her face.

I ran over to her.

"Mira!" She was honest-to-God wearing an apron and smelling like freshly baked bread.

Our strained relationship, our different interpretations of reality . . . none of it mattered in that moment. My best friend was in jail for murder, girls were getting abducted in and around my new hometown, and I needed my mom. I fell into her arms.

"Honey!" She patted my head, holding me awkwardly. "What's wrong?"

I couldn't tell her about the note. The further I fell into this mystery, the more it appeared as though my dad had been involved with some unsavory people, and possibly with sex trafficking. That wasn't the sort of thing you told your mom about her dead husband, especially since she was a glass-completely-full kind of woman, regardless of the truth.

"It's Mrs. Berns," I said. It wasn't exactly a lie. "She's not feeling well. I'm worried for her health."

"Come inside, sweetheart," my mom said. "I'll make you some hot chocolate with marshmallows and we can talk all about it."

But we couldn't, not really. My mom and I had *never* been able to talk all about it. We talked *around* it—my dad's drinking, his mood swings, the woman he'd killed in his final drunken driving escapade—but we never talked *about* it.

The back of my throat hollowed out. This time would be no different.

"Thanks, Mom. It's going to be a short visit, though. I just wanted to say hi, and maybe go through some old pictures?" Here I did straight-out lie. "I want to see images of you, me, and Dad when we were all happy together. It'll make me feel grounded."

Her eyes lit up. It hurt to witness the hope they held. She wanted so badly for me to have the same memory of our past as she did. "That's wonderful, honey. You know where the pictures are stored. I'll bring the hot chocolate on up to you."

The house appeared the same as it had my whole childhood, a tidy, outdated Midwestern farmhouse. Wait, that wasn't quite right. There were some new touches. Somebody had sanded and varnished the kitchen cabinets. They gleamed. It must've been her boyfriend. If so, he'd also set up a water-filtration system in the kitchen, replaced the worn carpeting on the stairs, and when I went to use the bathroom, I noticed he'd also swapped out the old 1960s-style faucet for a new, sleek chrome one.

He was a handyman. Maybe he could take that show on the road and visit me in Battle Lake.

The photo albums were stored on a dedicated shelf in the second story sitting room, next to my old bedroom, which my mom kept exactly as it had been in high school, down to the Jimmy Page poster on the wall. That was the room Johnny and I had first made love in, back in December. I kept my head down as I walked past it.

The photo albums were arranged in chronological order. I picked up the farthest left one, thick and white, its plastic sleeves yellowed with age. The first image was of Mom and Dad before they were married. They were barely teenagers, wearing their matching enormous, owl-eyed glasses. They were smiling so wide. They couldn't be much older than Peaches and her crew.

They'd met in high school, and if I did my math, it seemed likely that Mom had gotten pregnant with me right before they married. No quitter, she had stuck with Dad through the end. I flipped through pages of them getting married, going on their honeymoon to Disney World (my mom's idea), having friends over, all the pictures seemingly tinged with that odd orange light of the late '60s and '70s.

The next two photo albums were more of the same. It wasn't until the third one that I showed up. And it wasn't until the fifth one that I discovered pictures of me as a recognizable girl rather than a blobby infant. I smiled when I came across one of me wearing my favorite powder-blue jacket, my bony knees hanging out below and my pigtails hooking above. I was smiling, dimpled, all of seven years old.

On the next page, I found a photo of me sitting behind my dad on a motorcycle. I was holding tight to his waist. We both wore matching grins. It squeezed my heart, gazing at that picture and that faraway girl. I always forgot the good times. They were few and far between, but that didn't make them any less real.

"Your dad loved that motorcycle almost as much as he loved you."

I jumped. I hadn't heard Mom come up behind me. I reached for the mug of hot chocolate she offered.

"Thank you," I said.

Her hands free, she pushed her hair behind her ears. "Your dad was a good man," she said. "A good husband."

I felt the truth burble up. I didn't want to say it out loud, not in her house, not holding her hot chocolate, but I couldn't look away from the lie any longer, regardless of how she received the truth. "No, Mom, he

wasn't. In fact, he was a drunk who killed someone. He hurt all of us."
I was surprised that it came out without anger.

My mom's smile took on a clownish stretch, but she didn't give up.
"I didn't say he was *perfect*," she said. "I said he was a good man. I've
made peace with the mistakes he made. You should, too."

My impulse to be authentic with her dwindled as quickly as it
had sprung up. I couldn't make my mom see my truth any more than
she could make me fall for hers. She had her reality, and that's all she
needed.

"Thanks for the advice, Mom. I'll take it under advisement."

I took a sip of the hot chocolate. It was delicious, of course. I set
it down and gently peeled back the tacky plastic holding the photograph of my father and me in place. I removed the photo and turned it
around. *Mark and Mira, 1981* was written on the back.

"Did Dad write this?"

Mom leaned forward, pulling her glasses from the top of her head
to her nose. "Yep," she said. "That's his handwriting."

It was cramped and chicken scratchy, whereas the writing on the
note was looping and smooth. My dad had not written it. I flipped the
photograph back over and returned it to the plastic, sealing it in for
eternity. I felt a lonely pressure on my throat. I'd seen enough. This trip
had been a waste. More than a waste. I'd upset my mom and reminded
myself why she and I could never be close, not really, not if she thought
driving drunk was a "mistake" that could be forgiven when the killer—
my dad—had died without ever apologizing.

To anyone.

I was about to slide the photo album back onto the shelf when I
noticed a dark shadow in the spot where it had been. I reached in and
came out with a matchbook.

I turned it over. Mosquito Bay Lodge was printed in white ink
on a blue background.

My mouth grew dry. Mosquito Bay Lodge of Battle Lake,
Minnesota, the same location B. Janston and J. Guinn had attended a

Teen Mental Health conference fourteen years earlier. When my dad was still alive.

Mom leaned over and tapped the cardboard. "A friend of your dad's owned that place, maybe still does. Dad visited there a lot. He must have kept one of their matchbooks as a souvenir."

"Mom," I said, my words tumbling out before I lost my courage, "was Dad ever a private investigator?"

Her face went slack, like I'd shown her something ugly, but she quickly reassembled it into a bright smile, just like she'd done her whole life. "Of course not! Your dad was in finance. A private investigator. Next you'll be asking if he was an astronaut in all his spare time."

She was standing so close I could touch her, yet the distance between us had never been greater. I heard what sounded like a rumble of thunder outside, but it couldn't be. Not in April, not with a blizzard threatening. "Mom, I think I need to go. I want to get home before the storm hits. No telling what it's going to bring."

"But this is your home," she said, still smiling. She had to say those words, to keep up the pretense. She didn't expect me to respond.

"Can I keep these?" I held out the matches.

She closed my hands over them. "Yes, you may. I'll get you a to-go cup for the hot chocolate."

I thanked her, wondering whether I had time to reach Mosquito Bay Lodge before hell's weather broke loose.

Chapter 35

Mosquito Bay Lodge was north of Battle Lake on the way to Otter Tail. I'd ridden past its sign and driveway many times, but I'd never had a reason to pull in and check it out. The storm clouds were an eerie dark force as I neared it. The approaching storm was intensifying, gathering power, but it didn't look like it was going to break just yet. Still, the ceiling of the sky pushed down on my allergies, making my eyes itch worse than ever before.

I was rubbing them so fiercely that I almost missed the turnoff. I signaled left and veered in at the last moment, sliding on the ice. The driveway curved through pines and over a hill before opening to a gorgeous log building that appeared to be constructed of whole timber. On each side were less impressive, '60s-era hotel-looking buildings, but the lodge itself was magnificent.

Middle of the week and April, I wasn't surprised to see the parking lot nearly empty. I pulled my Toyota in, walked to the front counter, and dinged the bell.

A smartly dressed woman walked out, an expectant smile on her face. "Yes?"

"Can I speak to the owner?"

Her smile faltered. "Is there something I can help you with?"

"There's no problem," I said, hoping to reassure her. "The owner and my father used to be close friends and I have a message for him." At least I guessed it was him. I should have asked my mother.

The front desk person's face relaxed. "Well, he's not usually around, but you're in luck! He's here for a brief visit. I'll be right back."

I turned to study the lobby as she disappeared down the hall, appreciating the practicality of the dark-blue-and-maroon chevron-design carpeting. This main lodge was a two-story building, with the lobby a big open space encompassing both levels and featuring an oversize river-stone fireplace, tables hewn of whole pine logs, and rustic touches throughout, from the Ducks Unlimited paintings to the old-time blacksmith and farrier tools accenting the massive fireplace. A ledge above the foyer revealed what appeared to be meeting rooms on the second floor. I assumed there were more down the hall the woman had disappeared into. I was walking toward the magazines on a big log table when I heard a familiar voice.

"Mira James!" he boomed.

I turned. It couldn't be.

"I was wondering when you would finally show up," he said.

Chapter 36

"You're the spitting image of your father," Senator Janston declared. "I recognized you instantly in the woods the other day. I hope you don't mind that I did a little research to make sure it was you."

He'd led me to his private office, loving the theatricality of our meeting, waiting to tell me how he knew me until he was comfortable.

Some hotel owners might choose the most mundane spot for their office, leaving the nicest spaces for their guests. Not Barry Janston. His office was in a crow's nest at the rear of the lodge, overlooking the dark woods, all black and swaying evergreen trees. It was very private. The glowing mahogany bookshelves and rich leather furniture added to the feeling of luxury. Janston's feet were currently crossed on his desk, his hands laced behind his head in the picture of relaxation.

"My mom said you and my dad were good friends," I said, trying to get the upper hand in the conversation and failing miserably.

Janston's face slid a bit, but he caught it in time. "Something like that. Your dad and I met in college, both of us in the finance program. Banks, he used to call me back then. I guess it was prophetic, as I started out my career in the Glidder Bank system. Your dad and I reconnected later. He did some work for me back in the day."

"Some PI work?" I asked, as if it were the most normal thing in the world and I'd known my whole life that my dad had been a private investigator.

"Exactly." Janston smiled warmly, like he could still win my vote. "I had him investigating John Guinn. Can I say that your father's features look much better on a woman?"

I didn't bother acknowledging that last bit, too busy wondering why Janston was sharing this information with me. "Why would you have Guinn investigated? You said yourself when we first met in the woods that you two are good friends."

"We attended the same high school," Janston said, "but we weren't really close, not back then. That didn't come until later. Our paths crossed again when I got into politics and Guinn into therapy. Specifically, helping troubled teens. It was something that I wanted as a campaign platform. I needed him investigated to make sure there were no skeletons in his closet before I brought him on board as an adviser."

Well, wasn't that a neatly wrapped package? Janston had surely heard that Guinn had been detained last night, and what he'd been arrested for. And here he had a pat explanation for their whole relationship, including the fact that he'd had Guinn investigated, letting Janston off the hook for any indelicacies Guinn may have been involved in.

"Did my dad find any?"

Janston's smile was broad. "Not a one. Clean as a whistle."

I suspected that Janston was as good a liar as I was, maybe better, which meant that there was a shifting kernel of truth in everything he said. One of my least-likely theories surrounding the note was that my dad had been investigating the bad guys, not been a bad guy himself. Janston had neatly handed that theory back. *Too* neatly. Plus, I couldn't avoid the fact that I was getting this news from a man accused of sexually harassing or assaulting at least four women.

I decided to go on the offense. "Do you know Lou Banks?"

"The dentist?" Janston scratched his head. "Sure, I know who he is. Probably been at some of the same events around town."

"Did he know my dad?"

"You would have to ask Dr. Banks," he said.

I would. I still hadn't interviewed him since I'd discovered the note had likely come from his office. I also needed to return to the woods to figure out who I'd seen watching Guinn's place last night, check in on Mrs. Berns, make sure the library had gotten closed down properly, and I really should figure out what was up with me and Johnny. But suddenly, I wanted nothing more than to search the entire Mosquito Bay Lodge, top to bottom. I didn't know what to look for, but I was confident I'd recognize it when I found it.

There was no way Janston was going to let me do that, though. For all the smiling, he was studying me as closely as I was watching him. He'd been expecting my arrival, and not only because he thought I was the spitting image of my father. I was beginning to feel like I had been played from the moment I had "discovered" that note, but I couldn't imagine what the end game was.

"Can I ask how long you've owned this place?"

"Fourteen years," Janston said, smiling. "Came here for a conference and fell in love."

Well, that matched with what I knew. In fact, it lined up perfectly with the article I had coincidentally discovered at work today. "You've heard Guinn was arrested?"

Janston leaned forward, his face falling into a swath of shadow. "I heard he *wasn't* arrested."

There was no room for a follow-up question there. "Well, thanks for your time," I said, standing to leave. "Sorry to have bothered you."

"Not at all," he said, gregarious all over again. "I'll walk you to the door."

I bet you will.

And he did, leading me so aggressively to the exit that I didn't even have the chance to peek into any of the half-open doors on the way. I'd have to figure out a way to return, because this whole place was setting off my Spidey senses.

In the meanwhile, I decided to visit Maisy Kramer.

I had some questions for her.

Chapter 37

Karen did not want to let me into her house, but Maisy heard my voice.

"Is that Mira?" she yelled out from the middle of the one-story home. "Let her in, Mom!"

Karen glared at me. Fine by me. I didn't much care what she thought of me. I did care that my best friend was in jail for killing Guinn. When I brushed past Karen, I noticed her fruity scent again, like apples gone bad. Whatever her perfume was, I thought she should consider changing it.

I found Maisy in the living room, a cluttered space featuring Precious Moments figurines on one wall of shelves and books on the other. I was pleasantly surprised that Peaches as well as the blonde from the Chick Club meeting were present. I found out her name was Chelsea when she told me, and declared she was Maisy's best friend. Peaches didn't seem to mind.

After introductions, I asked Maisy how she was feeling.

"Fine," she said. Her eyes darted to Chelsea and Peaches, who both glanced down at their hands. I didn't know if it was because they were hiding something from me or if Peaches had told them that I knew about the racy videos they'd made.

"We heard Mrs. Berns was arrested," Peaches said. Her eyes brimmed with tears. "We're so sorry."

"Yeah, me too," I said. I stomped down all the painful feelings that threatened to burst through. "I want to help her. That's why I'm here, other than wanting to check up on Maisy. Is there anything more you girls can tell me about Guinn?"

The three of them tossed that same hot look back and forth. Peaches spoke first. "Nothing that we didn't already tell you." She widened her eyes and stared meaningfully from me to Karen, who stood at my shoulder. I understood. They didn't want her to know about the videos, and that made sense.

I suddenly felt bone tired. When had I last eaten? "If there's anything any of you can think of, you have my home and work numbers, right?"

All three nodded vigorously. I turned to Karen. "I need to ask you something. Can we go somewhere private?"

She stared down her nose at me. "I don't need to tell you anything."

I sighed. I'd had exactly enough. "No," I said, "you don't. But here's what I want to know. You and Barry Janston used to date. He's been accused of sexual assault. Did you witness any of that behavior when you were with him?" Janston might be off topic from Guinn and the disappearing girls, or he might not be. I needed to know for sure what he was capable of.

Karen turned the color of a potato and grew some scary-looking frown lines between her eyebrows. "That 'volunteer' who first claimed she was harassed? Do you know that she went willingly into a hotel room with Janston?"

"I read the article," I said. "They were traveling for work. They booked separate rooms, and according to the woman, who was an intern, Janston requested that she meet him in his to do some work. Being an employee, she did."

"Exactly," Karen said tartly. "What sort of girl walks willingly into a man's hotel room? If you do that, you get what is coming to you. There aren't any good men anymore, so it's up to us to conduct ourselves properly."

Dang, that punched me in the stomach. I knew what Mrs. Berns would say if she were here. *Screw that.* I glanced over at Maisy. She was holding herself still, as if she were carved of glass.

"If someone is attacked, there is only one person at fault: the attacker," I snapped.

I wanted to ask Maisy who she'd planned to meet yesterday for lunch, what her boyfriend's name was, but I wouldn't do that to her in front of her mom. What I would do was order Maisy a trusty Z-Force stun gun. No girl should be without one.

"We're going to have a Chick Club meeting again next week, same day, time, and location," I said. "You three will be there?"

"For sure," they said in unison. I noticed the first hint of a smile on Maisy's face.

"Good," I said, turning to Karen. "Because in times like these, women need to stick together."

If she heard what I was really saying, she gave no sign.

Chapter 38

Of all the things Karen Kramer was incorrect about, the one that most chapped me at the moment was her assertion that there were no good men. I knew plenty, one of whom I specifically needed to speak with immediately.

I made the short trip from the Kramers' to the Battle Lake Senior Sunset Nursing Home. I hit the post-dinnertime visiting hour perfectly. I sniffed. My allergies were out of control, but my best guess was that the residents had eaten tomato soup and grilled cheese sandwiches for dinner. It was wild how our lives were bookended by cafeteria food. Below that smell there was the unnerving scent of hospital. I signed the guest register and made my way to Curtis's.

His door was ajar. I knocked on it. "Curtis?"

There was no answer. The sounds of TVs filtered out of the nearby rooms, and the clicking of the kitchen staff cleaning up after mealtime created a pleasant backbeat. I knocked again. "Curtis?"

Still no answer.

I gently pushed open his door and peeked inside.

Curtis lay on his bed, his back to me, huddled underneath a blanket that was pulled almost over the top of his head. He wasn't moving. My mouth turned pasty. *He shouldn't be in bed this early.* I hoped he wasn't sick, or . . . something worse. I couldn't handle that on top of everything else.

I sucked in my lips, wanting to touch him but unable to think about what I'd do if he didn't respond. "Curtis?"

He sat up lickety-split. He held a book, and his eyes were bright. "Mira! I didn't hear you. I've got this great World War II read and I can't put it down."

I almost wept with relief. One thing in this whole awful day was normal, at least.

"Your hair is messed up." I smiled at him.

He ran his hands through his thick white mane. "Old habits die hard. When I was a boy, I always had to read under the covers at night. 'Course we read by candles back then. Made it a mite dangerous."

I didn't know if he was joking.

"Heard Mrs. Berns is in the clink," he said, cutting right to the chase.

"Yeah." This time I didn't try to stop the tears.

Curtis did not rush over and hug me. He also didn't try to tell me things would be OK. I appreciated both gestures. Once I had myself under control, I asked if he knew anything about the Perham girl disappearing.

"Nothing that wasn't in the paper," he said. He held a pregnant pause. I knew him well enough to wait for the rest. "Can't say the same for Janston," he finally said.

My interest perked up. "You know stuff about him?"

"I know he's dangerous. He's always been an empty kid, and now he's just a bigger empty kid with power."

It was funny hearing a man in his late fifties being referred to as a kid, but Curtis had the years to do that. "Empty kid?"

"You know the kind," he said. "There's nothing inside of them. They're all need and greed and meanness. No soul or heart. They make great politicians or CEOs, but terrible people."

I nodded. That sounded about right. "You know he owns Mosquito Bay Lodge?"

"Yep," Curtis said. "His parents opened it up. It was passed down to him over twenty years ago. He's mostly an absentee owner, though."

Janston had lied about buying the lodge fourteen years ago, then. I had a hunch he'd done it for no other reason than he could. It was a lie that wouldn't cost him, but it would confuse me. Empty kid indeed.

"Hey, Curtis. Have you ever met my dad?"

For the first time since I'd known him, Curtis looked away from a direct question. I couldn't see his face when he said no.

I found myself not wanting to ask any follow-up questions.

"All right," I said. "If you hear anything that can help Mrs. Berns, will you get a hold of me?"

He still didn't turn around. "You know I will," he said softly.

I walked out.

I was so tired I felt like a zombie, but I couldn't go home and sleep until I was sure the library was closed up properly. When I checked the front door, I was pleasantly surprised to find that not only had Kennie locked it, but when I unlocked it to go inside, I saw she had cleaned up.

That warmed my heart a bit. My bed was calling, even though it was ungodly early. The front desk computer was pleading more loudly, though. If I left a stone uncovered that could help Mrs. Berns, there was no way I could sleep anyhow. Since I was inside, I might as well do some more research.

I set my shoulders and powered on the computer. This time I searched for Janston without simultaneously searching for Guinn. I discovered Janston had voted along party lines on everything that came across his desk, including voting against a recent bill that would have increased funding for statewide law enforcement, with a chunk of that money earmarked for the attorney general's human trafficking division. That didn't tell me anything for sure except that Janston was scum.

On a hunch, I searched for Dr. Lou Banks, the dentist I still hadn't been able to meet with. I uncovered nothing there, either.

There was no more I could do tonight other than go home to my animals, more disturbed than ever.

I'd make time to grab some groceries on the way. The storm was almost here.

Chapter 39

The next morning, I woke up with allergies so fierce that I almost couldn't crack my eyes wide enough to see. I scoured them in the shower, doused them from a jumbo-size bottle of drops, made sure my pets got outside and into the crotchety air and had fresh food and water, then headed straight to the dentist. So much seemed to hinge on him. He'd had the book containing the note in his office. Immediately after I brought the note back to his office to show to Anne, the library was burgled.

Anne did not appear surprised at all to see me when I charged through the door for the millionth time this week. I was a new regular, the kind who never got her teeth checked.

"Morning," I said.

"Dr. Banks is in with a patient," she said by way of greeting. Her tone was professional.

I glanced around the empty waiting room. "I actually came to see you. Have there been any new patients the last couple weeks?"

She tapped her lip with a pen, a sparkle in her eye. It appeared she'd come to enjoy our visits. "There's always new patients."

"I'm wondering if there are any younger patients. Female." *Possibly girls who Janston and Guinn are trafficking and need dental care for on the down-low? Because that would surely explain everything going on, beginning with the note I discovered in a book that had last been in your waiting room.*

"Well, you know I can't give you any specific patient information." She fluffed her hair, glancing around the empty waiting room for imaginary eavesdroppers. "But I can tell you that we've had quite a few patients with limited English lately."

My pulse drum-rolled. "What age?"

"All ages," she said, vaguely.

Well, that told me next to nothing.

"Thanks," I said. What I really needed was to talk to Dr. Banks to see if I could suss out what kind of man he was. It looked like today would not be my lucky day. "See you later?"

At the library, I powered through the opening duties on automatic. I couldn't keep my mind on the job. I walked around like a robot answering questions, putting books away, and then just sitting in my chair staring blankly.

That was how Gary found me. I didn't even glance up when he walked in the door. It was only his intense energy standing near the desk that roused me from my funk.

I glanced over. I had no emotion to spare, not even surprise that he'd come by. "Yeah? What is it now?" I asked. "Do you want to arrest *me*? Or maybe it's been a full hour since you were a meanie to someone, and good old Mira James came to mind?"

His face was impassive. He still didn't speak. For some reason, his silence infuriated me more than anything. I hopped off my chair, walked around the front counter, and jabbed my finger into his chest.

"It's your fault that Mrs. Berns is in jail," I said. "If you'd kept Guinn in his cell where he belonged, she never would have gone out there. You know that."

I realized it wasn't fair what I was saying, but once I started, I couldn't stop. My voice was escalating. "*You* should be in jail, not her." I could hear the feverishness. I needed to get a grip. Patrons were staring at me.

Gary finally moved. He put a hand on each of my shoulders. It was a surprisingly intimate gesture. "I'm here as a courtesy. I want you to hear it from me."

He had my attention.

"Mrs. Berns has offered a written confession. Once I file it, she'll be spending the rest of her life in prison."

I'd known this was coming. Of course I'd known. But hearing Gary pronounce it here in the brightly lit library was too much. I collapsed into his arms. I couldn't imagine a life without Mrs. Berns. She was the piss in everyone's vinegar, the sparkle in our eyes, the love in our hearts. It wasn't that long ago she'd gathered up the courage to leave her terrible marriage and finally started living her own life. To have that stolen from her because she'd taken the law into her own hands to protect the vulnerable was unspeakably cruel. It was hard to breathe thinking about it. I felt like I kept falling, but Gary must have held me in place, at least until he grunted and moved to the side.

"What the hell are you doing?" Johnny demanded, his face screwed up in rage.

I blinked, confused. What was Johnny doing here? Why was he grabbing Gary, and what was he yelling about?

Gary shrugged off Johnny and held out his hands. *I mean no harm,* the gesture said. *I'm here on business.*

Johnny was angrier than I'd ever seen him. Actually, had I ever seen him angry?

Before I could speak, he took a swing at Gary.

Gary sidestepped it easily, tossed me an obscure look, and strode out the front door.

I couldn't process what I'd just seen. It was like all of Battle Lake was trapped in a snow globe, and some giant ninny was shaking it violently.

"What in the hell was that about?" I demanded of Johnny. The drama of my life was playing out on a public stage. I didn't like having the audience, but I couldn't seem to reel myself in.

"Are you serious?" Johnny asked, hand on his chest in a gesture I normally found sexy. "I walk in on you in Gary's arms and you want to know why I'm upset?"

Peaches and Maisy walked in the library door, torn jeans and hoop earrings and eyes wide. They clearly hadn't meant to stumble into an epic fight.

"I wasn't in his arms," I said to Johnny. "I mean, I was, but it wasn't what it looked like."

"Really? What about all the sexual tension between the two of you for months? I suppose that isn't what it looks like, either?"

I shook my head, trying to dislodge the confusion I was feeling. None of this made sense. Where had my calm and steady boyfriend gone? "Sexual tension? Between me and Gary? We hate each other!"

The anger melted out of Johnny, and he suddenly appeared devastated.

That expression was worse than any words he could have said.

"You need to pick, Mira," he finally said. He shambled out the door.

I stood, my mouth open.

"Haven't you ever seen a fight before?" Peaches demanded. At first, I thought she was talking to me, and then I noticed all the gaping patrons. Once Peaches called them out, they turned away, embarrassed.

"Thanks," I said to her.

"Your boyfriend is a caveman," Maisy said.

But he wasn't. He was the best man I knew. What was happening to my world? I was too numb to cry. "Aren't you girls supposed to be in school?"

"Sure," Maisy said. "Except we get work-experience days, and we decided today would be a perfect time to learn about running a library."

"What?"

"Yeah," Peaches said, grinning, absolutely pleased with herself. "We're here to learn about library operations."

"I'm sorry, girls. I don't have the time or energy to teach you." I didn't know if I even had the will to hunt down the aspirin I found myself desperately craving.

"That's what we figured," Peaches said. "So why don't you go do what you need to do, and we'll stay here and figure stuff out on our own?"

I finally understood.

They knew my friend was in trouble, and they were here to help. Lord, this poor library. It'd been babysat by everybody and run by nobody. But I needed to get to Perham, that was clear now. Everything else had dead-ended. I must find out what I could about Anita Juarez.

"Thanks," I said.

"No worries," Peaches said, smiling broadly. She had a star temporarily tattooed under her ear, and it made her look tough. "Chicks take care of each other, you know?"

Chapter 40

Serendipity was on my side. I pulled into Perham at noon, navigating the woods and then the prairie separating it from Battle Lake. A quick stop for gas and a question got me directions to the turkey plant on the northern edge of the town.

The plant was housed near the highway, an enormous block of a building, as big as three Costco warehouses stuck together. The front of the main building was a designated visitor parking lot, but I pulled around the back, driving through an open chain-link gate to park in the employee lot. I was hoping that at least some of the employees would be on lunch break.

My old Toyota fit right in with the battered pickups and sedans in the back lot. I tucked my car into an open spot and walked confidently toward the employee entrance. The plant's smell was surprisingly mild. I was sure the cold air cut it some, but I'd thought the gaminess would be stronger this close. A trio of men huddled near the back entrance, smoking, their hair covered by matching hairnets.

"Where's the break room?" I asked.

The man nearest hitched his thumb at the door. "Through here, down the hall, on your right. Can't miss it. Looks like you think it would."

I smiled. "Thanks."

The smell was stronger inside the factory, a thick odor of animal waste, wet feathers, and processed flesh. Rhythmic clanks and roars came from a far-off factory floor. Following the instructions the guy had given me, I quickly located a space approximately the size of a classroom with similar chairs and round tables. If I'd gone through the front door as a visitor, no way would I have gotten this far.

The people eating their meals glanced up at me and then returned to what they'd been doing.

I walked to the nearest table of women. "Excuse me?"

A couple of them smiled politely. Most kept eating.

"I'm a reporter from Battle Lake. I'm doing a story on the girl who disappeared. I heard she worked here. Her parents, too."

A dark-haired woman nodded and pointed at the next table over. I followed her finger. It had landed on a woman wearing a soft-looking blue denim shirt. She had food in front of her, but she wasn't touching it.

I felt like an ass for coming here. If I could help Mrs. Berns and the girl who'd been taken, though, I needed to ask questions, no matter how mercenary it felt. I walked over to the woman, intending to stick to my reporter story. "Excuse me, my name is Mira James."

When her eyes met mine, and I saw the bottomless pain in hers, something released inside me. Without warning, I found the truth tumbling out of my mouth. "My friend is in jail. I think it's somehow connected to the disappearance of Anita Juarez. Do you know Ms. Juarez?"

I realized the break room had gone quiet. Everyone was watching the woman in the denim shirt. She stared at me, her dark eyes unreadable. I was about to apologize from the bottom of my soul and slink out of there when she pulled out the chair next to her.

"Not good English," she said in a quiet voice.

A man who didn't look much older than twenty came over to the table. "I can translate. This is Anita's mother, Lupe."

My chin trembled. "I'm so sorry," I said. I couldn't imagine the depth of her pain.

She nodded, signaling for me to go on.

I pushed through the discomfort and took out a picture of Guinn that I had printed from the work computer. "Do you know this man?"

Lupe shrugged and spoke a flurry of Spanish to the young man who'd offered to translate. I felt like an idiot for knowing only my one language. When she paused, the translator turned to me, the shadow of a smile on his face.

"She says all Minnesotans look the same," he said, a note of apology in his voice.

I couldn't help but return the smile. "I suppose we do," I said.

"I recognize him, though," the translator said. "He's the man who is setting up the community center. John Guinn. The girls here don't like him."

I glanced around the room. All the women glanced down rather than meet my eyes.

I nodded. That was the general consensus about Guinn: he gave girls and women the creeps. I turned back to Lupe. "You haven't heard from your daughter since she disappeared?"

Her eyes welled with tears. "No," she said. "No call."

She returned to her native language, speaking to the translator.

When she was done, he turned to me once again. "She says that her daughter would never run away. She was responsible. She also said that she isn't the first to be abducted, either. One town over, Frazee? Another Mexican girl disappeared from there. A good girl. No one listens to her parents, like no one listens here."

"Do you know that girl's name?"

The translator and the women exchanged glances, and then the woman nodded.

"Talia Hector," the translator said. "She's sixteen, just like Anita."

Lupe nodded again, her face heavy.

"Thank you," I said. I didn't know what else to say. "I'm so sorry."

The woman tried to smile but couldn't.

"Gracias," she said.

◆ ◆ ◆

My trip to Perham convinced me more than ever that Guinn was a pervert or worse. It hadn't given me anything more concrete than that, unfortunately.

I was relieved to find the library in good shape when I returned. Peaches and Maisy were particularly proud of how they'd dusted and organized Jed's altar. Apparently he'd taken on a mythical quality at the high school. It made sense. He'd been one of the good guys, relatable, with a kind word for everyone.

I wished he were here now.

As soon as Maisy and Peaches left, I searched for information on Talia Hector. The *Fargo Forum* had run the only article about her disappearance, and it was short. It said she was missing, and that police were looking into it.

That'd been nearly two weeks ago.

I suspected her race, as well as that of Anita Juarez, had something to do with how little coverage their cases were getting. Maisy Kramer's abduction, on the other hand, was front page news across all major media outlets, that and John Guinn's murder. Mrs. Berns wasn't named in any of the articles, only referred to as "a likely suspect in custody." I couldn't read too many of those pieces.

Instead, I searched for more information on sex trafficking and found nothing new, nothing that would explain why a man like John Guinn would have been reckless enough to abduct girls so close to home. Given how little media attention the disappearances of the two Mexican American girls had generated, it was horribly logical for Guinn to have chosen them, if that was in fact what had happened. But Maisy Kramer? That made no sense, particularly if Guinn had been doing this for a decade and a half. What could have driven him to take such a risk? It was frustrating, this online search, when I didn't really know what I was looking for. That's when I remembered the file of Lartel's stuff that I'd lifted from Kennie's.

Time to go old-school again.

It was exactly where I'd left it in the library storage room. There hadn't been anything of note when I'd first riffled through it, but I hadn't known what I was looking for. I brought it to the front counter so I could keep an eye on patrons while I read through it more carefully.

I hit pay dirt in Lartel's bills: a fourteen-year-old receipt for a stay at Mosquito Bay Lodge. I checked the dates. They were identical to the days both Janston and Guinn had been there for the Teen Mental Health conference.

I'd bet my car that my dad had been there, too, that he'd participated in something so craven that he spent the next year drinking himself to death, finally succeeding. The light was dimming on Mark James as it became less and less likely that he had been "investigating" for Janston.

Curse words.

I snatched the library phone and dialed the number from heart. Gary picked up on the third ring.

"Chief Wohnt, it's Mira." The formality, and the distance it conveyed, felt important since Johnny's visit. "Guinn was the one who kidnapped the girl in Perham and the girl in Frazee and who tried to take Maisy."

It felt good to get all that out there.

Until it didn't.

"Hello?" I said when Gary didn't answer. I'd expected him to demand proof, and I'd been lining it up as best I could. I hadn't prepared for a nonresponse.

"That's great," Gary finally said. "Except another girl has disappeared, and Guinn has been dead for over twenty-four hours."

"Another girl gone?" I said. I'd heard him, but I couldn't get my head around it.

"Chelsea Cruise."

God, no. The sweet blonde from the Chick Club, Maisy Kramer's best friend. It knocked the breath out of me so hard that I almost missed the inspector walking toward me.

Chapter 41

"Did I hear you say another girl has disappeared?"

I swiveled toward the voice. Inspector Bob Hartman's expression was worried. Even through the shock, I knew I had to smooth this over. I gave a thumbs-up. Gary had already hung up on the other side, but Bob didn't know that. "That sounds like a fantastic talent show skill," I chirped. "I'll see you Saturday."

The inspector's glasses were doing that light-reflection trick that made it hard to see his eyes. I sure hoped he'd swallowed my lie. It'd be a perfect ending to a terrible week if the town swirled down the drain along with my life.

Bob took a step forward, allowing me to see his eyes. They appeared intrigued. He'd bought my lie. I let out a breath I hadn't realized I was holding.

"Is the girl disappearing part of a magic act for the talent show?" he asked.

I smiled wanly. "Yep. You're going to be there, right?"

"I'm not sure yet," he said with a mixture of suspicion and shyness. "I don't know how long I'll be in town."

That's when I remembered the book I'd overnighted for him. I reached under the counter. "I ordered this from another library for you," I said, sliding it toward him.

His face lit up when he saw the Midwestern-specialties cookbook. "I love to cook for people with special dietary needs. My mom had diabetes, you know. It killed her. I want to make sure that doesn't happen to anyone else. Not on my watch."

He spilled all that in an unguarded, from-the-heart release. I found myself charmed by his sudden honesty. I thought again about Karen's comment that there were no good men left. I had a hunch I was looking at one. He was a weirdo, for sure, but he was more than that. I made a mental note to order him a book on starting a small business. I suspected he'd be much more fulfilled running a specialized catering company than inspecting small towns.

After a little small talk, he checked out his book, plus a few others, and left.

Somehow, I got through the work day without being completely swallowed by depression at the thought of Mrs. Berns in jail and Chelsea captured, made time to order a Z-Force for every girl in the Chick Club, and then the minute I could close up shop, I rushed over to Chelsea's house on the edge of town.

Karen was there when I arrived, consoling Chelsea's parents, who were in terrible shape. With urging from Karen that surprised me, they told me what they'd already told the police: Chelsea had never returned home from school that day. She'd attended her last class, stopped at the gas station to buy a Coke, and no one had seen her since.

"Was she meeting somebody?" I asked.

Her mom and dad exchanged a pained glance, their faces swollen from crying. "We don't think so," Chelsea's father finally said. His tears fell freely. He didn't bother wiping them away. "We think she just went to get a pop."

"She wouldn't have run away," Chelsea's mom said.

"No, she wouldn't have," I agreed sincerely. "She's a good kid."

Just like the other two girls who'd disappeared. And Maisy.

I comforted them as best I could and then drove to Maisy's house. I needed to know who she'd been meeting for lunch when she was snatched, whether or not she felt like telling me. She wasn't home. She didn't answer the phone, either.

Same with Peaches.

I couldn't talk with Mrs. Berns. Gary wouldn't let me see her, and I didn't know if I could stand to see her locked up again even if he did. I didn't know who else to interview to uncover what was happening. Jed was dead. Kennie was a wild card. Curtis had told me everything he knew. Johnny wasn't talking to me. Gary was the enemy.

I was lost and alone.

Rattled, I drove home and tried to soothe myself by petting Luna and Tiger Pop, but I transferred my agitation onto them. I tried watching TV, but I couldn't focus. Even my plants didn't pacify me.

I was making Luna antsy. She was whining, twining herself around my feet. "I'm going to go for a walk," I said, tugging on my jacket. Her tail waved at the word, but I had to let her down. I was heading to Guinn's house, and I didn't know what I would find. No way was I going to put her in any danger.

I stepped outside into air as charged as I was.

I crunched through the woods. Dusk was settling, and my allergies had my face feeling like a big mushy swamp. But I kept walking. Took me almost twenty minutes to reach the clearing surrounding Guinn's house.

When I did, I realized something was wrong.

At first, I thought there was a tree in his yard where before there'd been none. It took me a moment to realize it wasn't a tree but a man. The same man I had seen spying on Guinn's place last night.

The rough, matted fur coat was unmistakable.

For a chaotic second I thought I was looking at Bigfoot.

But then he turned toward me.

It wasn't Bigfoot at all standing there.

It was Jed Heike.

Chapter 42

Clearly, I had lost my ever-loving mind.

It was the stress, the allergies, the lack of sleep, the poor food choices.

My entire body was fluttery, tingling. I rubbed my eyes and took a step closer.

"Jed?" I repeated.

The man staring at me looked exactly like my beautiful Jed, his hair gone wild and his beard scraggly. The funky Frankenstein coat appeared to be harvested and tied-together roadkill. But it couldn't have been Jed because he wasn't responding.

I kept walking toward him. My legs felt faraway, or maybe it was my mind floating free of my body. I expected him to disappear like a hallucination or a mirage, but he grew more solid the nearer I got. Finally, I was standing in front of him. He smelled terrible, like a man who hadn't bathed in more than two months.

A sob escaped my mouth.

I yanked off my mitten because I needed to feel him, skin to skin. I placed my hand on his cheek. He felt rough, warm.

Real.

"Oh my god, it's you," I whispered.

He held his hand over mine, but no light of recognition bloomed in his eyes. "I'm so sorry," he said, his voice coming out gravelly, "but I don't know you."

"It's OK," I said, the tears coursing down my cheeks. I didn't know how it had happened, but it was real. Jed was here. "I know you. You're home."

◆ ◆ ◆

Luna went insane when I brought Jed back. I led him into the house like a child. She jumped on him and sniffed him and tried to crawl into his lap when he sat down. His face lit up, but there was still no sign of recognition. I stayed only long enough to grab my car keys and call Sal.

I counted the rings. Seven. The eighth would send me to voicemail. "Hello?"

"Sal, it's Mira." Jed was a few feet away, Luna perched on his lap, licking his face. He was smiling, those familiar happy crinkles in the corners of his eyes just about breaking my heart.

"Jed's alive," I croaked. Saying it out loud brought a whole fresh wave of tears.

She was quiet on the other end. "This isn't funny," she finally said.

"No, Sal, it's true." My voice was shaking. "Jed is home. He doesn't remember anything. Meet me at the Fergus hospital. I'm bringing him in."

She was weeping when I hung up.

I bundled Jed into my car and drove him the half an hour to Fergus Falls. He watched the night race by out the window, oddly quiet. He answered my questions politely but all the same: *I don't know. I don't know.* His responses eerily paralleled Maisy's the night I'd driven her to the police station.

Once they'd hustled him into a private examination room, I returned to the lobby to meet Sal and Bill when they arrived. That's where I ran into Gary in uniform. A surge of anger exploded in me, but it wasn't sustainable, not with Jed safe.

Gary's expression turned to happiness when he spotted me, which was truly a first. Years fell off him. He must have heard about Jed. I didn't know he'd cared for him so much.

"You heard?" Gary asked.

"Heard? I brought him in."

Gary appeared confused. "Brought who in?"

I grew uneasy. "Wait, what is it that *you* know?"

Gary wanted to slide his cop face back on, I could see the struggle, but he couldn't overcome the grin. I'd never realized he had such a nice smile. "Mrs. Berns is free."

In books, I'd read the expression "the world shifted." I'd always thought it hyperbole, but then the floor moved underfoot. I held out my hands, wondering if I was caught in some sort of April Fools' loop.

"What?" I asked.

"The coroner called me in." Gary's grin nearly split his face in two. "Guinn had been dead for hours when Mrs. Berns shot him. Someone had strangled him and propped him in his chair by the window."

My brain was trying to piece that together.

Gary saved me the trouble. "You can't murder a corpse."

Chapter 43

Sal and Bill's reunion with their son was just as emotional as you would expect. The nurses had to finally pry Jed out of Sal's arms so they could wheel him down the hall for an MRI. I hoped a bath would follow.

Jed was game for all of it, as he'd always been, but he had no clue what was going on. He seemed cognitively fine based on the initial tests, but he suffered from profound amnesia. Searching through his pockets didn't provide any insight into how he'd survived since he'd been thrown out of the Valentine Train through the Rockies in February. The doctor's best guess was that Jed had hurt his head in the fall, but somehow made his way back to Battle Lake without understanding why, like a salmon returning to its birthplace.

I wanted to stay, but Gary told me Mrs. Berns was being processed out of her holding cell and would need a ride. As soon as I made sure Jed was in good hands, I raced to Battle Lake to spring my best friend.

She was waiting inside the station for me. She looked frail and disheveled, but she was still quick. She rushed at me. "I'm in jail for twenty-four hours and you find Jed? What the hell?"

Her words were harsh, but she and I were smiling so happily at each other that neither of us could say anything more. We hugged instead. She felt surprisingly light. Her skin looked papery up close, and her eye bags had bags, but she was free.

"You're coming home with me tonight," I said. "I have popcorn and wine."

"And a shower?" Mrs. Berns said.

"And a shower. You smell almost as ripe as Jed."

"A minute," the deputy called from behind us.

Both Mrs. Berns and I tensed. I turned, standing in front to shield her. "Chief Wohnt said she could leave with me."

The deputy smiled. "He also said to give this to Mrs. Berns. Just in case."

I took the envelope he was holding and handed it to her, afraid that if he got near her, he'd find a reason to lock her back up.

Mrs. Berns opened the envelope on the way to the car.

"What is it?" I asked.

"A light goose hunting license, backdated to last week."

On the drive to my place, I filled her in on what she'd missed: Jed had complete amnesia but was alive! Janston owned Mosquito Bay Lodge, and my instincts were telling me it was a central site for sex trafficking. She cursed at this bit of news, but didn't interrupt my update. I also knew in my gut that my dad was involved and that he'd been there at that conference fourteen years ago, the same one Lartel, Guinn, Janston, and likely Penetal had attended. I knew but could not prove that at the meeting, they had either formulated or ramped up a sex trafficking operation, and that the numbers on the note were connected to that. They may have been kidnapping immigrant girls for a while, but something had made them reckless, driven them to abduct two local girls.

"I suspect that the dentist, Banks, is involved, too," I said. "That would explain why the note was tucked in a book that was in his office. One of the kidnapped girls must have found an old slip of paper belonging to Guinn or Janston and scribbled 'help' on it."

Mrs. Berns, bless her, dived right to the heart of it. "You sure your dad was involved?"

"Yeah," I said, "I am. I know what kind of man he was: unprincipled. My mom will never accept it, and I didn't want to, but the truth is, he was always shadowy."

"We aren't the sins of our parents," Mrs. Berns said firmly, rephrasing an earlier comment of hers. "If your dad was involved in sex trafficking, that's on him. But I wouldn't spend the emotions on that until you're sure. No reason to borrow that sort of pain."

She was right, probably, but I'd never been much good at turning off worry.

When we reached my double-wide, Luna was almost as excited to see Mrs. Berns as she had been to see Jed. Even Tiger Pop padded out of the bedroom to say hi. I got us settled in, making popcorn and pouring wine while Mrs. Berns showered. I let her borrow a pair of thermal long underwear and fleece-lined slippers.

When she came out dressed for comfort, we fell into the couch and started fleshing out theories of who had really killed Guinn and why.

That's what we were doing when a knock resounded at my door.

"Given how your day is going, that's either Elvis or the FBI," Mrs. Berns said, tossing a fluffy white kernel into her open mouth.

When I reached the door and opened it, I saw that she wasn't far off.

Chapter 44

"Slumber party!" Kennie squealed, pushing past me to get inside. "I heard on the police scanner that you'd found Jed and that you brought home Mrs. Berns, though I have no idea how you freed a woman accused of murder. In any case, I'm here to celebrate."

I glanced at Mrs. Berns.

Kennie needs to leave, her eyes said. But then they widened.

I turned back to Kennie, who was holding out a Ziploc bag of amazing-looking chocolate chip cookies, each perfectly round and golden with a generous sprinkling of chocolate. My stomach gurgled. I hadn't eaten anything but wine and popcorn all day.

"Those look good," Mrs. Berns said. "Bring 'em on over."

And that's how the strangest slumber party of my life began.

"I'll grab milk," I said.

"Be a dear and grab me a wineglass, too," Kennie said, plopping on the couch next to Mrs. Berns and handing her the cookie bag.

Luna and Tiger Pop had both retreated to my bedroom. Smart animals. I emerged from the kitchen with three cups held by the fingers of one hand, waitress-style, and a carton of rice milk. "Pour what you like in your cup."

Kennie reached for the wine. "I heard something you might be interested in," she said archly.

"On the scanner, too?" Mrs. Berns asked, a cookie in each hand.

"Nope. This is from a friend at the capitol. Sounds like those charges against Janston are being dropped. He's only going to get a very private hand slap."

Mrs. Berns coughed on her cookie, but took another bite like a champ, speaking around her chewing. "Didn't *four* women accuse him of illegal behavior?" she asked.

I bit into my own cookie. It was delicious. No, it was better than delicious. It was *exquisite.* I finished it and reached for another before I spoke.

"That's bullcrap," I said.

"Yep," Mrs. Berns agreed. "If four accused him, there are likely more. How did we let the dum-dums run the world?"

"Cheers," Kennie said, holding her cookie out to Mrs. Berns so they could clink them in a toast.

"These are amazing cookies," I said. "I didn't know you could bake."

"I can't. Brad made 'em."

I nodded, and the movement made the lights in the room sparkle.

"You know Brad cheated on Mira, right?" Mrs. Berns asked Kennie. "If he was a fish, he'd be a shitty-mouthed bass."

That made me giggle. Once I started, I couldn't stop.

Even Kennie began laughing. "What kind of fish would I be?"

Mrs. Berns thought on that. "Probably tuna because you smell like one?"

That sent me and Kennie over the edge. Like, we literally fell off the couch laughing.

"What about me?" I asked, gasping for air.

"You wouldn't be a fish," Mrs. Berns said sagely, digging in the bag for her third cookie. "You'd be something large and elegant. Like an elk."

This time, cookie sprayed out my nose. "I don't think elks are elegant," I sputtered when I was finally able to speak.

"Shows what you know," Mrs. Berns said.

"Gary took me elk hunting once," Kennie said. She was staring off into the distance, her face grown soft.

I stopped laughing. I always forgot that they used to date. I reached for a mug and poured myself some milk. I was suddenly terribly thirsty.

"How'd it go?" Mrs. Berns asked.

"Not well. I was in charge of using the elk bugle to call them in. I wasn't very good at it."

Mrs. Berns patted her knee. "Elk bugling isn't something you get right the first time."

That reignited and then elevated my laughter to the stratosphere.

Kennie nodded. "I mentioned that Brad packed these cookies with marijuana, right?"

And it was in that state of mind that we decided it would be a brilliant idea to break into Guinn's house and snag the concealed laptop I'd seen the day he'd let me inside his house.

Chapter 45

It took my threesome far longer to navigate the woods to Guinn's than it would have taken me alone. Mostly because heavy clouds had obscured the moon, allowing only a dim illumination to guide our way. That, and Mrs. Berns and Kennie kept pausing to remark on how beautiful the snow was. It didn't help that Mrs. Berns legitimately stopped to full-on hug four different trees.

Our appreciative mood stilled when Guinn's house came in sight. Police tape ringing the front porch was visible from our angle.

"What was it like to shoot somebody?" Kennie asked.

Talk about a buzzkill.

But Mrs. Berns was all there for it, per usual. "It was awful," she said. "But not as terrible as it would have felt to hear that he'd hurt another girl."

"You didn't kill him, though," I said, patting her shoulder.

"True dat," Mrs. Berns said, a smile lighting up her face. "In that case, it was like shooting a bag of potatoes!"

Kennie smacked her lips. "Wouldn't some potato chips taste excellent right now? And what's this about him already being dead?"

"You better not tell anyone," I said, "at least not until the police officially announce it. I don't want to hamper their investigation. But yeah, somebody got to Guinn before Mrs. Berns. That's why she was released tonight. He was already gone when she shot him."

"Don't tell anyone what?" Kennie asked, kneeling in the snow. "I'm really thirsty. Think I can eat this?"

Confident that Kennie's swiss-cheese marijuana brain was the safest home for the secret, I tiptoed toward Guinn's, motioning for the women to follow. "We are sneaking in through that back window," I said as I moved. "This whole house is a new-build, which means all the windows are probably tightly sealed. Our only hope is that he didn't lock one of these—"

My breaking-and-entering speech was interrupted by a crash. The window I'd been leading us toward disappeared in front of my eyes, its broken, double-paned glass raining onto the snow.

I turned on Kennie, my eyes wide.

She stood with her hands on her hips, a satisfied expression on her face. "That summer softball league sure is paying off," she said.

"What did you throw?" Mrs. Berns asked, high-fiving her.

"My phone," Kennie said. Her brow furrowed. "But now that I think about it, I maybe should have chosen something else?"

I shook my head. I was in a gang with the Keystone Cops. "There's no turning back now."

I plucked out the glass shards still clinging to the frame, grateful that I'd worn leather gloves rather than mittens.

"Kennie," I said, "you hoist me in. Then I'll pull the two of you in after me."

"I'm the lightest," Mrs. Berns protested. "I should go in first. Also, I am currently constructed of love and illumination, so I won't need a flashlight."

This was good pot. Maybe too good. I was feeling a bit slow and stupid myself, two qualities you do *not* want on a B and E adventure. Fortunately, they were balanced by the sense that I was indomitable.

"You *are* made of love and light," I agreed. "However, I've already been inside this house. It makes sense for me to go first." I didn't want to tell her the rest of my reasoning, which was that I was sure there would be ghosts and other terrible things inside, and I didn't want her to encounter them first.

I hoisted myself over the windowsill without a hitch. First thing I did was grab Kennie's phone and hand it back to her. "Put your gloves on," I told her. "We don't want to leave fingerprints."

Mrs. Berns was already wearing hers. I pulled her inside next, and then she and I both tugged in Kennie. Once she was on her feet, Kennie switched on her phone and pushed a button. Immediately, a bright beam of light shot out of it.

"Your phone turns into a flashlight?" I asked. "I really need to get me one of those."

"You think?" Kennie asked. "You're the only person in the county who doesn't own a cell phone."

"It's true," Mrs. Berns said. "We all talk about you. It's embarrassing."

"I can't afford one," I said. That was mostly factual. More true was that technology intimidated me. But now that I'd learned phones could double as a flashlight? Spygirl me wanted on board.

"Here's the plan," I said. "The two of you are going to make a quick sweep of the house to make sure there's nothing obvious the police may have overlooked. You will avoid any areas surrounded by bright yellow tape, and you will touch nothing with your bare hands. Meanwhile, I'm going to search for Guinn's laptop."

Mrs. Berns saluted me. Kennie was already making her way to the stairs.

Half of me wondered if the three of us coming here was the worst idea ever.

The other half was positive it was.

With Kennie's light gone, I had to allow my eyes a moment to adjust. Fortunately, the moon had tipped through the clouds. The clear bit of sky made me wonder if the storm of the century was ever coming, except my ramped-up allergies told me it was just around the corner.

I rubbed my itchy, dark-adjusted eyes and made my way to the bookshelf. There was a good chance the police had not thought to even look there. Their goal was to find out who'd killed Guinn now that they knew Mrs. Berns hadn't, and so why bother scrutinizing bookshelves? I discovered the laptop on the third ledge. It was nestled in the same deep maroon case I'd spotted next to Guinn's chair the day he'd invited me in, the one designed to look like a tall book.

I fell into the couch. I unzipped the case and flipped it open. Guinn's computer lay inside. It was a Mac. My technophobia ramped up. We had PCs at the library. I hoped the two had similar set-ups. The Mac's power button was easy to locate, anyhow. I turned it on, steeling myself for what I might discover. Guinn was a pervert, a monster, a man who'd likely been running a modern slavery ring before his death. That knowledge made his computer feel hot and oily on my lap.

The screen lit up, greeting me with a tiny, circular headshot of Guinn above a box with the flashing request for a password. *Dangnabbit.* I typed in his name. No go. I typed in the name of the community center. Dead end. I glanced around the room looking for any clue. If we couldn't access Guinn's laptop, this trip was a bust.

Mrs. Berns appeared in the doorway, a slip of paper in one hand and an open bag of potato chips in the other.

"You took food from his kitchen?" I asked, incredulous.

Mrs. Berns shrugged. "Sorry. By which I mean, I'm not sorry. You need this?"

I took the slip of paper that she was offering. The word "passwords" was scribbled across the top.

"Found it stuck to the side of his fridge," she said, munching chips with all the finesse of Cookie Monster.

I studied the slip of paper. I couldn't judge Guinn on this point. I would've done the same if I had passwords to remember. Fortunately, I found all other sorts of things to judge him on once I accessed his home screen using a random string of letters and numbers that he'd scribbled next to the word "laptop" on his passwords list.

The folder labeled MISCELLANEOUS was the worst. I could stomach only the first two images before I closed it out, wishing I could scrub my eyes and also that I could bring Guinn back to life so I could torture him for a while before killing him again.

Inside the folder titled BATTLE LAKE COMMUNITY CENTER, I uncovered funding tables, bills, schedules, and the videos Peaches had told me about. I deleted the girls' videos and then emptied Guinn's trash. I didn't care if they were evidence. There was plenty of other stuff on here without those images.

"Check out the name of this," I said, calling Mrs. Berns and Kennie over. I pointed at a folder I'd discovered within a folder. It was called BANKS.

"More financial records?" Kennie asked.

I opened it. Inside were the only encrypted files I'd come across. "I don't know," I said. "But I know someone by that name."

"The dentist who'd checked out the book you found the note in?" Mrs. Berns asked.

"Bingo," I said.

"Check his internet search history," Kennie said, tapping the computer screen with her gloved finger.

"Good idea," I said. I clicked on his browser. It'd been cleaned out a week ago, but since then, Guinn had visited some innocuous sites as well as a place called Secretdoor.com. I opened that last site up. The first page cautioned me that it was an adult-only page. I clicked past that warning and was brought to a log-in screen already populated with Guinn's name and password.

I had only to select "Enter."

The moment I did, Kennie and Mrs. Berns sucked in their breath so sharply I felt my hair move. Secret Door was a site men visited to find "judgment-free companionship." The home screen was peppered with ads featuring women who would provide this companionship, but they didn't look like women. They looked like teenagers, or younger.

But that wasn't what had my heart pounding and what had made Mrs. Berns and Kennie intake so loudly. We were all three looking at the "newest arrival" box featured in the center of the screen. Inside was a picture of Chelsea Cruise, the girl who had just been abducted from Battle Lake. When I clicked on it, I saw that Guinn had made the entry himself. The ad promised that Chelsea would provide "special, never-before-experienced services."

It did not describe what they were, but the implication was clear: Chelsea was a virgin.

I felt sick to my stomach. A snap behind me told me Mrs. Berns was taking a picture of the screen. She was smart, but she wasn't immune. When I glanced at her face, I saw she was as green as I felt.

"Think his phone is still hooked up?" I asked.

Kennie's voice came out strangled. "I imagine so. The phone company won't turn off his service until they're asked."

"Good," I said. I powered down the computer, closed the case, and slid it back into place before dialing 911. I told them exactly what I'd discovered, starting with Chelsea's photo on the website and the laptop itself, plus its password and location on John Guinn's bookshelf. When the operator asked for my name, I hung up the phone.

"Time to run," I said.

We helped each other out of the window and then hightailed it back to my place, moving so fast that the cartoon, coconut-drum sound of Scooby-Doo fleeing a monster would not have been out of place.

Chapter 46

We reached my house in record time. When we got inside and caught our breath, I said out loud what I assumed all three of us were thinking.

"You know we're not done," I said, looking at both of them.

"Yep," Mrs. Berns said. "We also need to put our own ad on that gruesome site and catch every bastard in the county who's using it."

"Exactly," I said. "With luck, one of them will be the person who killed Guinn."

"How do you mean?" Kennie asked.

"No reason to off Guinn unless you were worried about what he'd tell the police," Mrs. Berns answered for me. "He was on their radar after Mira found Maisy in his shed. He could have done a lot of damage, spilling names to keep himself out of jail."

Kennie pondered that. "Not many people would kill to protect their reputation."

"Someone with a lot to lose, like a politician or a dentist, might," I said. "Especially if they were found to be running a sex trafficking ring."

Kennie hauled out her phone. "Point taken. Let's cast our web, spiders."

We searched online for photos of women we could use in the ad, but in the end, we decided we didn't want to put anyone in that position without their permission, even a stock photo model. We settled for pulling loose hair close to my face, holding it in place with a beanie, and taking a digital photo of my profile in dim lighting using Mrs. Berns's camera.

We all agreed I looked much younger in the pic and that you couldn't tell it was me, not even if you squinted. Still using her phone, we styled the ad after the one Guinn had created for Chelsea, using the same vague language and making sure to underscore that I lived in Otter Tail County.

Once the ad was uploaded, there was nothing left to do but wait.

I expected to wake up with a hangover given how much marijuana I'd ingested, but instead I awoke feeling like I'd had the best night's sleep of my life. Mrs. Berns and Kennie were already gone, so I showered, ate a big breakfast of oatmeal doused with brown sugar and cream, fed and played with my animals, and called Sal.

I was delighted when she answered.

"How's Jed?" I asked. "Can he have visitors at the hospital?"

"He's at home with me right now," Sal said. "He's watching cartoons and eating a pizza for breakfast, just like always." Her voice was pure satisfied happiness.

My heart leaped. "Is he starting to remember stuff?"

"Not yet," she said. "But the doctor said he could at any time. We need to surround him with familiar settings and people to jog his memory. She said it's either that, some big shock, or another conk on his head that's going to bring him back." She chuckled. "Bill and I voted for the familiar settings and people."

"Can I stop by later?"

"Of course! Johnny will be by over his lunch hour, if you want to come then?"

I didn't like the twinge that mentioning Johnny's name gave me. It wasn't the thrill of anticipation I'd grown used to. It was a paranoid, sloshing feeling. There was something for him and me to deal with, and

I had been putting it off. Well, another few days of that couldn't hurt. I had bigger fish to fry.

Driving into work, I made the executive decision to ask for Gary's help. The idea was bananas, but I figured it would clear Mrs. Berns, Kennie, and me of any suspicion regarding who had called in the tip last night. I would be the last person they suspected of the B and E at Guinn's if I showed up at the police station today, right?

Maybe even more importantly, something had shifted between me and Gary. Or maybe just inside Gary. He'd presumably never filed Mrs. Berns's confession, or she wouldn't have been released so easily. Then he'd put his name on the line to procure a backdated hunting license for her to protect her from any fallout from shooting Guinn. Maybe I hadn't been giving him enough credit for being human.

I could fix that now. I could tell him about the plan to trap the sex traffickers using Secretdoor.com.

But when I pulled open the police door and stepped inside the station, I realized I had been foolish to come here.

Gary sat behind his desk, doing his best impression of Man with a Head Full of Stinging Bees. The sparks of concern and kindness he'd recently shown? Aberrations.

"What the hell do you want, James?" he grumbled.

His anger hit me like a shove, which momentarily froze me in place. Why was he so mad? The door closed behind me, its soft click breaking my paralysis. I glanced to my left, where a deputy stood at the filing cabinet. He threw me a brief, down-low *probably best to turn around* look.

But it was too late. I was in for a penny, in for a pound.

The speech I'd rehearsed on my drive over spilled out of my mouth. "On Monday, I found a note in a library book that Dr. Banks or his receptionist had checked out. The note contained four names, Mark James, John Guinn, Jefferson Penetal, and Lartel McManus, plus numbers after each, all written in the same handwriting. There was also the word 'help' written in a different hand.

"I think that Banks, Janston, Guinn, Penetal, McManus, and probably my dad, Mark James, were working together to run a sex trafficking ring out of Battle Lake, and specifically, out of Mosquito Bay Lodge. I have good reason to believe they're using the website Secret Door to market the girls they kidnap, children of immigrants from around the state, mostly, but now, Battle Lake girls, too. I want your help in putting up a fake ad and entrapping them."

No way was I going to tell him we'd already done that. I couldn't tip my whole hand. Old habits died hard. But if he agreed, which was a to-the-moon-and-back long shot based on his seething expression, then I would show him our ad.

"That is a slim accusation," Gary said, his words falling like knives. "Besides being a *ridiculous* one."

I couldn't reveal anything else without compromising myself or my friends, especially the fact that I had seen Guinn's laptop. I imagined when the state police located it—if they hadn't already—they would send it over to their forensics department, which would find the same troubling images I had as well as Guinn's search history. By then, though, it could be too late. Anita, Talia, and Chelsea were running on borrowed time.

"Cat got your tongue, James?" Gary said. His tone was cruel. "Battle Lake's favorite know-it-all has nothing else to say?"

"Actually, I *do* have something to say," I said, my voice shaking, "and it's this: you're mean."

Not my best comeback, but I was trapped. I'd given him too much information, but I also couldn't give him any more. I stuck out my tongue before turning on my heel and stomping out. Score one for the kindergartner.

When I reached the library, Mrs. Berns was already there, having opened it up early. She was peering at the front computer.

"Any hits on our ad?" I asked.

"None," she said. "But boy did I sleep well last night."

"Yeah, me too."

A good night's rest wasn't enough to prepare me for the library's first visitor, though. I hadn't even had a chance to remove my coat.

"Good morning," I said to Karen Kramer, who strode through the door looking like she definitely had *not* slept well. "Something we can help you find this morning?"

"I am fine by myself," she said, stomping toward the reference section.

I should have just let her go, but I was gunning for a fight, and so I followed, removing my jacket as I did. "How's Maisy doing?"

"Fine," she said, stopping short of the stacks. "She wanted to stay home for some alone time today, and I let her."

I looked for something to argue with, but I couldn't find it. It didn't help that Karen's ripe-fruit smell was even stronger today than it had been yesterday.

The door announced another visitor. Bob Hartman, the inspector.

All the aggressiveness drained out of me. He and I seemed to be getting along better now, but I imagined he would still do his job. He was required to report on Battle Lake and maybe shut down our tourism business. Chelsea's disappearing was a tragedy all its own, and it would also make it that much harder for the inspector to do anything but tank us.

"Morning," Mrs. Berns said to him, too cheerfully.

He tipped his hat and then made his way to Karen and me.

"Thank you for the book," he said shyly. "I really enjoyed it."

"You read it already?"

"That happens when it's a subject I'm passionate about."

I found myself smiling. Except I didn't understand why Karen wasn't speaking. She surely had already met the inspector at the chamber meeting. I glanced over at her. She did not look well and was suddenly glassy-eyed, with a sheen on her skin.

"I love marshmallows," she said.

"Excuse me?" Did I still have marijuana in my system?

She fell to the floor with a thump, legs crossed like she was ready for story time. "Marshmallows. I really, really love them. Everyone should have a marshmallow."

I pinched myself to see if I was dreaming. Nope. Before I could decide how to respond to Karen, the inspector leaned over and put his hand respectfully on her shoulder.

"Are you all right?" he asked. His nose crinkled. "Sweet cherry," he said.

I glanced at Mrs. Berns, hoping she could explain what was happening. She already held the library phone in her hand, worried eyes pinned on Karen and the inspector.

"Does she have diabetes?" the inspector asked.

"I don't know," Mrs. Berns said.

"I think she's falling into a diabetic coma," the inspector said, his voice growing suddenly urgent. "Can you please dial 911?"

Mrs. Berns was already doing it.

I was leaning over to help Karen when Dr. Banks strode into the library.

Chapter 47

The ambulance arrived in minutes. The inspector explained to the EMTs what he believed was happening. After the medics administered a shot to Karen, she started becoming coherent almost immediately. Her vital signs stabilized, but the EMTs took her to the ER to be safe. The inspector said he'd follow along to give her a ride home after, which I thought incredibly kind.

"I heard you wanted to see me," Dr. Banks said when the EMTs and Bob left with Karen. He'd offered his help and then stayed out of the way as the drama unfolded. "Anne told me you've been in nearly every day this week! I had a morning cancellation free up my schedule, so I stopped by. Quite an exciting day at the library."

"I guess," I said.

Dr. Banks was a bland-looking guy in his late fifties or early sixties with smile lines at the corner of his eyes. He was tall, maybe six feet even. Just as Mrs. Berns had said, he had washed-out hair and a matching mustache the same color as his skin. He also had a great smile, which was no surprise considering he was a dentist. That didn't mean much, though. Guinn had been opening community centers, for Pete's sake. Predators could hide in any form. I'd never have guessed in a million years that Banks would come to see me, though, and so I hadn't prepared what to say to him.

"I heard you found Jed Heike, too," he said.

Something closed inside me. Turned out I was protective of that information. "Yeah," I said, "or he found me."

I expected Dr. Banks to inundate me with nosy follow-up questions, but he just smiled and said, "I'm so glad to hear it."

My brain scrambled for a game plan. If Banks truly didn't yet know about the note, it would be stupid to tell him. Or maybe it wouldn't be a bad idea, if only to see his response. If he was a skilled liar, though, showing my hand would lose more ground than it would gain.

Across from me, Banks's expression was beginning to wilt. I'd waited too long to respond.

"The book, *Minnesota's Hidden Treasures*," I blurted. "Have you read it?"

Dr. Banks appeared genuinely confused. "No, I haven't. Is it good?"

I'd been watching his face. He genuinely couldn't recall the title. However, that didn't prove anything. If my hunch was right that a girl or woman had successfully hidden the note in the book, then Dr. Banks wouldn't have seen her do it.

"Yeah, it's a real page-turner," Mrs. Berns said. "That's all we wanted to talk to you about. See if you wanted to read it."

"Well," the dentist said, clearly not knowing how to respond. "I guess I could check out some books while I'm here to bring back to my office. Usually my receptionist does it, but she's such a hard worker, I could save her the trouble."

He made his way to the stacks. I leaned over to Mrs. Berns. "I don't get any bad vibes from him," I said. "And I don't like that one bit."

Mrs. Berns flicked my forehead. "Trusting your instincts isn't just about knowing who's bad. It's about trusting who's good, down in your belly, even if your brain isn't on board."

I wasn't ready to trust at the moment, but I also wasn't selfish enough to let that stop me from helping kidnapped girls. I walked back to where Dr. Banks was perusing the books. He jumped when I appeared. If he was an actor, he was a good one.

"Are you Barry Janston's dentist?" I asked.

"I can't tell you that," he responded, his face smooth.

"How about Guinn's?"

This time he couldn't hide a reaction. If I was reading him correctly, the name made him angry. Maybe Guinn had double-crossed him?

"I also can't tell you that."

I exhaled loudly through my nose. "Then you probably can't tell me this, either. Did Guinn or Janston ever drop off girls to get their teeth checked, girls he knew from the community center?"

Dr. Banks opened his mouth, then closed it. I expected another demurral, but he surprised me. "Yes," he said, "Guinn did. Immigrant girls, some of them who didn't speak much English. And it will forever haunt me that I didn't go to the police about it."

My breath hitched. "Did you tell them now?"

"Yes," he said. "As soon as I heard you found Maisy Kramer in his shed. I turned over the records on the girls Guinn brought in, but I assume the names were aliases. Guinn paid in cash. He told me he was helping them, and I believed him because it was easier than making trouble where there might not be any."

Dang, did I know that impulse. "Thank you," I said, grudgingly.

He went back to his book search. "It's not enough," he said softly. "It never will be."

I still wasn't sure whether to put Dr. Banks into my good or bad file, so I walked away. That was the problem with interacting with enough criminals. You never knew who to believe. Except I could always trust Mrs. Berns.

"I'm going to run over to Maisy's house to check on her," I told her. I hadn't even hung up my coat yet, so I just tugged it back on. "I'm no fan of Karen's, but I want to make sure her daughter's OK."

Mrs. Berns made a scolding noise. "You know how I told you Karen had a bad divorce and has to serve on the chamber of commerce alongside her ex's relatives? Well, she was married to a cheating preacher, and all his family sided with him."

"Maisy's dad is a cheating preacher?"

"Obviously, pudding head. Karen Kramer has had bad luck with men and with life in general. That's why she said those stupid things about Janston on television. It's easier for her to be on his side than admit she'd exposed her daughter to a real creep. You walking around judging her isn't going to do anything to fix that. She's a complex person, you know, just like the rest of us. She even let Chelsea live with her and Maisy, back after the divorce, when Chelsea's parents weren't doing so well."

The shame was immediate, a branding iron held to my sternum. I considered defending myself, but a quick scan revealed that Mrs. Berns was right. Karen had rubbed me the wrong way because she was so stiff and rigid and had been defending a bad man. But I'd never stopped to ask myself why a woman would do that. Besides, she'd helped me to interview Chelsea's parents.

"You think she's a decent person, deep down?"

"I think she deserves a second chance to prove it one way or the other. I think everyone deserves a second chance."

"Really?" I asked, my heart warming.

"No," she said. "Some people are pure a-holes, top to bottom, and there's no point in wasting time on them. But it was still a nice thing for me to say."

Chapter 48

Maisy was fine. Her mom had called her from the hospital, assured her that her blood sugar levels were again in line, and promised her daughter to do a better job watching what she ate. Maisy's love and worry for her mother thawed my heart even more. The woman had issues, no doubt, and I didn't agree with everything she did, but she'd raised a cool kid, and that counted for something.

After I assured myself Maisy was OK and that Peaches was on her way over so Maisy wouldn't be alone, I discovered that I was starving. I stopped by the Fortune Café to grab lunch for me and Mrs. Berns. The powerfully comforting smell of freshly roasted coffee, baking bread, and cinnamon cookies washed over me just inside their door. It absolutely relaxed me, which was why I was not prepared for the running, tackling hug Sid gave me when I approached her counter.

"You found Jed! You brought our boy home."

I stayed snuggled in her arms for a full thirty seconds before I corrected her. "I didn't find him. He walked all the way back here to find us."

Nancy showed up from the kitchen wearing an apron that read I'M NOT GAY, BUT MY GIRLFRIEND IS.

"Learn to take the love," Nancy said, chuckling and wiping her flour-covered hands on her apron.

I smiled a sideways grin. That was good life advice. "I talked to Sal this morning, and she said that Jed has total amnesia but there's hope he can recover his memory over time."

Sid slung her arm around Nancy. "We can do you one better. We brought them fresh doughnuts and coffee before we opened. Jed looks weak and skinny, and they had to shave off his hair because it had grown so matted, but it was still him. It's our boy," she said, using the back of her hand to wipe away tears.

"I don't know if Sal told you," Nancy said, "but Jed has taken to wandering a bit. They let him, Sal and Bill, because it's that rambling that brought him home. But we need him to remember who he is so he doesn't disappear again."

"I didn't know about the wandering," I said, troubled. "I'm going to stop by the Heikes' later today. I'll bring some of the memorabilia from the altar. Maybe looking at some of his old stuff will help jog his memory."

"I bet it will," Sid said, smiling. "Now what can I get you for lunch?"

"I'll take an everything bagel, toasted, with Greek olive cream cheese." My mouth filled with saliva thinking about it. Nancy's home-made bagels were warm and chewy, and the salty creaminess of the olive cream cheese was a slice of heaven. "And for Mrs. Berns, a ham and swiss on a plain bagel. I'll do a green tea for me, and hot chocolate for her."

Sid wrapped up my order and took my money. I grabbed both drinks and the bag of food, ran them to my car, and decided to stop and poke my head into the newspaper office rather than heading straight to the library. I had a couple questions for Ron.

I found him at his desk, typing up an article. His news wasn't good.

"Yep," he said, not pausing his typing. "You heard right. Janston is for sure getting off easy. Just another guy doing his thing."

"You wouldn't do that thing," I sputtered. "Neither would Johnny, or Curtis, or Jed."

Ron held up his hand and gave me his full attention. "Not saying it's right. Matter of fact, I think the system is broken. I'm saying men like Janston getting off scot-free happens all the time. And by the way, great job on Jed. You'll write an article about his return for Monday's paper?"

"Only if Sal wants me to. And I think you can retire the story on Bigfoot. It was Jed, blundering around in the woods."

Ron chuckled. "Only in Battle Lake."

"I don't want to ruin your sudden good mood," I said, "but I believe that Janston is a sex trafficker. Guinn certainly was, and the two of them were connected."

"That's quite an accusation," he said. "You have any proof to back it up?"

It was a version of the same question Gary had asked. It didn't make me nearly as angry when Ron tossed it out, however. Before I had a chance to answer him, his phone rang.

He picked it up.

I knew him well enough to recognize when he'd been thrown a curveball. He had a good poker face, but his nostrils flared when he heard something he didn't like.

"Yep," he said. "Yep. Yep."

He hung up the phone.

"Guinn's body was stolen from the morgue," he said, rubbing his face. "Around midnight last night."

Chapter 49

It took me all of four minutes to reach the police department. If earlier Gary had looked furious, he'd probably grown nuclear by now. I didn't care. If Guinn's body disappearing meant Mrs. Berns was back on the line, I needed to know.

We were alone in the police department when I barged in for the second time that day.

"Who else knew about how Guinn actually died?" I demanded.

I certainly hadn't expected Gary to be meek, but his rage and speed caught me off guard. He flew around his desk and came at me, his finger pointing at me like a sword. He stopped just short of touching me, panting.

"You. And that's it. I never should have told you. Dammit, what was I thinking?"

"It can't just be me," I said, stumbling backward. No way was *I* on the hook for Guinn's missing corpse. "The coroner knows, obviously. Did you tell your deputy?"

He turned so I couldn't read his eyes. "Yeah, my deputy knows, but he wouldn't have told anybody. I can't say the same for you. Or Mrs. Berns."

Or Kennie. This had become a loose ship. Except Mrs. Berns had hardly been out of my sight since I'd sprung her from jail, and in the short period between Kennie showing up at my house and midnight, when the corpse vanished, she'd been glued to my side. No, Gary was missing the big picture, and I was here to fix that.

"Whoever stole Guinn's body didn't want anyone to find out that he was already dead when Mrs. Berns shot him. They wanted her on the line for the murder. It all squares right up with my sex trafficking theory."

"Get. Out. Of. My. Police. Station."

His cruel tone made me want to cry. And when I felt that miserable, I attacked. "It must be a bummer to have somebody remind you how much you suck at your job," I said through gritted teeth. "You let all these murders happen under your nose, and sex trafficking is going down on your doorstep. And now a body that's part of your investigation is missing. Some police chief you are."

I didn't know which one of my mean accusations struck home, but suddenly, all the rage drained out of him. I hated to see it, hated to know I was responsible. I wanted him to fight, not quiver.

"Just go," he said quietly.

I returned to the library and ate lunch with Mrs. Berns. My bagel, which looked delicious, tasted like dust. I struggled through the rest of the day. When my shift ended, I drove straight to Jed's.

My visit with him was a mixed bag. I felt the absolute joy of seeing him and knowing he was alive, but it was more apparent than ever that the Jed I'd known wasn't there anymore. I hoped my friend still lived inside this Jed-shaped man, but when I showed him pictures of us together and had him hold his stuffed shark, he only smiled pleasantly, distantly, the same confused, blank way he'd been smiling since I'd discovered him at Guinn's.

I didn't bother showing him the glass ornaments I'd also brought, the very first ones he'd blown. They were the size of marbles and just as pretty. It would have broken my heart to witness that same empty stare.

Seeing Gary crumble followed by spending time with a Jed who didn't recognize me sent my mood to a basement low. Johnny and I were at a weird spot, but I was desperate for comfort. Still, I sat in my car outside his house for a full twenty minutes before I rang his doorbell.

Chapter 50

He opened the door wearing low-slung Levi's and an unbuttoned white linen shirt. I smelled his homemade fresh tomato sauce bubbling on the stove. His beauty and comfort made my heart ache. He was my safe haven, always had been. I'd known that in my most true center, but I was scared—terrified, in fact—that if I let myself fall all the way, Johnny would turn into my dad, and me into my mom. He wouldn't, though, not Johnny. Right?

But rather than hug me, or step aside to invite me in, he put his hand on the top of the door and filled up the space between me and his living room.

"Hey, Johnny," I said, my mouth dry. He wouldn't dump me now, not when I needed him so bad, when I'd finally realized how much he meant to me and what was holding me back. Life couldn't be that cruel. "How's it going?"

"Not great," he said.

Heat crept up my neck, and I felt my armor going up in response. Normally, he would have asked me how I was doing. Suddenly, I didn't feel like asking him about himself, either.

"It's been a bad week," I agreed, vaguely.

This was the spot where he usually folded, giving in and wrapping me in his arms, easing the distance between us so I didn't have to, taking care of me.

"Yeah, Mira, it really has."

I closed my mouth. For the first time in our relationship, he wasn't giving an inch. Usually he gave the whole mile.

Not today.

"You take me for granted," he continued. "And you don't admit that Gary is attracted to you and you to him."

I shook my head vigorously, my heart sick-thumping in my chest.

He continued as if he didn't see it. "I can handle anything but secrets, Mira. I'm a grown man. But you need to treat me like one, or it's over."

God, I wanted him to slam the door in my face. Because then he wouldn't see my mouth opening and closing like I was a landed fish. And I would never have seen that horrible, terrible sympathy in his eyes. Sympathy and pain.

He wanted me to say I chose him. Or that I chose healthiness for us.

Instead, I chose to turn on my heels and head home.

Once there, for the second evening in a row, I decided to head to Guinn's place. I was past crying. I was past numb.

I was a machine.

I didn't intend to sneak inside his house again. His place would be too hot now that I'd called in the laptop. But I could search the shed one more time. I'd barely peeked inside when I found Maisy. There might've been something I'd missed. Something that could definitively tie Banks or Janston to all this.

The weather was finally, finally starting to break, the steel-colored clouds swirling angrily across the stars and full moon. By the time I bundled up and grabbed a flashlight, the wind was screaming. It brought the most unsettling smell of tropical tundra. I didn't know what that sort of dangerous, push-pull weather meant for us mortals below, but the weight of it seemed appropriate at the moment.

Judgment Day.

Putting my shoulder into the biting wind, I trudged through the woods, following a now-familiar path until I reached Guinn's shed. It was unlocked. I entered. I played my flashlight around the first room, the one I'd found Maisy tied up in. The wind howled through the eaves.

I dropped to my knees.

Usually, the thing I was searching for was the last thing I found, if it revealed itself at all.

Not this time.

In the corner, underneath a raised filing cabinet, I spotted it immediately.

Something the police had missed.

I scrambled forward, grasped it, pulled it toward me.

I smiled, darkly.

It was a retainer case.

Chapter 51

"Yeah, that's mine," Maisy said.

Karen perched on the couch next to her. She was acting much mellower toward me.

Note to self: stop judging people and they might be decent around you.

"Why didn't you tell the police it was missing?" Karen asked.

"Cuz I hate my retainer," Maisy said, as if leaving it behind were perfectly logical.

"Do you remember losing it?" I asked.

"Yeah. When I came to in Guinnie's shed, I saw my retainer on the floor by my feet. It must have fallen out of my pocket when I was getting tied up. I kicked it underneath that cabinet. I figured if something happened to me, the police could find it and nail whoever had kidnapped me."

"Smart girl," I said. "Can I ask who your dentist is?"

But I knew the answer.

"Dr. Banks," Maisy said, smiling. "I like *him.* I just don't like my retainer."

"Do you know who Chelsea's dentist was?" I asked.

Maisy shook her head.

"I don't, either," Karen said. "But most of the moms around here bring our kids to Dr. Banks. He's good with them."

That's what the adults had thought about Guinn, too.

I didn't have much more to say. I hugged Maisy, tossed her mom a smile, and pushed against the shrieking wind to return to my car. I sat in it for a full five minutes, the impending blizzard throwing its smothering blanket over Battle Lake, before I decided that I needed to visit Mosquito Bay Lodge, and quick, before the full weight of this storm bore down.

Once I arrived, I realized I had a real dilemma on my hands. I couldn't leave my car on the county road, where it could be spotted and called in. I also couldn't park in the lodge's driveway, because that would be some weak spying.

I compromised by parking at an empty-looking cabin about half a mile up the road. I hoped it was a summer-only residence. It appeared that the driveway and walkway hadn't been shoveled since the last snow, which reassured me. I took off into the woods, where I was pleasantly surprised to discover that because of the curve of the lake, it took only ten minutes to reach the lodge's perimeter.

The parking lot held half a dozen cars. Who was staying here in April?

When a red sedan pulled in, I got an answer.

Dr. Banks stepped out of the car.

I was leaning forward to get a closer look when a hand clamped over my mouth.

Chapter 52

"Jed!"

His face was pale where his beard had been, and his eyes carried that same wandering oddness.

"You can't go in there," he said.

"Why?" I asked.

My question made Jed agitated, and his mood was contagious. I shifted my weight from one leg to the other, the wind's probing fingers slipping and crawling under my clothes.

"I don't know," he finally said. "Just don't go in there, OK?"

I pulled us back into the cover of the woods and then faced him toward the lodge, so the yard light reached us through the buffeting wind. I tugged off my glove, reached into my pocket, and came out with a blue-green sea ornament he'd made, his first glassblowing project. It was a little bit blobby, and it was full of accidental bubbles.

It was also the most precious thing I'd ever held.

"You made this, Jed. Do you remember?"

I tugged off his gloves and rested the bauble on his palm. I closed his hand around it so he could warm it with his body heat. I was desperate. I needed him here with me, real Jed, not Jed-shaped man.

I looked into his eyes.

And I saw a miracle.

His awareness shifted. Something was emerging in his face, some focus, some words that belonged to my Jed. I put my hand over my mouth, my pulse drumming, my eyes growing wet.

"Jed?"

A car door slammed shut.

Jed's eyes did the same. His blank stare returned.

I'd seen something below it, though. Hadn't I?

I glanced at the parking lot. Another car was pulling in.

"I need to get you home, Jed. There's a storm coming."

Because he didn't remember anything, and he didn't have much to say, I found myself spilling everything to Jed on the ride home, the wind buffeting my tiny car from one side of the road to the other. No precipitation had started falling, but the gray clouds bulged with ice and snow.

"I think Johnny and I are done for," I said, the words breaking my heart as they tumbled off my lips. "He needs me to be softer, and I need him to have more of an edge. It's not that I want him to be violent or anything, I just want him to fight for me, just once. And to stand up to me.

"And that's not the only problem," I continued. "I think there are three girls in awful danger, and I'm helpless to save them. If I don't find them soon, I don't know if they'll ever return to their families, or even if they do, that they'll be whole enough to go on."

I drew in a big, shuddering breath. "I want to save them while they're still girls, you know? I want to save their innocence."

"Did anyone save you when you were a girl?" he asked.

I jerked away from him. It was the same vacant tone he'd used since I'd found him, but there was something powerful in those words.

I looked over, studying him through the hot tears that were sheeting down my face. He watched the swirling weather like it was the best show he'd ever seen, oblivious to his own wisdom.

"I love you, Jed," I whispered, grabbing his hand.

He didn't answer.

Chapter 53

I spent all day Sunday feeling like a hamster on a wheel, but I had no better plan when I woke up Monday morning than to drive straight to Dr. Banks.

I'd liked him when I'd finally met him.

Yet finding Maisy's retainer had further connected Banks to the abducted girls. Plus, I'd seen him pull into Mosquito Bay Lodge. Everything I'd learned about him made this more confusing, not less. Didn't the universe know how discovering clues and interviewing suspects was supposed to work?

And I didn't exactly drive *straight* to his place.

I slid all over the road in near-blizzard conditions.

Snow had been falling for hours. The wind wasn't shrieking anymore, but at least six inches of the fluffy stuff had accumulated overnight, and it showed no sign of slowing.

The radio announcer concurred.

"They are calling it the snowpocalypse," he said. "We're predicting up to twenty-four inches of snow in the next twelve hours in some parts of northwestern Minnesota. Snowthunder is all but guaranteed to accompany the snowfall."

I realized I still wasn't exactly sure what snowthunder was. I supposed I should, given that I chose to live in Minnesota. I clicked off the radio and drove the rest of the way listening to the mouse feet of falling snow and the swish-crunch of my tires grabbing at sheets of ice.

I parked the car in the dentist's lot and peeked into the empty storefront out of habit. Except it was no longer so empty. There were footprints across the dusty floor that had not been there last time I was here, and it looked like new boxes were stacked in the corner. Maybe somebody was going to rent it out. That gave me a spark of hope for Battle Lake.

I entered Dr. Banks's office. Anne spoke before I had a chance.

"He said he stopped by to see you yesterday."

I couldn't read her tone, but if I had to guess, I would say she sounded exasperated.

"He came by the library," I agreed. "Thank you for letting him know I wanted to meet with him. I'm actually here today to speak with you."

She quirked an eyebrow. "Yeah?"

"Yeah," I said, casually throwing out the gambit I'd rehearsed on the drive over. "I wanted to know if you were organizing the get-together at Mosquito Bay, or if Dr. Banks was doing that on his own."

The ploy paid off.

"That's me," she said, flipping her hair. "Dr. Banks is technically in charge, but I'm the one who reserved the lodge for the retreat."

"What kind of retreat?"

"For Dentists Without Boundaries. They gather once a year. This round, it's in Battle Lake."

Boy, did they need a different name. "When's the retreat?"

"Weekend after this."

I nodded as if I'd expected this, the wheels turning in my head. Dr. Banks might have visited the lodge because he wanted to survey the setup before hosting a large event. That would be a totally reasonable move. Or he might have visited Janston to make sure there were enough girls for his retreat. That ugly thought did not settle well. I had truly liked Dr. Banks. I couldn't let that interfere with all the evidence piling up against him, though.

"Thanks," I said. "That's all I needed to know."

"For the paper?" she asked, smiling brightly.

"Totally," I said, making a note to work on my backstory. I was sliding in old age.

I made my way to the library. This morning, before I'd left the house, I'd slipped on my favorite pair of Levi's and my age-worn Led Zeppelin T-shirt. The beauty of running the library was I got to wear what I wanted, though I usually dressed professionally. Today, though, I was wearing comfort clothes because it felt like it was all going to break, and not just the storm.

For that reason, I'd also slathered on dark eyeliner and lipstick in Throwdown Red. I rarely wore makeup, but the extra level of armor felt good. I also slid on the poison ring I'd bought from Kennie. It looked badass. Only I knew it was full of iodized salt, not arsenic.

I wasn't going to tell Kennie that I thought the rings were her best idea yet.

While I appeared rock and roll on the outside, I was still dweeb on the inside, so I'd slipped a full bottle of jumbo eye drops into my back pocket, too. The storm exploding had, surprisingly, eased up my allergies, but I didn't want to be caught unprepared if they returned with a vengeance, instigated by, say, snowthunder.

"Hey, Mrs. Berns," I said, walking through the door and stomping the April snow off my boots. "Is this going to be a new thing, you opening the library?"

"I should think not," she said. "Not unless we're going to be going undercover regularly."

My heart lurched. "Did someone answer our ad?"

"Not yet," she said. "But it's only a matter of time."

I shook the snow off my coat, my mood darkening. "That's the thing we don't have: time. Those poor girls are waiting on us."

Mrs. Berns didn't bother to answer. What could she have said?

A pall lay over the library, and it wasn't just the cloud cover strangling the morning light. As soon as I had my opening duties out of the way, I went online to research Dr. Banks's upcoming retreat. I didn't find anything on his business website, so I hopped over to the Mosquito Bay Lodge one.

Their homepage trumpeted the upcoming Dentists Without Boundaries Retreat, the dates lining up with what Anne had said. (Really, though. That name.) I started feeling down before I realized the timing of the retreat might work to my advantage. If Dr. Banks was who I thought he was—the king of this area's sex trafficking, paying Janston to do business at his lodge and Guinn to bring him teenagers—he'd need a whole influx of girls for the upcoming retreat.

That demand would make my ad even more appealing.

As if the universe were finally paying attention, the computer dinged. Secretdoor.com was open on another screen, and a message had just landed in our inbox. I clicked on it, feeling meat-sweats sick. I wanted this to work, but I also didn't.

The message was short, and it was not sweet.

> You look gorgeous. Meet you tonight at Halverson Park. 8 p.m. I'll bring cash, and you bring your cute smile.

I hadn't been smiling in the photograph, but I don't suppose that mattered.

Halverson Park was the home of my glorious Chief Wenonga, the twenty-three-foot fiberglass statue. It was also less than a block from the Urho Gas Station, the last place Chelsea Cruise had been seen.

I called Mrs. Berns over. She bent toward the computer and read the message.

Then she turned and looked me up and down. "We've got to figure out how to make you look like a teenager before eight p.m."

"I know just who to call," I said.

Chapter 54

Peaches and Maisy showed up as soon as school let out, alarmingly prepared.

"I'm not going to dye my hair," I protested.

"It'll look great," Peaches said, holding up the box. "Please? You'll make a stunning redhead."

"It's true," Maisy agreed. "With your pale skin and gray eyes, you'll look *hawt.*"

"More importantly," Mrs. Berns said, "you'll be harder to recognize if the man you're meeting already knows you."

"But in the photo of me we posted with the ad, I didn't have red hair," I said. I'd had dark hair my whole life. The shining, smiling woman on the box Peaches held had wavy tresses the color of raspberries.

"Mira," Mrs. Berns said, "that photo was so dark, it was almost a black and white. Your hair could have been any color. Would you prefer blonde over red?"

I would not.

I glanced at the box again. I might look ridiculous as a redhead, but I'd look even more ridiculous if I showed up looking just like me, and a library regular or some guy I'd played pool with at Bonnie & Clyde's was the one responding to my ad. If he recognized me, our single shot was blown. Was I going to let vanity stand in the way of potentially saving Chelsea, Talia, and Anita?

I was not.

That didn't mean I was going to be gracious about it.

"Fine," I said, letting them lead me into the library's back room, where we had a full bathroom, including a large sink. "But I'm not wearing those color contacts. My allergies are too severe to stick something in my eye."

Peaches and Maisy both clapped their hands in glee. "That's OK!"

After they dyed, blow-dried, and styled my hair into waves, I could hardly believe it was me staring back from the mirror. The raspberry looked more bruised, darker on me, and it turned my eyes hazel and made a rosiness bloom on my cheeks.

My hair perfect, they moved to my face, rimming my eyes with kohl, clipping on fake magnetic eyelashes that made me look like a Disney princess, and painting my fingernails pine-forest green. They let me keep my Levi's, but against my protests tore some rips in the knees and tugged down the button-fly front so you could see my belly button.

I refused to let them rip the Led Zeppelin T-shirt I'd scored in a Minneapolis Ragstock a few years earlier. It was authentic, from one of their last concerts with John Bonham still drumming. Their compromise was to leave the shirt intact but tie a knot at the front. I didn't know how my Nut Goodie pudge was alluring, but they assured me that feminine curves were all the rage.

I didn't mind wearing the black Converse high-tops that Peaches had brought, and I was a little more than excited to slap on the Pretty in Ink tattoos. I stuck a bumblebee on my neck, right below my left ear, and a moon symbol on the inside of my right wrist.

"What model of phone do you have?" Peaches asked, fussing with my hair even though it looked better than it had my entire life. "If it's not up to date, you'll stand out like a sore thumb no matter what we do with your makeup and hair."

Mrs. Berns snorted. "She's got the Flintstones' Horn Bone Flip Phone. Will that work?"

"No way, dude," Maisy said. "You don't own a cell phone?"

"All I have is the phone attached to my wall back home."

By their expressions, they would have been less shocked if I'd told them that I ate nail clippings for breakfast.

"Here," Maisy said, not looking straight at me. "You could borrow mine."

"And you can use my car," Peaches said, handing me the keys. "Everybody in town knows your Toyota."

The weight of their gifts—the most precious a teenager could bestow—landed heavily on me. "Thank you," I said, sincerely. "We couldn't do this without your help."

"What about that?" Mrs. Berns asked, pointing to the poison ring on my finger.

"Oh my gosh, we love that!" Peaches said. "For sure keep it on. Where'd you get it?"

"The mayor is selling them," I said. She might have a whole new audience for her jewelry if we all lived. *Hmm.* Except I didn't know if I wanted to encourage these girls to hang out with Kennie, unsupervised.

I'd worry about that later.

"I think I'm ready," I said, grabbing my coat and walking toward the library's main room. "And just in time. It's seven thirty."

"Hold up," Peaches said. "You can't walk like that."

"Like what?"

Maisy appeared perturbed. "Like you're not afraid of anything. You need to move with your shoulders hunched. Look down at your feet. You're a teenage girl in this world."

As she demonstrated, Mrs. Berns and I exchanged a glance. I knew what she was thinking cuz it was the same thing I was: forget Chick Club. When this was all over, we were going to start a Reverse Fight Club, where rather than fight each other, they turned their incredible power on the world.

But we had urgent matters to attend to now.

"Like this?" I asked, emulating Maisy's walk. It wasn't hard to slip back into it. After all, it was the same gait I'd shuffled through high school with after my dad had killed himself and the other driver in the car accident.

If I was honest, it was the walk I'd sported even before that.

I'd been brought up on the same contradictory rule for girls as Peaches and Maisy had: *don't invite attention, but make sure that you're pretty enough to deserve attention.* It had taken me years to unlearn that, and sometimes I still forgot.

"You're doing it perfectly," Maisy said. She looked as sad as I felt. "And one other thing, when you get there, to the park? While you're waiting for whatever guy to show up, be staring at your phone."

"What? I would never do that. Somebody could hurt me if I'm distracted."

Maisy nodded. "Exactly," she said. "Look like you're not paying attention, but always pay attention. That's the way things are these days."

I had that thought running around in my head as I braved the howling blizzard and climbed into Peaches's car. I blinked heavy flakes off my fake eyelashes as I fired up the Buick. The radio came on with the engine. I didn't recognize the singer, but I liked her wail and the driving beat.

The park was near enough to the library, not even a mile up the road, but I had to drive well under the speed limit because of the thick, swirling snow. Another ten inches had dropped since I'd arrived at the library that a.m. The flurries were constant, but at least they were pure snow. Icy rain laced in would be deadly.

The snow was soft, too, so it was drivable (more like sleddable). Yet I worried that whoever I was meeting wouldn't show up because of the weather.

Part of me was even more worried that he *would* show up.

The plan was that if I didn't text back within half an hour, then Mrs. Berns would call Gary and tell him what was up. Maisy assured me that as long as I had the phone on my person, I would always be traceable.

It wasn't a great plan, but it was the best we had.

I parked in the Halverson Park public lot and tried to look around. The snowflakes swatted at my eyes. They were coming down so hard I could only see a foot or two in front of me. Remembering how I was supposed to walk, I put my head down and shambled toward the shelter. I wanted to run over to Wenonga and say hi, but I didn't want to stand out.

So I plopped myself onto a picnic table bench.

I tugged Maisy's phone out and stared at the bright light. The home screen featured an image of her, some boy I didn't know kissing her cheek. I smiled. She looked so happy.

I tried listening for someone approaching as I pretended to study the picture, but the snow warped noise. All those sound waves bouncing off those flakes. Two blocks up I spotted a murky brightness that might be headlights and heard the far-off crunch of tires, the first car I'd seen in the snowstorm besides my own.

My heartbeat quickened.

This just might work was the last thought I had before I was struck in the head and everything tilted black.

Chapter 55

I came to in surroundings so dark that I wasn't sure I was conscious.

When we traveled over a bump, I realized I was in the trunk of a car. I gurgled, unable to inhale. I was trapped, being driven away from safety, toward . . . what? I felt around frantically in the murky ink, struggling to take calming breaths to ward off the panic threatening me. Thank god whoever had knocked me out hadn't tied my hands or feet. I searched the back of my head, gingerly, and discovered a nice-size goose egg but no stickiness. At least I wasn't bleeding.

Better yet, I discovered, as I felt in my coat pocket, my phone was still with me.

Another bump, this one a doozy, lifted me off the floor of the trunk, and I dropped the phone trying to steady myself. A moan escaped my lips. That's when I noticed the smell, so unsettling that it made the hair on the back of my neck rise. It was a metallic scent, fierce ozone combined with the softer smell of snow. I'd never encountered any scent like it, a dangerous mix of thunderstorm and blizzard. My lizard brain did not like it one bit.

Then I heard a muted, percussive bang.

I yelped, despite my best intentions.

It'd sounded like a gunshot, close and everywhere at the same time.

The sound came again, simultaneously high-powered but muffled. A pressure constricted around my chest like a rope being pulled tight as I realized what I must be hearing: *thundersnow*. Christ on a cracker, it really was the snowpocalypse, and I was trapped in somebody's trunk.

I located the phone just as the car slid to a halt. The air in the trunk around me grew thick and liquid, and I felt lightheaded. I had only seconds to call 911 before whoever had stuck me in this trunk opened it up. I flicked on the phone. My eyes couldn't immediately focus. When they did, I saw a flurry of texts from Mrs. Berns.

Before I could do anything else, I heard a key in the trunk.

I jammed the phone into my pocket and readied my hands to punch and legs to kick.

The first object I contacted was a stun gun, business side aimed at me.

I realized it as soon as the golden jolt of pure electricity zipped through my body, charging the fillings in my teeth. My muscles spasmed, locked tight for a millisecond, and then began twitching.

I couldn't control any part of my body.

Z-Force traitor.

A bag was yanked over my head. I clenched and shivered, clenched and shivered, unable to move, feeling like I'd been buried alive in my own body. I heard a grunt as I was hoisted unceremoniously out of the trunk and lifted over someone's shoulder. My mouth opened to yell, but I couldn't even make a noise. I began hyperventilating, trying to blink away the stars inside my eyelids.

Calm yourself. If you lose it, you can't help anyone.

Breathe.

Breathe.

Through sheer force of will, I dragged myself back from the edge of Losing It Lane.

In through your nose, out through your mouth. That's it. You got this, Mira. The stun will last for ten minutes, tops. Let it run its course. Prepare to fight when you're back in control.

I caught a glimpse of snow through the bottom of the bag. It was about six feet away. The man carrying me was tall. I listened for anything that would give away my location. Another *whomp* of thundersnow resonated close by.

"Some damn weird weather," the man holding me said.

"I think it makes it more festive," said another man to my right.

So, there were at least two of them. I recognized neither voice.

The man carrying me slipped, momentarily losing his grip on me, but he regained his footing before he reached the ground. The lurch drove his shoulder into my stomach, and I *oofed*. Good. My diaphragm was relaxing enough to make noise.

A square of light appeared beneath me. A door opening. We were inside. Heat and brightness surrounded me, trying to comfort me, but I was still twitching. I focused on my breathing, on testing my body parts, small movements. I could only blink. I knew I must fight back as soon as my muscles were mine again.

A moan fled my lips. *Damn.* I hadn't meant it to.

The man holding me slapped my butt. "Don't worry, sweetheart. This is exactly what you signed up for."

Fury burned through me. At least that part of me still worked.

Another door opened, and I was roughly dropped to the floor. I landed on my tailbone, the pain knifing through me. But the shock of it stopped the twitching, and I realized I could now squeeze my right hand. The door slammed shut. The bag was yanked off my head, and I found myself gazing into the most caring brown eyes I'd ever seen.

They were in a familiar face.

I searched my brain for the name of the girl who'd been abducted from Frazee. "Talia?"

She sat back on her heels. "You know me?"

"Mira?" Chelsea ran over and held me where I lay. She looked tired but unharmed. "You're going to save us!"

I was able to turn my head, which was new. I counted six other girls in the room. Talia from Frazee, Chelsea, Anita from Perham, and three unfamiliar girls, none of them older than sixteen. Thick blankets had been nailed to all the walls, apparently for soundproofing. I shuddered, almost intentionally. Cots lined the walls, and from the pungent smell, I guessed the five-gallon bucket in the farthest corner was their bathroom.

"Help me sit up," I said.

Chelsea bent me at the waist, propping my upper body against hers. Both my fists clenched when I told them to. My head could move side to side, forward and back. Best of all, I could awkwardly tuck my legs underneath me. Pins and hot needles pierced every inch of my flesh, but it was a million times better than feeling nothing at all. "Help me stand, please."

Chelsea grabbed one arm and Anita the other, and they hoisted me to my feet. My legs were trembly, sort of new-calf-like, but they held me up. The stun gun must have been on its lowest setting. I suppose the creeps didn't want their merchandise to be off market for too long.

The men also hadn't bothered to check my pockets. I sent a prayer to whoever was listening and patted my jacket pocket. The reassuring rectangle of the phone was still there, which meant that the police knew where I was.

I grabbed the phone and held it up.

"We really *are* going to be saved," Talia whispered, as if she couldn't quite believe it.

I was working up the fine motor skills to dial 911 when the door slammed open.

A man built like a silo, probably the one who'd hauled me in on his shoulder, lunged for the phone. "I'll take that."

He slid it into an interior pocket before I had a chance to protest. The girls started wailing, rushing him.

"And I'll take you, too," he said, pushing them away like they were made of paper and tossing me over his shoulder again. "Time to do what you came for."

Chapter 56

Without the bag over my head, I easily recognized the blue-and-red chevron-pattern carpeting of Mosquito Bay Lodge. I didn't know what section I was being carried through, though, and I couldn't risk screaming because for all I knew, the hotel was full of only bad guys. Yelling for help would need to be my last resort.

Before I had time to formulate a plan, the goon opened a door and steered me into a new room. This one was decorated like a library, with shelves full of leather-bound books and rich, gleaming furniture. He dumped me on the nearest couch. I had a moment to study his features. He was tall, hulking, and bald. He looked for all the world like a Bond villain. He surely had never been to Battle Lake, at least not in the daylight. He would have stood out like a sore thumb, which, frankly, was exactly what he looked like.

"Here's how it works. You see those drinks over there?" he grunted, pointing to the other side of the room at several liquor bottles and a heavy, ornate decanter surrounded by a set of expensive-looking crystal glasses. "You're going to serve them to the fellas who come into this room. If you're good at it, we might not have to use those other girls. Got it? All you gotta do is waitress."

"Yeah, that makes real sense," I said to him, venom dripping from my words. "That's how most people get their servers. They kidnap them."

"So, you're a smart one?" he said angrily, pumping his shoulders.

I looked around the room, scowling. "I'm not feeling particularly smart at the moment."

He got a chuckle out of that. "Look, all I'm saying is that the better you do now, the better it is for those other girls. Got it?"

I nodded. "Yeah, I got it."

He walked his sticky eyes up and down me. "You're a real pretty one. The guys are gonna like you."

Even though I felt like throwing up, I steeled myself, not moving, checking the urge to launch myself at him and make him eat his own fingers. If he came near, I'd fight him, using everything I'd learned in Tae Kwon Do, but I was still weak from the stun gun, and he was huge. It would be way better if he didn't come at me. My tongue tasted tacky, sour with fear. I was careful to not so much as twitch.

When I didn't respond, he clucked his tongue. "All right then, if you wanna be quiet." He turned, had a second thought, and turned back, his glance flying to my hand. "That one of those poison rings?"

"No," I said, covering it with my other hand. "It's just a ring."

"I ain't that dumb," he said, putting the immediate lie to his words. He came over and twisted the ring off my finger, tearing my skin. He flipped the lid on the ring, his eyes growing angry.

"See," he said pointing inside. "Poison."

"It's salt," I said.

He smelled it. "Right, and then you get me to taste it and I die, yeah?"

I wished more than anything it were poison, or that I knew how to throw knives with deadly accuracy. And had knives with me. "You got me," I said, hands up. "It's poison."

He grunted. "I'd smack that smart mouth of yours, except the customers'll be here any minute, and they don't like their girls crying, at least not right away. Run your fingers through your hair or something and get those drinks ready. You and me'll square up later."

He walked out the door. The sound of tumblers falling into place told me he'd locked it from the outside, but I ran to check just to be sure, my legs quivering.

Yep. Locked.

At least I could move quickly. My body was mine again.

The bad news was that I had no phone and no plan. I looked around for a clock, but didn't see one. My best guess was that I'd been in the lodge for seven minutes or so. I had no idea how long I'd been out before that. I hoped that a half an hour had passed, and that Mrs. Berns had called the police.

Regardless, I had only one option: stall for time.

That realization made me feel hopeless. A gaggle of men could inflict a lot of harm before the police arrived. I swallowed. Better me than the teenage girls down the hall.

A rapid-fire round of sneezes caught me off guard. When they subsided, I rubbed my eyes. Man, they were itchy. *I wish I had my—*

I paused. *Eye drops.* In my back pocket. A full bottle, in fact.

I yanked it out.

Just don't get any in your mouth, Mrs. Berns had said. *As little as a teaspoon will make you so sick you'll wish you were never born.*

I glanced over at the glittering, crystal lowball glasses and back at the door. I didn't have much time. I ran over and distributed the drops equally into four glasses before pouring the golden liquor over the top. I sniffed the results. It smelled like bourbon only.

I shoved the empty bottle back into my pocket just as the door unlocked, then opened. Four men walked in. They all had bland, forgettable faces, the types of faces I could encounter in any grocery store or bar or church in the region.

Ten minutes. I only had to occupy them for ten minutes.

Except I couldn't stop shaking.

Chapter 57

I didn't know what they'd been told to expect, but two of the men appeared uneasy, while the other two were smiling like this was not their first rodeo.

"Drinks?" I asked, balancing the glasses on a tray and walking toward the men. The two who'd been grinning stiffened. I realized I was carrying myself like an equal. I drew my shoulders toward my ears and stared toward my feet.

I sensed them all relax.

They each took a drink from a tray. They sipped.

"Cheers!" one of the more confident men said. He was dressed professionally in a sports coat over a button-down shirt, belted blue jeans, and loafers.

I risked a flirtatious smile in his direction, but made it clumsy, like I was a teenager or just me, who was terrible at flirting. "Your fee includes top-shelf liquor. I say slam that first one," I said, giggling and hoping I was conveying the proper subservient party-girl aura.

It hurt adult me to behave like this, but it was not lost on me that back in college, I had fantasized about being "forced" to cater to the needs of powerful men just like this. I blamed it on the film *Pretty Woman*, which had messed up a whole generation of girls. I wondered if it had been toxic for boys and men, too, if it had contributed to the sense of entitlement these four were displaying.

I shook off that thought. In showing up for a night with a girl they had surely been told was a minor, these guys were demonstrating they were a special breed of evil. It made it difficult not to hurt them—I mean, physically, and immediately, rather than waiting for the eye drops to kick in.

In that moment, I was overwhelmed by the sense of how lucky I was to have found Johnny, a kind, loving, and gentle man. I'd been childish with him, so cavegirl in my desire that he drop down to the knuckle-dragger level to please me. If I made it out of this nightmare, I would grow up for him, on the spot.

"She's right!" said the man wearing a lilac cashmere sweater as he raised his glass. His hands were smooth, his fingernails so shiny they indicated a recent manicure. "Bottoms up!"

They all chugged their drinks, puffing up as they inhaled liquid courage. I guessed these creeps were all in their fifties. Chances were strong they had daughters of their own.

"Let me get you refills," I said, keeping my eyes demurely lowered as I took their glasses.

"Make it quick, will you," the man in the light-purple cashmere said. "Banks is coming, and if we seem greedy in front of him, he won't invite us back."

Beads of sweat broke out on my upper lip. Lou Banks! He *had* been running this all along. It made me sad to discover he was as warped as the evidence suggested. It also made me wonder what Janston's role in all this was. Maybe he just provided the lodge, and got kickbacks? No way he didn't know what was going on under his roof.

The room grew blindingly bright for a moment, followed by that distant, haunting thump.

We all jumped.

"Damn," one of the two more timid men said, glancing nervously toward the wall of windows. "It's a snowpocalypse."

But I wasn't listening. I was watching the doorknob, which was turning.

Banks had arrived.

Chapter 58

Barry Janston strutted into the room wearing a three-piece suit and looking for all the world like he was about to accept an award.

"The banker is here!" he said, his smile wide.

Realization pressed like a bear trap around my throat. Too late, I recalled what Janston had told me in his Mosquito Bay office a few days earlier.

Your dad and I met in college, both of us in the finance program. Banks, he used to call me back then. I guess it was prophetic, as I started out my career in the Glidder Bank system.

I was trying to catch up. Before I had a chance, Janston's eyes landed on me. It took all of three seconds for him to recognize me, red hair or no.

He froze at the same time the man in the lilac cashmere doubled over, making a wet herking sound way back in his throat. The eye drops were kicking in. There was no better time. I gripped the heavy, leaded crystal decanter by its neck and leaped toward the man in the sports coat, cracking him on the back of the head. He fell like a tree. I spun and took out the man in cashmere with a kick to his pork and beans.

He dropped with a thud.

I turned on the third, one of the quieter perverts. If any of the four hadn't just slammed a healthy shot of tetrahydrozoline, I wouldn't have stood a chance, but they were all struggling with their own bodies, and so a one-two punch to the face and then stomach sent him to the ground. My adrenaline coursed through my veins like mercury, giving me a superhuman strength and speed I'd never experienced before. I should've been short of breath, but instead, I felt like I could fly.

I swiveled to the fourth man. He toppled over on his own, landing with a sickening *thunk.*

I spun on Janston.

Unfortunately, he had not ingested any poison. He launched himself at me and trapped me in a crushing grip, his elbow crooked around my neck. He pulled me close, squeezing, stopping my breath and blood, forcing my face into his chest.

His voice came hot in my ear. "It's easy to make girls like you disappear. Your father did it all the time."

My vision blurred. There it was. The confirmation I had dreaded but somehow knew was coming. I was the daughter of the worst sort of man, worse than I'd even imagined. I went limp in Janston's arms. What right did I have to fight for myself? I was the daughter of a monster.

My limpness increased the pressure at my neck, which made stars shoot across the back of my eyelids. This seemed like a fitting end, dying at the hand of the state senator from Battle Lake. After all, I'd brought nothing but terrible luck to this beautiful town. They deserved to get in the last word. The stars were fading, replaced by slashes of red and black, blood thumping as my heart knocked up against the block at my throat, unable to send oxygen to my brain.

I was grateful it was happening without pain.

I was facing a merciful ending, even though I'd been cursed most of my life.

I'll curse you if you don't *fight,* came Mrs. Berns's voice, deep in my brain. *You are not the sins of your father, so stop being such a baby and get to it.*

I blinked, letting in some light. *Too late,* I told the voice. *I'm on my way out.*

I'll say this only once, came Mrs. Berns's voice in my head again, strong and angry, just as she'd be if she were standing next to me: *There's*

terrified girls down the hall who need you right now. So fight back. Now.
You can feel sorry for yourself later.

That last part got me. This wasn't going to end well for me, certainly, but at least I'd had a chance to live a better life. Those girls hadn't had their opportunity yet. Against all instincts, I turned toward Janston, shoving my face deeper into his chest and buying myself a blessed quarter inch of relief at my neck. I sucked in a scream of air and readied my legs. My donkey kick caught Janston off guard. He let me go and stumbled backward, but he was up in a shot, swinging.

His fist connected with my cheek before I could block it. All my Tae Kwon Do fighting had been orchestrated, a flowing dance, but this was street fighting. I fell to the floor, bracing myself for the next blow, struggling to regain my bearings. I didn't have long to wait. Janston kicked me in the stomach with a sickening crunch.

The force of his front kick spun me onto my back. I could taste my own blood, but I couldn't breathe. I couldn't catch air. I clawed at my throat, my mouth, my stomach, but it was no use. My body was locked up.

Janston was rolling up his sleeves and stalking toward me, hate igniting his eyes. I was on the same level with the miserable men, all four of them retching and moaning. But I couldn't speak. I could only open and close my mouth, chewing the air, dying to draw it in but unable to.

My vision was narrowing. The adrenaline had used up much of the oxygen in my blood, and I couldn't replace it. My fingers and toes grew cold. Still, Janston advanced. I tried to roll away, but the movement awoke a piercing pain in my rib cage.

This was how it was going to end for me.

I couldn't say I was surprised, given how the past year had gone. Only brokenhearted that I couldn't be held by Johnny one last time, educated again by Mrs. Berns, scolded by Gary once more, entertained by Curtis, harassed by Kennie. At least I would go knowing that the girls would soon be safe. Surely a half an hour had nearly passed since

I'd left the library. All cell phones were trackable, that's what the girls had said. The police would be here soon.

I'd stalled long enough.

A tear slid down my cheek and my diaphragm relaxed for a millisecond. I sucked in a wheezing, delicious sip of air.

Janston stood over me, his glare venomous. "Your dad never liked this work, I'll give him that. That's why he drank, you know? Drown out all his guilt. Well, you'll see him soon. You can ask him about it yourself."

"Why?" I asked. Or, I meant to. No air, no words.

Janston read my lips. "Why the sex trafficking? That's a long story, but I'll tell you the short version: four bored men, playing cards late at night after a conference fourteen years ago. I can't remember if it was money or women we wanted more of, but we figured a way to make both happen. Probably you'd like an explanation that was something more momentous, but that's not how it works, ever. Crime is just regular people, deciding the rules don't apply to them. Or maybe you mean why'd I go after Maisy and Chelsea? Well, I'd developed a fancy for them when I was dating Karen. You regularly see two girls flouncing around you every day, and you develop a hankering.

"Or maybe why did I have Guinn killed? No, you're smart enough to have figured that one out. He'd borrowed Maisy for me, but then he'd gotten busted with her. Idiot. I couldn't risk him blabbing what he knew to save his own sorry ass. That about covers the whys."

He knelt and tossed his tie over his shoulder like a man about to dig in. His hands circled my neck, the embrace almost tender, like he was feeling for the latch on a necklace. But then he started squeezing. And squeezing harder.

Any chance at a second drink of air had vanished.

My vision was fading, fireworks at the perimeter dimming to dying stars to pinpricks. I swatted at Janston, but my weak efforts were no more troubling than rain on a mountain.

In my final moments, my life didn't flash in front of my eyes like I expected.

Instead, my last vision was of Jed.

I smiled through the pain. If I had to die, that was a good way to go.

Except Jed looked so worried. And then angry. And then he had his hands on Janston, pushing him off me. When Janston's grip fell away, I inhaled air through my nose, my mouth, every pore of my body. I drew it in so fierce and fast that I choked. I turned over, throwing up and coughing, gasping, retching.

But I could breathe.

A crash to my left drew my attention. Janston stood over Jed as he'd just towered over me, a vase raised above his head. It looked exactly like the scene on the train in February just before Jed had been thrown off. He'd been coming to save me then, too.

No way was I going to let that happen twice.

I swiped my mouth with the back of my sleeve and launched myself at Janston with everything I had, shrieking like a banshee, ignoring the weakness in my limbs and the excruciating pain in my chest. My weight and fury pushed him into the far wall. He dropped the vase. I picked it up and smashed it over his head, knocking him out immediately.

And then I kicked him in the gut, exactly where he had kicked me.

Not my proudest moment, but I wasn't exactly ashamed of it, either.

I helped Jed up, checking whether he was OK before returning to frisk Janston. I located his phone in his front right pants pocket and dialed 911. The operator assured me officers were already on the way and would arrive within moments.

I dropped the phone on Janston.

Jed smiled goofily at me. "You really saved my beans, Mira."

Time stopped. I studied his sweet face. "What did you say?"

"Mira, dude, you saved my beans!" Jed held up his hand for a high five. "That guy was going to knock me out. Who is he, anyhow?"

My Jed was back. Tears flooded my face, but I didn't have time for much else.

"Come on," I said, holding out my hand. "We've got some more beans to save just down the hall."

Chapter 59

T and A inspector Bob Hartman appeared with Karen Kramer on his arm. They were both beaming. The inspector was dressed as a chef and Karen as an apple.

"Thank you so much for introducing me to this remarkable woman," he said after he'd threaded the crowd to reach me. "And this wonderful town. I have never felt so welcomed!"

I glanced around the community center. The decorations—part hoedown, part nondenominational Easter—were festive, and the turn-out great. At the Fergus Falls hospital the previous night, as I was getting my broken ribs x-rayed, Johnny had confessed that tonight's party was always intended to be a surprise celebration of my one-year anniversary in Battle Lake. Not an intervention or a marriage proposal after all.

When I confided that I'd lied to the inspector about tonight being a costume party, Johnny had instantly pivoted to turn it into exactly that, getting all of Battle Lake involved. A small-town miracle happened; a couple hundred people volunteered to decorate the center overnight, donate food, and dress up in creative costumes, twenty-two inches of fresh snowfall be damned.

Battle Lake had shown me this generosity before and was demonstrating it again. The town might have had lousy luck when it came to corpses piling up, but no place had better living, breathing, salt-of-the-earth people.

No place.

"It really is a great town," I told Bob. I considered avoiding the elephant in the room, but subtlety had never been my strong suit. "All the dead bodies I've come across don't bother you?"

"It's not my favorite aspect of Battle Lake," he said, frowning and patting Karen's arm. "But it seems like you also have a remarkable record of catching the bad guys, and that counts for a lot. Besides, the property values here are reasonable! That's why I've decided I'm going to rent out that storefront next to Dr. Banks. I'm opening a catering business that specializes in serving those with special nutritional needs. Karen said she'd help me get my feet off the ground."

Judging by the look Karen rolled his direction, I *bet* she was getting his feet off the ground. And good on her. She'd finally found a decent man.

Speaking of good men, Dr. Banks truly was one. He was completely innocent of all charges. He'd treated Talia for an impacted tooth, just as he'd cared for so many young immigrant girls Guinn had dropped off, not knowing that they'd been kidnapped. Talia had been too afraid to tell Banks who she was—Guinn had threatened to harm her family if she did—but she'd found a scrap of paper in a storage room Guinn had locked her up in, had just enough time to scribble the word "help" on it in the dentist's office, and slid it into *Minnesota's Hidden Treasures* in Banks's waiting room.

Afterward, Guinn suspected she'd signaled someone and had threatened her into confessing. Deciding he couldn't be sure what she'd written in the note, he returned to the dentist's office to retrieve it. The books had just been brought back to the library, though, and so he had to break in and steal the book.

Of course, I'd already removed the note.

Talia couldn't have known that the scrap of paper was a record of how many girls my dad, Guinn, Penetal, and Lartel had procured for Janston's trafficking operation, one of many discovered tucked in a safe in the attic of Guinn's workshop.

Ah, Janston.

He'd regained consciousness in the back of an ambulance. He sported a bump on his head, broken ribs, and a bruised kidney to match mine. He would never again get off with a mere slap, if today's St. Paul *Pioneer Press* headline was to be believed: **State's Largest Sex Trafficking Ring Busted, with Senator Barry Janston Found at the Helm.**

He'd limited his operation more or less to Minnesota, his henchmen preying on the state's large immigrant community as well as buying girls from out-of-state rings. He might have gotten away with it for much longer if not for Talia's courage in hiding that note. According to the *Pioneer Press* article, the FBI was just beginning to understand the scope of Janston's operation, using warrants to locate and free trafficked girls and women all over the state. The article also outlined how Minnesota authorities were working with the FBI and other agencies outside the state.

Below the headline and a stock photo of Janston was a picture of the giant-thumb man who'd hauled me into the lodge, that guy's partner in crime, and mug shots of the four men I'd happily poisoned. They would recover physically, but their public shaming and their guaranteed jail sentences would serve as a warning to any other monsters who were considering feeding their demons. Plus, the records uncovered on the laptop Janston kept hidden at Mosquito Bay promised many more arrests to come, many of them high-profile customers.

"Have you checked out this party's hottest costume?" Mrs. Berns said, appearing next to me, a grin the size of Lake Superior slapped on her face.

When I'd left for Halverson Park, she hadn't waited thirty minutes to call the police after all. Thank god. In fact, she'd decided about five minutes after I'd pulled out of the library lot that our plan was stupid, even by our usual standards, and she'd called Gary to let him know what was up.

He was furious, of course. The problem was, it turned out you *couldn't* trace a cell phone. So the police didn't know I was in the back of a trunk, or even that I'd been driven to Mosquito Bay Lodge.

Gary called in the state police, who split up their forces based on educated guesses, sending cars to the lodge, to Guinn's, to Banks's, and even one to my mom's place in case she'd been carrying on the tradition after my dad's death. My 911 call confirming I was at Mosquito Bay allowed them to pull back the other officers and focus all their efforts on raiding the resort. It turns out Janston had been holding one of the monthly parties he ran for his "elite recruiters," who each brought a friend. It was a pyramid scheme trading in girls. That explained why two of the men I'd poisoned seemed confident—sports coat guy and lilac cashmere sweater guy—the other two less sure of themselves.

What that meant for the authorities was that they were able to nail the main players all in one location, red-handed.

"I haven't," I said, looking Mrs. Berns up and down. I laughed out loud, even though it hurt my ribs. She was wearing a ripped pair of Levi's with a Led Zeppelin T-shirt knotted at her tummy and black Cons on her feet. She stepped aside. Behind her stood Peaches, Maisy, and Chelsea, all of them wearing the same outfit.

My heart swelled so big it almost cracked. "May I ask what the four of you are dressed up as?"

"Superheroes," Chelsea said, grinning.

I'd have teared up if it didn't feel so good to see Chelsea able to smile. She and the other girls had been terrified when I first saw them at the lodge, but they'd also been untouched. They were being intentionally "saved" for this weekend's party.

"I'd like you to meet my boyfriend, Deke," Maisy said, stepping aside so I could shake hands with an obviously college-age man.

"The one you were meeting for lunch the day Guinn took you?" I asked. If so, his age explained why Maisy had been so protective of his identity.

She nodded, then pointed over my shoulder. "Hey, is that the police chief?"

I turned to see Gary Wohnt standing in a clot of people about thirty feet away, near the DJ table, and dressed as a police officer.

My chest tightened. "Will you excuse me?" I said to Mrs. Berns and the girls.

I had something to tell Gary. It was long overdue.

I made my way through the crowd as quickly as I could, but Johnny, across the room and dressed as a gladiator, was faster. He reached Gary first. Every nerve went on high alert, but it needn't have. Johnny was using his words, at least for the moment, which was one of the many reasons I loved him—even if it meant he didn't always have an edge.

"Mira is mine," I heard him say to Gary, firmly. "I will fight you for her if I have to, but I prefer a gentleman's agreement."

I reached his side and stood, unsure, heart thudding.

Gary's inky eyes flicked to me. "What makes you think I want her?"

His words should have embarrassed me, but I read it in his eyes, the truth of his attraction. I didn't know how I'd missed it before.

The feeling was not reciprocated, though. Johnny was the only man for me, had always been my guy, even when I was too self-involved and immature to realize it.

"Nobody needs to fight over me," I said, winding up for a grand speech.

Before I could get out another word, Jed appeared alongside me, not dressed up at all, which was to say, he looked exactly like Shaggy from Scooby-Doo, right down to the bag of cookies he held.

"Hold up," he said, crumbs tumbling out of his mouth. "Didn't you tell me during that car ride that you wanted Johnny to fight for you? You wanted him to be more edgy, you said."

A fiery blush crept up my neck. "I thought you didn't remember anything from then."

"I guess I do," he said, smiling sweetly. "How cool is that? Hey, Johnny, you want to go sledding with me later?"

Johnny smiled, too. "You bet," he said. "Anytime."

I wanted to melt into the floor. Instead, I decided to try out a new version of the more mature me, the one I'd promised myself I'd be if I survived Janston strangling me. "I'm sorry I blabbed that to Jed," I said to Johnny, my voice quavering. "I'm not perfect. In fact, I know I'm a lot of work. But it turns out I don't need you to fight for me. What I would like is for you to stand up to me every now and again."

"I can give you lessons," Gary said to Johnny. "It's very satisfying."

I turned on him, ready with a searing comeback until I noticed the laughter in his eyes. I couldn't help but smile. We were going to be OK, Gary and me.

"Come on, Johnny," I said, looping my arm through his. "Let's grab some punch."

As we wove through the crowd, I inhaled the clean scent of him, the strong heat of his arm against mine. If I was going to live by my words, I couldn't just be a grown-up every now and then. I needed to make it a habit.

"Hey," I began hesitantly. "I've been worried about something, and maybe you can help. Do you think I should tell my mom what I found out about my dad? That he was the worst sort of criminal?" I usually saved these questions for Mrs. Berns, but if this was going to work, I couldn't always leave it up to Johnny to be the vulnerable one.

He remained silent for so long that I wondered if he'd heard me. Mrs. Berns always had a quick and snappy response to my questions. Were all guys so slow?

But it turned out Johnny was worth the wait.

"I think your mom already knows," he finally said. "And she's committed to whatever story she needed to stay with him all those years. So I don't think you need to tell her anything. But I do think you should forgive your dad. Not excuse his behavior." Johnny's voice grew solemn. "Never that. But let go of your anger toward him as soon as you're ready."

I hugged him. The deep-hearted grief I felt for my father would always be with me, but when Johnny's arms slipped around me, the grip of shame I didn't even know I'd been hoarding released ever so slightly.

"Thank you," I said.

"You're welcome." He kissed the top of my head.

And then he stepped back and crouched down on one knee.

"Not yet!" I blurted. "Too soon!"

He cocked an eyebrow, confused, and then began chuckling. He finished his movement so he could scoop up the dollar that someone had dropped. He held it up to reassure me. "I'll put this in the community center fund."

I would have eaten my own hair if it would have allowed me to disappear in that moment. Before I could find a way to rescue my pride, the liquid, rich opening strains of Etta James's "At Last" poured from the speakers. Johnny had hired a good DJ. Tamping down my embarrassment at misjudging his movement for a marriage proposal, I locked eyes with Johnny, ready to declare my love.

As usual, he was way ahead of me. He leaned in, his hot breath working like a mouth along my neck. "I think you're the most beautiful woman I've ever seen," he said.

I pulled back, ready to thank him, but he held me close, firmly, his lips brushing along my hairline, sending delicious quivers shooting through me.

"I love your hips, your lips, the way your stomach curves," he said, his voice a growl in my ear. My heartbeat thudded between my legs. The rest of the world fell away, the community center, my friends, the ache in my ribs and back. Johnny and me pressed close were a world all to ourselves.

"You make me laugh so hard I forget to worry," he continued, his voice still so close, so intimate. "You love your friends so deeply that you make us believe we're capable of anything. You're brave, and silly, and the smartest woman I've ever met."

I melted into him, our bodies merging in a way that was so natural, so comfortable, I wondered how I'd ever lived without it. Without us.

"You're my home, Mira," he said, echoing the thought I'd had when I believed I was about to die. "And nothing is more important to me than your happiness. That's why I got you and Mrs. Berns a present."

His tone shifted, and he stepped away. I fell forward, feeling an ache where his body had been. Talk about blue (cheese) balls.

"Yeah?" I said, trying to get hold of myself. He'd said everything I hadn't even known I needed to hear, let alone deserved. I couldn't process all that, not right now, so I'd best figure out what was happening. He'd just said something about Mrs. Berns and me and a present. I shook my head, trying to chase out the cobwebs. I couldn't imagine what she or I needed that wasn't already in this room.

"Yeah," he said, steering me toward the corner nearest the punch bowl. Jed was already standing near it, along with Kennie and Brad (dressed as Bonnie and Clyde, natch), Mrs. Berns, Curtis (in a Moses costume), and the whole Chick Club. Sid and Nancy were there, too, costumed like the *American Gothic* couple, complete with Sid holding a pitchfork. Next to them were Sal and Bill Heike, wearing Raggedy Ann and Andy costumes; the Senior Sunset sisters, Ida and Frida, made up as Laura and Mary Ingalls; and my friends Gina and Leif Hokum, dressed as Betty and Barney Rubble.

I suddenly grew embarrassed. I didn't deserve all these amazing people in my life. Plus, I didn't want them all to witness me getting a present, even if it was for me *and* Mrs. Berns.

Johnny pointed at a blanket draped over an easel.

"It's under there," he said.

"Do you know what this is?" I asked Mrs. Berns accusingly.

"Nope," she said, stepping forward and yanking off the blanket with a flourish. "But I know how to find out."

Underneath was a shingle, the type mercantile owners would hang in front of their shops back in the day. It read:

Mira James and Mrs. Berns
PI Services

The girls squealed, and Mrs. Berns clapped her hands in delight.

My heart swelled with gratitude, and then shrank. I didn't want to burst Johnny's bubble, but I had to state the obvious. "We're not licensed private investigators," I said, my voice low.

Of course Kennie heard me.

"No," she said, her hand on her chin, "but who dictates that's the only thing *PI* stands for? Maybe here in Battle Lake, it means you're a Personality Instructor. Like a life coach who uncovers secrets. You take their money and do some investigating to lead them toward a better life. You don't need a license to do that, do you?"

Her grin was wicked, her words true, and I saw all the possibilities unfurling in front of me. Mrs. Berns and I could rent a space, hang our sign, and work as investigators without ever calling ourselves that. A smile twitched at my lips, then grew until it about split my face. I turned to Mrs. Berns, who was smiling the same wide grin, standing among our circle of friends.

We were going to do it.

I finally understood that the future was full of rich possibilities.

But then, it always had been.

A Personal Note

April Fools is the twelfth and likely last (I think) book in my Murder by Month mysteries. It's been a wild ride. I wrote *May Day*, the first in the series, back in 2002 as a way to heal from my husband's suicide (full story over at my TEDx Talk). At the time, I needed to stop my spinning brain, but I also needed humor, justice, and closure.

I think a lot of us do, and that's why we turn to romances and mysteries. They distract us when life gets hard and connect us to larger truths, but also, I think they (and all good fiction) rewire us, organizing our brains and hearts to work together.

Plus, the villain *always* gets it in the end and there's *always* a happily ever after, and dangit, is there anything more satisfying?

I don't know if I can say goodbye forever to Mira or Mrs. Berns, and so, if a story strikes me, look for a future novel, novella, or at least short story featuring these two women I've come to love. Sign up for my newsletter on my website to be the first to hear should that happen and to automatically receive a free Mrs. Berns short story.

In the meanwhile, I hope you check out some of my other books. I'm particularly proud of *The Quarry Girls*, *Salem's Cipher*, and my deeply personal suspense novel, *Unspeakable Things*.

Thank you for reading.

Acknowledgments

A huge, heartfelt thanks to Thomas & Mercer for picking up the Murder by Month series and giving the books a warm new home, including providing gorgeous new covers and tireless editing across all twelve books. A special shout-out to Jessica Tribble Wells and Miranda Gardner for guiding this ship so deftly, and to my agent, the amazing Jill Marsal, for making this deal happen. But all the Nut Goodies in the world go to Kellie Osborne, a copyeditor sent by the angels, for wielding her red pen with wisdom, humor, and the occasional sprinkle of magic. Her support, research, and gentle guidance (monthly, for the past year!!) turned chaos into clarity and plot snarls into legit timelines. Thanks also to the series cold reader, Heather Rodino, who made sure we didn't miss a trick. For just a hint at how amazing Heather is, check out this recipe she invented for Battle Lake Bites. Cheers!

Frozen Nut Goodie-tini

Ingredients

    1 ounce Godiva chocolate liquor

    1 ounce Skrewball peanut butter whiskey

    2 tablespoons maple syrup

    1 cup ice

    Nut Goodie for garnish

Place all ingredients in a blender and blend until smooth. Pour into a martini glass and, using a Microplane, shave Nut Goodie on top as garnish.

About the Author

Photo © 2023 Kelly Weaver Photography

Jess Lourey writes about secrets, fosters kittens, and travels. She's surpassed a million readers, been short-listed for the Goodreads Choice Awards and the Edgar twice each, and won the International Thriller, Anthony, and Minnesota Book Awards. For more information, including a link to her TEDx Talk, in which she discusses the surprising inspiration for the first Murder by Month mystery, visit www.jesslourey.com.